Kick Back

Alec Munday, Volume 1

Phil Savage

Published by SBC Media, 2020.

To Jessica for all your patience

Readers Club Download Offer

Free bonus book. **Give Back** is the next episode in the Alec Munday series and is available to you now as a free download. Get your copy of **Give Back** by Phil Savage absolutely FREE

Get your free no-obligation download today. Find out more from www.philsavage.org

Chapter 1

With hindsight the champagne jacuzzi was a mistake. In fact, they're always a mistake. Nine times out of ten, everyone ends up cold and sticky and arguing over the repair bill. But when it's hot, the music's pumping and you're off your face, caution is always a casualty. This crowd didn't even notice when the water started to turn red. Until, that is, one of the girls began to scream, and the evening unravelled.

The source of the blood was identified later as the abductor hallucis muscle in the foot of João Ramos Rodrigues, known to most of the world as Diego, the English Premier League's most expensive-ever Brazilian import. One of the partygoers, in a rush to get to the jacuzzi action, had followed through with the glass as well as the champagne and the result was clear for all to see. The player felt nothing, but Alec Munday saw the future and it wasn't good.

He summoned party host, Blandine, whose team quickly got everyone out of the water and away from the area leaving Alec to assess the damage. He was no medic, but he'd seen plenty of footballing injuries in his time and this had all the hallmarks of a total loss for the star's insurers. He laid Diego on a lounger, pushed the gaping wound together and pressed a towel hard against it. As the player giggled and tried to get up, Alec yelled for an ambulance and paramedics were called. While Blandine phoned ahead to reserve a private room in the Helicopteros Sanitarios, Alec rode shotgun to downtown Puerto Banus trying to get some sense out of the player, while the sirens blared outside.

'Who am I going to call, Diego? Vic Vickers? He's still Player Liaison at the club, right?'

'Not the club, man' said the footballer, coming round slowly to the trouble he was in. 'I can't tell them. Call my agent, call Totò. He'll sort it out.'

'Listen, Diego,' Alec said, trying to keep the player calm and focused. 'What we do in the next ten minutes is going to be the difference between an awkward conversation at the start of pre-season training and the end of your career. Do you understand? You Need to Get your Shit Together.'

'Totò's a good guy, and he knows plenty of people. Call him and tell him he has to get me on a plane outa here.'

Alec knew it was pointless trying to keep the club out of the loop, but Diego would discover that for himself soon enough. He found Totò's number in the player's phone and made the call.

'Ei, Diego. Como você está? Estás bem?'

'Totò, this isn't Diego. I've got him with me but he's not in a position to talk. I need you to listen to me very carefully.'

He had the agent's full attention. Kidnap was rare outside Brazil and security wasn't normally a problem. Until it was.

'Who are you? What do you want?' said the voice 5000 miles away.

Alec outlined the situation briefly and gave Totò the benefit of his first-hand assessment of the injury. The agent was all business and took down details of the hospital without enquiring how and why they had ended up there. This wasn't his first player to get into trouble and no doubt it wouldn't be his last.

'Can you make arrangements to get your boy out of here and back to London? He's looking at emergency surgery if you're going to get any more cash out of him. We're going to be at the hospital in the next five minutes, so I'm going to need a surgeon to call me back with instructions for the local guys here. The paramedics have stopped the bleeding and given him some painkillers, but believe me, you cannot afford to leave him to a duty doctor with a scalpel.'

As the ambulance pulled into the casualty bay, Alec went to work. He pulled out his wallet and extracted eight €50 notes. He handed four each to the driver and paramedic with instructions to tell no one what they had seen, at risk of a slow and painful death. Whether or not they understood him, Alec knew from experience that he was just buying some time, but he hoped that Diego would be on a plane and out of the country before the media scrum descended. Once the player had checked into his room, Alec called Blandine.

'Ok, here's the plan. You have to get someone over here sharpish with Diego's passport. They need to mind him until he's on a plane and not our responsibility anymore.'

'I don't have anyone I can send to you,' came the reply in a husky French accent.

Bloody typical, he thought. She was happy enough to pour petrol on the fire, but he was the one left manning the pump when it got out of control.

'Whatever your guys are doing, it can wait. If we don't get fully across this situation right now, your days as party host to the Premier League are over.'

In the end it was more than an hour before one of Blandine's team arrived with the Brazilian's passport, enough time for Alec to take a call from a rather bewildered Mark Templeman-White, surgeon to the stars. His regular clientele was more interested in boob jobs and butt lifts than foot reconstructions, but he manfully gave instructions to the Spanish clinician and assured Alec that he would call a colleague with 'a more appropriate skillset' to prepare to receive a new patient.

Alec had no time to speculate where Totò had found him as his phone buzzed again. It was Blandine and she sounded worried. Reading between the lines he got the message that the party was reaching that inevitable moment when someone shouts, 'Let's hit a club'.

He had spent the past 48 hours in Marbella preparing for just this eventuality. The girls were Blandine's responsibility and her boss fixed the drugs, but Alec had the relationship with the footballers who were their paying guests. Back in London they were his mates and clients, but here on the ground he was their media minder, anticipating situations that could put the boys in the public eye and taking steps to avoid or at least manage them. None of their clubs knew they were here, and their partners had mostly been fed a line about a golfing trip or something similar. Alec had insisted on a social media blackout and wasn't about to be undone by 'events': there would be some major personal and professional fallout if the full details of their time in Marbella ever came out. Yes, he was their mate, but he was working, and they depended on him being sober and capable of bailing them out if the need arose.

Considering their youth, immaturity and spending power, the number of times that footballers actually end up in the papers for the wrong reasons is remarkably few. For every nightclub altercation, high-speed collision, or bedroom bust-up that makes the tabloids, there are a dozen others that simply disappear in quiet testimony to the work of a good media fixer working the channels behind the scenes. And Alec Munday was as good as they got. A former player, turned journalist and PR man, he knew both sides of the business and was adept at working each one. He might not be able to play anymore, but he was still good friends with a lot of those that could and trusted by members of the inner circle of the English Premier League. Once his fellow journalists grudgingly acknowledged that his writing was halfway decent, his footballing credentials gave him a huge amount of kudos. He was generous with introductions to his contacts and earned a reputation as someone who could provide access to players and managers alike. His mates in the game introduced him to the up and coming talent and new foreign imports, and his network of clients now rivalled that of any super agent. And just because they didn't make the papers, that didn't mean his players stayed out of trouble. There was always a demand for the kind of services he had to offer.

Normally Alec liked to control situations personally, but just because he wasn't on the scene this time there was no immediate cause for concern. Everything would be fine – that's what they paid him for.

'Don't panic,' he reassured Blandine. 'I've got an arrangement at Olivia Valere. The guys are expected, and I've paid off the paps so there shouldn't be an issue. Get them to sit tight for five minutes while I arrange the cars, then make sure one of your boys is down there ahead of the party to smooth the way in.'

Halfway into a conversation with the transport company, his phone beeped to indicate another call coming through. He glanced at the screen; Blandine again.

'I couldn't stop them, Alec. They just grabbed a bottle each and are out on the strip heading for Tibu.'

'Fuck! Fuck, fuck, fuck! Right, damage limitation. Call Tibu and let them know who's about to descend on them. The transport'll be with you in five, so get as many of your team on the street as possible. I do not want to read about this in tomorrow's papers so keep the paps back and get the boys inside. I'm on my way.'

For the Brazilian beside him, the shine had well and truly worn off this evening and Alec was about to make it worse. 'Diego, I'm sorry, man, but duty calls. You're in good hands and everything's set up in London. We'll catch up soon, yeah?'

With that, he was out the door and back on the street. The club was a ten-minute walk from the hospital, but he made it in under four, his lungs bursting as he sprinted his way along the Marina in the shadow of billions of dollars-worth of super yachts. His choice of outfit – slim-fit Hugo Boss suit, tight white shirt and shoestring tie – was fine for the club but hardly the ideal running gear in the warm Spanish evening. The heels of his brown Berluti shoes (Oxford's not brogues) beat a rapid tattoo on the pavement and Alec wished, not for the first time, that he'd done more to keep up his fitness.

The scene that greeted his arrival was carnage. If he had been simply a casual observer Alec would have found it amusing. As it was he could only stand there trying to get his breath back, watching a slow-motion car crash as a dozen of the most recognisable footballers on the planet hit party central fuelled by enough cocaine to make them unstoppable. To make matters much worse, their arrival coincided with that of a tri-decked mega yacht which was disgorging its payload of glamour models, aspiring actresses and reality celebrities. They'd been partying since Cannes as guests of a media tycoon, and none of them was in the mood to slow down.

The waiting paparazzi couldn't believe their luck. A battery of camera flashes lit up the chaos as the snappers captured the scene in its full glory for the insatiable readers of the Sunday red tops. The yacht girls made a beeline for the footballers, drawn by some primeval instinct to their next meal ticket. Fortunately, the players came to their senses and realised just in time how exposed they were. *Un*fortunately, their excitable female companions were not so restrained.

The line between model and escort is physically and philosophically wafer thin and, seeing their prizes about to slip through carefully manicured fingers, the girls unleashed a spectacle that would provide clickbait for the Mail Online's sidebar of shame for months to come. Hair flew, nails ripped and heels broke as the girls bit, kicked and screamed their way into every photographers' personal showreel.

In the mayhem that ensued, Alec took his chance. He grabbed as many of the players as he could and yelled over the approaching sirens for the rest to follow. Bundling them into the waiting people carriers, they sped away to the relative safety of Olivia Valere where they would spend the rest of the night under his watchful gaze. For now, at least, he could relax in the knowledge that the guilty-looking faces of his players would not be staring at him from the front pages of the papers in the morning. And even if the boys were in the background, the action was such that not even the sharpest-eyed picture editor would spot them and make the connection.

The end-of-season energy was still burning bright though, and the coke rush needed somewhere to be released. By the time he had scored some bottles of Dom, the boys had already made a move on some of the female clubbers. Alec called Blandine and let her know the change of plans. She was with the police bailing out her girls who had suffered the multiple indignities of being assaulted, arrested and losing out on a lucrative night's work. It was going to take some doing, but Alec insisted they were squared away tonight.

'I don't care what it costs or how you do it. I can't run the risk of a bunch pissed-off hookers out there with stuff they can sell to the papers. You know the drill: wipe their phones of any awkward selfies and point out to them in words of one syllable the career benefits of keeping their mouths shut. Then, when you're done, the party's back on. The boys and girls are going to be back at the hotel by around 2.30 so you need to get the suite cleaned and restocked ready for our guests. The only thing that's changed is some of the faces. I'd say not all of them are working girls but who am I to judge? That's your department.'

'Fuck you, Alec,' she started, but he'd already hung up. The group had got its hands on some more of Columbia's finest and was starting to get its mojo back again. An hour or so of throwing dubious shapes and the pleasures of the dance floor were giving way to a desire for something more intimate: it was time to go. Alec went ahead to check that a bank of camera flashlights wasn't about to explode in their faces, then ushered the players and their new friends into the waiting vehicles.

Back at the hotel they weaved unsteadily into the party suite ignoring an extremely frosty-looking Blandine. She nodded imperceptibly at the girls she knew and fixed the others with a stare. She would need to keep her wits about her tonight.

Alec had been in the game long enough to know that footballers do everything as a team. The jacuzzi was soon the centre of the action again, this time with even fewer inhibitions. He'd seen enough rutting and roaring to last him a lifetime so this was the point where he drew a line. He let the boys knew they were on their own among the hyenas if they left the suite, then retreated to the sanctuary of his room.

It was 3.45 and, cracking open the minibar, Alec hooked a miniature of Grey Goose which he mixed with a diet coke. He reckoned he'd earned a drink, his first of the night. He pulled out a tiny bag of white power picked up from the nightclub table and inspected it. He could probably scrape a line together but he needed to sleep. As he slumped onto the bed, he felt a lump in his jacket pocket. It was Diego's phone. He hadn't meant to keep it but, in the confusion, had forgotten to give it back. He thought about calling Totò to find out what had happened to his player but decided against it. The long-term results of Diego's unfortunate incident would become clear in time whatever the agent might have to say about it. From Alec's perspective, none of the other players in the party would reveal the cause of the injury, so he was as sure as he could be that details of the evening's events would remain a mystery. Job done, until tomorrow.

Chapter 2

Alec woke up a few hours later momentarily unsure whether it was day or night. He lay there for a few minutes getting his bearings as memories of last evening came flooding back. He had seen it enough times to know that the final whistle of the season marks the start of a month of hedonism for some players, but he was still capable of being surprised by the extremes to which they would go. Most, of course, are quite restrained: some of the more committed even use the summer break to work on their fitness, returning to their clubs in better shape than when they left.

Of the others, those without young families typically jet off somewhere exotic with an equally exotic partner who pauses just long enough at the airport to make sure she's snapped with 'her beau', as the tabloids will inevitably call him. The family men usually de-camp to a luxury villa on one of the Costas where their worn-out bodies and fractured relationships get chance to recover from the de-mands of a playing schedule that has been relentless since Christmas. While they are there, their social scene relocates with them. It may not be Love Island exactly, but it's not far off. An idyllic oasis but without the unblinking eye of the Premier League's ever-rolling TV cameras.

Some, though, struggle with the lack of routine; for them there is no off switch and they bounce restlessly from one hotspot to anoth-er. There are the young foreign players who have effectively been traf-ficked from Africa or Latin America. They've been hawked around football clubs since they were teenagers and have lost contact and connection with their roots. They have nowhere that really feels like home anymore and are surrounded by people who flatter their egos while helping them spend their money. During the season the clubs are all over these prize assets like a second skin, but, for a few weeks in the summer, they are footloose and ready to party.

Then there are the senior players, the hellraisers who are old enough to know better but are either slow learners or past caring. They are addicted to the dopamine hit they get from pushing boundaries on and off the pitch. Once they've shrugged off the straight jacket of the season, they set their course for where the flame burns brightest. In this exposed state, the players are at huge risk of a kiss and tell especially when the tabloids will pay big money for a story. Unless they are doing something completely outrageous, journalists aren't usually that interested in the singletons, but once there's a permanent WAG on the scene, it's a different story. The glamourous wedding photos and glossy home feature in *Hello!* sell magazines, but so does the tabloid sting when our boy comes stumbling out of a nightclub with a new gold digger on his arm. And these days there is always somebody around with a smartphone ready to record their moment of madness too.

Alec Munday numbered both young and older players among his clients whom he coaxed, cajoled and bullied into forming a profitable relationship with the media. With the smart ones, he would use the press to raise their profile, making their money back through lucrative endorsements, media opportunities and even transfer offers which sometimes came in as a bi-product. For the wayward ones, he would cultivate a wild child persona which they were usually only too happy to live up to. He knew well the reasons why players tried to transfer from the back pages of the papers to the front, but he always warned them what would happen when they grabbed the tiger's tail.

'The British press don't play by any fair rules of engagement,' he counselled. 'It's a question of whether they'll shaft you, but how far they'll stick it in.' Even the most irreproachably clean living found themselves shafted at some point. When they did, Alec's experience meant he could often kill a story, but if that wasn't possible, he was on hand to steer his footballing clientele through the occupational hazards of life in the public gaze.

He had seen enough players struggle to cope with the trappings of fame not to judge them, but the one thing he asked for from his clients was honesty. The press couldn't abide a hypocrite and a particularly hot corner of media hell is reserved for the apparently clean-cut Roy-of-the-Rovers type if he is caught betraying his wife, his club or his country. He had seen more than one player lose sponsors, career prospects, family and reputation almost overnight and was determined it wouldn't happen to any in his care. Had things worked out differently with his own playing career he would have been in their position and glad of the help. As it was, he turned his skills to working on their behalf and his task for these few days was to keep the party on course which meant avoiding any more disasters.

As details of last night's incident loomed larger in his mind, Alec reached reflexively for his mobile phone. He would have been called if the story was out there, but he quickly reviewed the websites of the British tabloids and *O Dia* in Brazil just in case. He found no reference to Diego or the events at the nightclub and, by the time *Hola! Brasil* was published, the trail would be well and truly cold. For now, at least, the story was contained.

He made himself a double espresso from the in-room coffee machine then checked his overnight emails. There was nothing that couldn't wait, so he picked up Diego's phone and saw a stream of Instagram notifications, texts and WhatsApp messages that would be a red-top journalist's wet dream. In among the many messages was a one-liner from Totò addressed to him simply asking him to arrange to return the phone. No thanks and no news, but Alec expected nothing less. When their cash cow was at risk, guys like him were nothing if not focused. Diego had a day-to-day point of contact assigned to him by his agent, but Totò was almost certainly on a plane to London by now to take charge of the situation himself. There would be some difficult conversations with the club in the weeks to come and the intermediary would not leave that to his minions. Alec also suspected he had a personal hold over the player, an interest that went beyond football which he would try to shore up at all costs. The world Totò operated in was infested with sharks and there was too much of a feeding frenzy around Diego for him to risk anyone else getting a bite.

Alec showered quickly glancing sideways at his reflection in the full-length mirror. This morning was not the moment to dwell on the slightly loose skin around his middle, the puffy red eyes or the journalist's pallor. He would need to put in a serious shift at the gym and use some of those miracle lotions the players were always promoting to keep his youthful footballer's looks. For now, though, he just splashed cold water on his face, slicked back his hair and pulled on jeans and loafers. A polo shirt completed the sports-casual look: classic but anonymous. Before he left the privacy of his hotel room he put calls through to a couple of British media contacts. News of an incident involving a player of Diego's profile would soon leak and he had to fill in at least the basic gaps to stop the pack sniffing any more of a story.

He told them 'off the record' that Diego had picked up a minor foot injury whilst on holiday. Doctors were still assessing, but he was expected to make a complete and rapid recovery although there was a chance he would not be fit for the start of the season. They pushed him for more details, but he shut them down and promised he'd talk to them first if there were any developments. With no juicy details and most of the club's management unavailable for comment, there was a decent chance the story would make no more than a couple of lines in the news-in-brief columns. Getting it out in a controlled way was also Alec's chance to give Vic Vickers the heads up as he would be left to pick up the pieces for the club.

He took the lift upstairs to the party suite where Blandine was busy mopping up, both physically and emotionally. The pros were easier, of course: for them last night had been a transaction and they had recognised the dollar signs early on. Blandine told them in no uncertain terms that this was not going to be their Pretty Woman moment, then softened the blow with a handout of either cash or coke, whichever was going to buy their silence. As well as the working girls there were two English teenagers who were fast waking up to the reality they were about to be parted from the footballer of their dreams. The disappointment and wounded pride combined to produce floods of tears as Blandine gathered up soiled knickers and got ready to bundle them out of the door. She promised she would personally make sure that Stevie and Silvan got their numbers and would call them the following evening but, for now, she just needed to check their phones.

By lunchtime her work was done and the players were ready to reconvene for the main order of business; a day on a racetrack and a drive through the mountain passes of the Sierra Blanca. It would be more Top Gear than F1, but it was still the reason why the boys had agreed to shell out ten grand each for the privilege.

It's an uncomfortable truth that the smooth-talking salesmen of Ferrari, Bugatti and McClaren tend to gloss over, but there is practically nowhere in Europe to drive their supercharged toys to anything like their full potential. The cities are clogged, speed cameras lurk on every stretch of open road and, with smart motorways spreading like an oil slick, it is increasingly difficult for a red-blooded male with 600 or more wild horses under the bonnet to have any fun at all. All of which is massively frustrating for the young thrill-seeking footballer. The older players have worked out that a high-spec Range Rover Overfinch provides if not a thrill, then at least street cred, comfort and anonymity. But it's a different story for the newly arrived Premier League sensation who has parted with north of

£200k for his first set of racing wheels. The frustration builds to the point where they are a danger to themselves and everyone else, at least, that's what Alec told himself. By giving the lads the chance to let off steam he was doing a favour to their families, other road users and the emergency services everywhere.

Down in the hotel reception the footballers had shrugged off any lingering effects of last night and were ready to roll. Liverpudlian Steven McBrien a.k.a. Stevie Mac, one of the older players, had a well-deserved reputation for signing as many personal endorsements as his agent could squeeze onto his tracksuit. Ignoring the battering he got from the rest of the lads, he strode across the lobby in full racing leathers sporting logos from at least a dozen household brands including Nivea, Persil and Durex.

'Hey, look out lads. Here comes Logo Man,' said Danny Duckham. 'If this was boxing, Stevie, your agent would get you a decent fee for putting logos on the bottom of your boots.'

'The only place he needs a logo is underneath his car,' said Premier League journeyman Nikolai Ruslanov, his accent a curious cocktail of Russian with a hint of Mancunian after eight years playing in the North of England.

'Alright, Metro,' Stevie shot back at Duckham, well aware that the best form of defence was attack. 'Got your moisturiser packed?'

Metro, (a name of Stevie's own invention and short for metrosexual), tried to shift his manbag out of view, but it was grabbed by the Logo Man and soon an assortment of luxury grooming products was flying between the players. A cheer went up as Alec arrived at just the right moment to catch a tube of collagen and marine serum anti-aging cream.

'Morning boys. All well, are we? Plenty of coffee on board? How's it going Danny? The last time I saw you, you looked like you'd grown a third leg,' he said, as the rest laughed. 'Anyway, what goes on tour and all that, yeh. It'll take around 15-minutes to drive to the

compound where your cars are parked up, so if everyone's ready, let's
go.'

Three people carriers ferried the players to a dusty enclosure a
few miles out of town to connect with probably the most expensive
concentration of road-legal supercars in Spain. They had been
shipped to Bilbao by ferry then ridden on transporters the length
of the country to await their impatient owners. Alec stood back as
their host and guide, former F1 driver Pedro de la Rosa, came to
meet them. The players listened with grins on their faces as de la Rosa
described the white-knuckle drive through the mountains that lay
ahead of them. He lowered his voice to a conspiratorial whisper as
he let them in on the 'exclusive raceday experience' that would come
later at the Circuito Ascari.

'This is "money can't buy"', said the Spaniard, looking around the
group.

Alec begged to differ: it could, and it had, but fortunately the
point was lost amid the anticipation of a day spent in their personal
version of Fast and Furious. Despite buying ever more expensive and
impractical vehicles, most footballers struggle to bay park in a supermarket, so there was every chance half the cars would come back
with some improvised body styling. Be that as it may, the players
were buzzing and high-fived each other at the end of the safety briefing before clambering into their Lambos, A8s and AMG GT R Mercedes. The engines roared, rattling the windows of the briefing hut,
and the smell of exhaust fumes filled the air as they eased out of the
parking garage and onto the road.

Alec allowed himself a wry smile as he watched the cars disappear into the heat haze. Was he jealous? Of course he bloody was, but
he had no time to regret what might have been. With the boys out of
the way, he was due a conversation with Blandine. The fact that last
evening had not been a complete disaster was no excuse and largely
down to him. She had been in charge when a top international foot-

baller had been badly injured, she had allowed the party to spiral out of control and into the street, her girls had unleashed fury outside Tibu and she had had the nerve to complain when he'd got things back on track.

He tracked her down outside the Portside bar, his anger building all the while. When he saw her, smoking and sipping Perrier, he paused taking in the view whilst mentally rehearsing his speech. She was in her early 30s and effortlessly chic in that way which requires an immense effort and the kind of wardrobe budget that French women seem to accept as the price of aging. Moving closer he admired her tanned legs, short silk shift dress and flawless makeup. She had tousled beach-toned blonde hair but enough steel behind her eyes to leave no one in any doubt that she was well able to keep a rash of working girls in order. He felt his resolve slipping.

When challenged, Alec Munday was not an aggressive man, preferring to rely on his natural affability rather than risk confrontation with the ever-attendant possibility of violence. He would have hit Blandine with both barrels but, in truth, she was just the help. The real discussion would have to be had with her boss, Marko, when he got back to London. Last night's escapade had very nearly blown the entire enterprise out of the water and it couldn't be allowed to happen again. Alec's relationships in the game were pivotal to his livelihood and his highest-profile contact had just been badly burned. Marko needed to know that his golden goose had almost got the chop and to take his responsibilities more seriously next time. Or at least pay Alec a lot more for his trouble.

As he approached the table Blandine looked up, smiled disarmingly and Alec folded. He slumped into a chair opposite her, the long night suddenly catching up with him.

'You look like shit,' she said laughing. 'How can I make it better?'

'You know exactly how, Blandine.'

This was their third time of working together in various locations, and Alec still wasn't sure whether she actually liked him or simply used him to satisfy her own physical needs. Either way, at this moment he didn't care. An afternoon of uncomplicated sex was just what he needed. He ordered coffee and a bocadillo de jamon serrano and felt himself relaxing for the first time since the party had arrived in Spain the previous afternoon.

'Do you know what I think, Blandine? I think you love winding me up just so that you can unwind me afterwards.'

'I never heard you complaining up to now.'

'Maybe, but last night was a close one. You know that at least three of our boys have got problems at home. A roasting in the media would finish off their marriages and their sponsors would be running for the exits in short order soon afterwards.'

'What's this, mon cheri, a conscience?' She pouted, blowing smoke towards the street, her expression drowsy with ennui.

'Maybe, but this is a decent gig, and it won't last five minutes if the papers catch our clients with their pants round their ankles.'

'Then they are very lucky to have you looking after them, and you are very lucky to have me looking after you.'

He finished his sandwich quickly, rose from his seat and made to pay the bill.

'You're in a hurry,' she said, still laughing at him.

'And you're starting to wind me up again. Let's go.'

They walked back to the hotel with Blandine lingering tantalizingly in front of each designer store they passed, but back in his room it was a different story. She slipped quickly out of her dress before turning to undress Alec with practised efficiency. She had always been more than happy to make the running, but this afternoon she left him scratched and bitten as she took her pleasure.

When they had finished, he slept deeply, waking four hours later to find her gone. Feeling a pang of guilt, Alec fished out his phone to call his girlfriend, Sophie. Looking at the screen, he saw seven missed calls: two from one of the players, one from de la Rosa and four from Vic Vickers. Sophie forgotten, he was back on duty and it looked like he was in for another long night.

Chapter 3

The black BMW parked on Threadneedle Street was indistinguish-
able from dozens of oversized German saloons carefully depositing
captains of industry and commerce at their City offices. Its engine
had cut out, without a trace of irony, as a consideration of the health
of passers by. All around it, luxury sedans came and went. Once their
cars were empty the drivers headed either to one of several transport
cafes to the east of London to await further instructions, or to the
five-star hotels of the West End to ferry a steady stream of the super-
rich to Heathrow's first-class lounges. But the black BMW was on
a different mission. Its occupants were hidden behind privacy glass
and it remained still, silent and brooding in its place. Not that anyone would notice and it was too early to attract the attentions of the
City's army of traffic wardens

A mile away, Michaela Dagg was alone on the street walking
briskly through the crisp spring morning. She was slim and athletic
and every inch the City professional with clear blue eyes, alabaster
skin and a brittle confidence to match. Her only concessions to the
business of the day were patent leather lace-up shoes in place of her
usual low-heeled court shoes and a warrant card in her pocket. She
had seen the sunrise from her flat in Shoreditch then left at 7.00 to
take the short walk down the Bethnal Green Road towards the tem-
ples of glass and steel that made up London's financial district.

For officers in the neighbouring Metropolitan Police, a dawn
raid meant exactly that: forced entry at the time when a drug den
or terrorist lair was at its most vulnerable. But for the City of London Police, dawn, which in March was around 6.15, was a time when
their criminal element was at its most impregnable. The global markets may never sleep, but City banks remain firmly shuttered behind
bombproof doors until at least 7.00. In the case of Pepys Lyon it
was even later. An elderly porter in morning coat and grey striped

trousers would open up reluctantly to employees at around 8.20 and never to members of the public without prior appointment. The moment of his appearance was the time chosen by Detective Inspector Dagg and her team to make their move.

Notorious US criminal, Willie Sutton, when asked why he robbed banks, replied "Because that's where the money is." The City of London accounts for the largest volume of financial transactions and is home to the highest concentration of financial institutions anywhere on earth. The sheer volume of capital is enough to attract criminals from all around the world although not for reasons Willie Sutton would have recognised: it is simply the perfect place to hide the proceeds of criminal enterprise in plain sight.

While the appeal is obvious, those looking to put The City's institutions to work to shelter ill-gotten gains face considerable obstacles. It is governed by some of the tightest regulatory controls of any global financial centre and the City of London Police are world leaders in fighting financial crime. UK Border Force grabs the headlines with its drug seizures, but behind the grimy windows of a nondescript office building on the borders of the Square Mile lies an operation which, although modest in scale, regularly unearths financial crimes accounting for millions if not billions of pounds.

For criminals, their first challenge is to persuade banks that their money is clean enough to accept and that means money laundering. It was DI Dagg's job to put as many barriers in their way as possible, and as she did so, she gained a certain notoriety among the banking professionals which whom she mixed day to day. Bankers view money laundering as the purview of compliance departments staffed by spectral individuals kept far away from public view. They detest these fastidious phantoms who seem hell bent on capping their bonuses by turning away perfectly good customers or asking them to jump through small and awkwardly shaped hoops before accepting their business. The police rely on these very same bankers to give them access to information and client data and, with such an arrangement, it is almost inevitable that a certain amount of what both sides liked to call 'flexibility' will be shown.

For Michaela Dagg, flexibility started and stopped at the door or her yoga class: as far as police work was concerned, it simply wasn't in her vocabulary. Combine that with a forensic attention to detail and doggedness bordering on the bloody minded, and she became a thorn in the side of any banker whose customers were less than forthcoming with details of their true identities or source of their wealth. Not that this affected her standing in the Unit, quite the opposite. The Proceeds of Crime Act meant that uncovering dirty money was a nice little earner for the CoLP and Dagg was one of its top providers, which in no small part accounted for her rapid promotion through the ranks. She was the youngest member of the team she led which might in other Police units have caused her problems, but she had earned the right to be called ma'am and no one disputed it. She was also a natural at managing the bankers she encountered who treated her much like they would Pope's ring: they all lined up to kiss her but none of them knew what she might catch. Always ambitious, at her first Nick in Tottenham she had taught herself Turkish to stand a better chance of disrupting the local gangs. Now, she had learned a new language, that of the City, and she spoke it like a native.

Pepys Lyon had been providing discreet merchant banking services in the Square Mile since the 1740s when two of the original financiers of The East India Company formed an alliance by marriage. The arrangement proved fruitful in all aspects but one and the elderly partners were beginning to despair that their bond would not survive more than a generation. A baby boy did finally appear, but the habit of male Pepys Lyons putting off for as long as possible the tiresome business of siring an heir, became ingrained. Hence there were only six generations spanning the 280 years of the bank's existence and, despite his father dying well into his 80s, the current Chairman was barely 30 when he took over. Sir Edward Pepys Lyon – nicknamed Sextus – had little experience and even less interest in banking, so when a friend from Eton recommended he fund a government-backed hospital building project, he agreed. The project promptly collapsed leaving a tidy hole in the bank's capital and earning the novice banker a reputation as an extremely unsafe pair of hands. A suitably chastened Sextus was modest enough to accept his fellow shareholders' suggestion that his become a more titular role and he went back to what he loved doing most; being a self-styled adventurer. With the Chairman effectively side lined, the board instituted a series of changes of direction which profoundly altered the nature of the bank's business. One by one the old money families, who had banked with Pepys Lyon for generations, took their money elsewhere while Sir Edward ran the Marathon des Sables or road horseback across the Hindu Kush. As his bank was taken captive, Sextus wasn't so much asleep at the wheel as freediving off the side of the boat.

He was greeted by obsequious flunkies when he attended quarterly board meetings and blinded by glitzy powerpoints showing the bank's finances were in rude and rosy health. Reserves had been rebuilt, the loan book was small and practically risk free and fee income was soaring. Had Sir Edward chosen to turn over a rock or two, he would have found things rather murkier. The rise in fees was due entirely to an unprecedented amount of money washing through several recently opened accounts the beneficial owners of which were opaque to say the least. One of the departing family trustees chose to tip off the regulator and Pepys Lyon was flagged up by the FSA to Dagg's unit for investigation.

Its banking licence listed owners in Luxemburg, but it took Dagg just twenty minutes to establish that it was highly likely Pepys Lyon had been hijacked by a third party and put to use as an industrial scale money laundering factory. It took another three months of painstaking work to amass enough hard evidence to persuade her superiors and a reluctant judge that one of the City's most venerable institutions should be raided, but in the end, the case was overwhelming. Ordinarily, when she needed something tying criminals to the movement of money, Dagg would arrange to serve notice on the bank concerned and be given access to their records. In the case of Pepys Lyon, she could prove that, rather than the bank's clients, it was the bank itself that was corrupt. The institution had become a front for a collection of financial interests linked directly to Serbian organised crime. She was convinced that it was at the heart of a criminal network and persuaded the Common Serjeant of London, the City's second most senior judge, that the usual courtesies allowing the board to get its house in order should be withheld. She got her warrant on Shrove Tuesday, Mardi Gras in many countries and, although she wasn't religious, Dagg was looking forward to bringing the Pepys Lyon party to an end. There was a ripple of excitement as she briefed her team most of whose memories of kicking down doors were distant at best. No resistance was anticipated and they would be supported by a dozen uniformed officers, but it would be different from the keyboard war they were usually engaged in. The obligatory drink after work was kept to a single pint but otherwise the prospect of a raid was seen as no more than a welcome distraction.

Now, at 7.45 on Ash Wednesday, they were reconvening, hot beverages in hand, in two unmarked vans parked in a quiet side street. By sheer coincidence, Sextus was also in the City that morning. He could have been in Laos or Liberia and probably had been recently, but last evening he had been staying in rooms at his Livery Hall on Threadneedle Street in preparation for a Pepys Lyon board meeting. As Michaela was walking down Bishopsgate, he was among the early morning joggers having completed a 5-mile circuit south of the river. He returned across London Bridge, passed up Gracechurch

Street and turned onto Bishopsgate. Not being a fan of the coffee at the Hall, he ducked into a branch of Costa to pick up a takeaway.

Less than 200 yards away, DI Dagg was nearing her destination and using the rhythm of her steps to tick off the details of the raid in her mind. Alert and focused she perceived nothing to set alarm bells ringing as she entered Threadneedle Street. The police officer's legendary instinct for danger is in reality more street sense than sixth sense. There are those who swear that a highly attuned cerebellum has kept generations of their evolutionary forbears alive despite the best efforts of dinosaurs, devils or deviants. But, when science interrogates their claims, the reality turns out to be more prosaic: an unfamiliar car parked in the wrong place, an unconscious gesture or a glance exchanged between persons of interest which put the already wary copper on the alert.

Police officers in the Square Mile are blessed with an abundance of data, almost none of it of any significance. The streets around the Bank of England are a complex system of activity that is hard to get a feel for, even for a foot patrol. For someone whose investigations are conducted by mostly by computer it is impossible. Michaela Dagg was not inattentive but the hair on the back of her neck never once prickled as she passed the black BMW and strode on purposefully. She failed to register any threat as its engine coughed into life and was therefore taken completely by surprise when, as she crossed Finch Lane, it appeared as if out of nowhere and mowed her down. By the time Sextus had paid for his flat white and rounded the corner, the car was gone and the only indication that anything had happened was a small crowd gathered a hundred yards or so ahead of him as he re-entered the Hall.

Chapter 4

The crowd at an FA Cup game is as tribal as they come.

'Run it. Tackle 'im. Chase 'im, you lazy bastard.'

'E don't like Munday, 'e don't like Munday, 'e don't like Munday, 'e's gonna shoo, ooh, ooh, ooh, ooh, oot, the whole day down.'

'Get on 'im. Fuckin' tackle 'im. Take 'is fuckin' legs out.'

'E don't like Munday, 'e don't like Munday, 'e don't like Munday, 'e's gonna shoo, ooh, ooh, ooh, ooh, SHOOOOT. GOOOOOAAAAAL!'

'E's comin' again. 'E's takin' the fuckin' piss. Fuckin' get 'im. Take 'im out, you fat cunt.'

'E don't like Munday, 'e don't like Munday, 'e don't like Munday, 'e's gonna shoo, ooh, ooh, ooh, oooooaaaaggggghh, fuckin' 'ell.'

The tackle, when it came in, was as bad as anyone in the stands had ever seen. Two footed, off the ground and totally out of control. Alec Munday went up in the air and when he landed, his left ankle was facing in completely the wrong direction.

The lads were sympathetic and the club did what they could. He got the best medical care and they kept paying his wages but, after months of treatment, it was clear there was going to be no way back. He had injury insurance which gave him a year free of any financial worries, but then Alec needed a job. Like many young players before him, he had spent most of his school days playing football rather than studying, but his teachers had said he had a good brain and a flair for English. He started writing to fill the empty hours although in those early months his copy could most kindly be described as functional. What he did have was what many aspiring sports journalists lacked – access to footballers and football managers – and, with plenty of time to practice, he was soon scratching a living serving up interviews for some of the many fanzines and football websites.

Most of us can look back on pivotal moments when an apparently random event changes the course of the rest of our lives. Alec's first came when he suffered his injury just as he was playing his way into the starting line-up. His second came in the form of a chance encounter with the sports editor of *The Guardian* newspaper, Dominic Fordyce. It was early one weekday evening in July, and Alec was in a pub in Mayfair waiting for a couple of his former teammates who he was joining for the Professional Footballers' Association annual awards dinner. The pub was a popular hangout and filling up with the usual after-work crowd who spilled out onto the street. The journalist was there too grabbing a pie and a pint ahead of a long and probably fruitless evening trying to secure interviews with the winning players. He would normally have sent a junior reporter, but his budget had been cut and he was already in a foul mood when Alec backed away from the bar and knocked his drink over. Fordyce cursed as the beer soaked into his shirt and disappeared between the keys of his laptop. The drink was easily replaced but Alec could see the damage he'd done and wanted to do more to make amends.

'Oh look, I'm really sorry mate. Can I give you something for the dry-cleaning bill?'

Fordyce's instinct was to chin him, but he had been around enough footballers to recognise the type, so he chanced his arm and said: 'Don't worry about it. If you can get me into the PFA dinner, we'll call it quits.'

'No problem. You might need a clean shirt though,' came the hoped-for reply, and the two were destined to be friends from that moment on.

Although their style, tone and economy with the truth may be different, journalists who write for tabloid newspapers are in almost every respect the same as those whose wordier prose fills the columns of Her Majesty's so-called quality press. A paper like *The Guardian* may sneer at The Sun's boobs and bold headlines, but its sports editor shares the same unhealthy obsession with the inner workings of the football industry as his red top counterparts. Alec worked his mag-

ic with the organisers and Fordyce found himself in the middle of
his own personal fantasy league sitting at a table with nine Premier League footballers and surrounded on every side by the biggest
names in the English game. Completely star struck, he didn't get so
much as a soundbite from any of the players, but he was totally sold
on Alec who he knew was his key to unlocking the sport.

At the end of the evening, the two shared a taxi together and
Alec's story came out. The journalist listened intently and promised
he'd be in touch as he climbed out of the car and staggered into the
night. Alec didn't think much more about it, but by the time he
opened his eyes blearily the next morning there was a text message
waiting for him.

'Hi mate, give me a call. I've got a proposition for you. Dom.'

Direct From The Dressing Room was the column the two came
up with at a meeting in *The Guardian*'s offices a couple of days later.
The idea was that Alec would use his privileged access to go beyond
the usual pundit's blather and get the scoop on the stories behind
each round of Premier League games. Just why had the manager left
out his star player? What was that melee in the players' tunnel all
about? And what was really in the mind of the normally rock solid
striker as he skied that penalty? *Guardian* readers would know and
everyone else would buy the paper to find out. It would have to be
written anonymously so that the players could speak without fear of
recriminations, but for Alec it was the perfect opportunity. He could
stay in regular contact with his mates in football and get some journalistic experience with one of the national dailies, even if he didn't
get a byline. Keeping the column anonymous suited Fordyce who
privately had his doubts that Alec would be able to deliver for more
than a few weeks but, in the end, he was pleasantly surprised. The
former player worked hard and his writing improved under the guid-
ance of one of the paper's sub editors. The new column gained a huge
readership and was regularly referred to by TV and radio pundits for

the accuracy of its revelations. It also performed a genuine public service by giving insiders the chance to correct some of the more persistent myths around the game.

Alec found it took him a bit longer to be accepted by the other journos but, using his contacts as currency, he found his place. His writing style may never have reached the heights of some of his new colleagues, but he had a popular touch and an intuitive feel for a good story. That natural flair meant he was as successful at getting a piece into print as he was at getting it hushed up, and he did both with skill as the situation required.

He found his credibility as a former player and now media expert was useful to the sport as well, and he developed a profitable side-line running media training on behalf of several Premier League clubs. His favourite trick was to plaster the walls of a conference room with large posters of topless glamour models. He would then invite the players in, leaving them for a few minutes to appreciate the view. Having got their attention, he would deliver his payoff line: 'Any one of these girls could wreck your career and your life.' It was corny, but it gave him the chance to help the younger ones understand the predatory nature of the world they were entering.

He was a natural with the younger boys and many, especially those brought in from abroad, saw him as someone from outside their club who they could confide in. He was soon advising some of the biggest names in English football including some high-profile Latin American and African players which was how, a couple of years into his new career, he managed to take on Diego.

He had just wrapped up a training session at one of the London clubs and was chatting with some of the team who he had been working with. A shock of platinum blond hair caught his eye and he glanced over to the corner of the room to see a pale, diminutive boy who didn't look much more than fifteen years old. Alec knew who he was, of course; you don't get to sign for a new Premier League record without the world knowing your name. Diego was a rare and mercurial talent with the kind of lightening pace and poacher's instinct for goal that strikes fear into the hearts of defenders. For now, though, there was none of the usual swagger typical of someone with his exceptional talents. Beneath the confident spikes of his electric Mohican, the young man looked haunted and miserable.

'We're a bit worried about him.'

The voice belonged to Danny 'Vic' Vickers, the club's player liaison officer, and it was quite an admission from the ultimate behind the scenes man. Vickers was a warm and cuddly character who, although he wore the club's training kit, looked like he'd not kicked a ball in anger for a many a long year. He took a lot of stick from the youngsters over his lack of fitness but underneath they all adored him. Like all PLOs, he was a vital lubricant in the club's machine. Whether it was sorting out a rented house for a new signing or telling him where to park his Ferrari when he arrives for his first training session, Vic was the one whose job it was to surround the club's most expensive assets with the love and attention they needed to give their best on the pitch.

A club man through and through, Vickers had been part of the inner circle for decades and was fiercely loyal, but his real gift was as a father figure to players who can be notoriously hard to handle. After the hairdryer treatment from the manager, Vic would have a quiet word, nurse bruised egos on both sides and, more often than not, find a way back into the fold for someone whose every instinct is to walk away. But this time he looked a worried man.

'I've not seen it before,' he said. 'Normally if their personal life's in a mess, we all know about it when they're on the pitch, but Diego's doing well in training and he's started scoring. It's just when he's not playing, he's like a ghost. No one can get a word out of him and he's not mixing with the rest of the lads. I got Darren to have a chat with him, you know as a senior player, get him to open up a bit, but he got nowhere either. I wouldn't trust that agent of his as far as I could throw him, but he insists it's just a bit of homesickness. The boy says he's fine, of course, but you and I both know that, with a high-profile player like him, it's not going to be long before his mood starts having an effect on the dressing room.'

'Do you want me to have a go with him?' Alec offered. 'He might respond to someone who's not directly connected to the club.'

'I'm not keen, Alec. Obviously, it doesn't reflect well on me, but I don't think the chairman would be too happy either, knowing someone who's not on the team is working with him.'

'It doesn't need to be anything official, mate. I'll just have a friendly word and see how he reacts.'

Alec had spent his two years in journalism honing his interview technique, not that anyone would call it that. He had just developed a knack for getting players to relax, and before long they were telling him things they would have kept secret from even their closest friends. He never betrayed their confidence unless someone asked him to work it into the Direct From The Dressing Room column, but by now he had more than enough material for at least one sensational book.

There has long been speculation around gay players in football, but Alec Munday was one of the few in the game who knew more than one or two personally. Drugs in the sport? Not too much in Alec's experience, but he could tell you who was taking what and probably who his dealer was. He knew intimate details of infidelities and family breakdowns, and he had seen enough to know that good mental health didn't automatically come with a huge pay packet. He found it was good for business to do a bit of research into any new players on the scene, so he wasn't entirely working blind as he poured two coffees and sat down uninvited next to Diego.

'What do you think your brother's going to be doing around now?'

The player looked up, immediately reticent, then shrugged and said in heavily accented English, 'He'll for sure be racing today.'

The myth that all Brazilian players have come from the favelas of Rio is in most cases a long way from the truth. Diego's family were from a middleclass suburb of Brazil's largest city, São Paulo, where his father worked for the local government and his mother was a dental technician. As young teenagers, both he and his younger brother Luiz were sports mad, splitting their affiliation between the Corinthians Paulista football club and an addiction to go-karting. The family celebrated when Diego was signed at fourteen as by Corinthians' Youth Academy but, quietly, Luiz was also carving out a sporting career following in the footsteps of the boys' childhood idol, Felipe Massa.

The brothers followed parallel tracks in their respective sports until Corinthians revealed their full intentions. In common with many top Brazilian clubs, one of their biggest money spinners is the export of promising young players. Corinthians greased the right palms and got their boy a berth in the national team although, in truth, a star like Diego was always destined to be play on the biggest stage for his country. And so the same conveyor belt that brought Neymar and Dani Alves to Barcelona saw the 23-year-old come to London. None of this bothered the player; he was ready for the move and happy to take his chances. Several of his fellow Canarinhos had made the switch to London, and his young wife was also excited at the prospect.

No, his problem was much less complicated. At the very moment he was signing his life away to make the move to London, brother Luiz was winning the annual Felipe Massa charity go-karting race, The Challenge of the Stars.

'When I think what my brother is doing, I think I did the wrong decision,' he told Alec, his body language revealing the depth of his misery. 'He's gonna be soon driving in Indycar and I wish it was me.'

Alec thought for a minute then said: 'Ok, what we're going to do now is probably against every rule in your club handbook, but let's get out of here. I can't get you into Indycar, but we can at least give you a reminder of what it's like.'

He winked at Vickers as the two left the conference room and took Diego's Maserati from the training ground to an indoor karting centre north of London. Two hours later the player came off the track saying, 'This is the worst go-karting I ever did.' But he had a smile on his face when Alec delivered him back to the club. With a bit of string pulling and arm twisting, Alec engineered a couple of sessions with a Formula 4 team where the player could really let rip. The two became firm friends from then on and, although the quality of the racing improved, Diego would always refer back to that first time spent dodging the corporate team builders and local boy racers at Full Throttle Karting. A couple of drives later, Vickers pulled Alec aside.

'I don't know what you've done with him, but Diego's like a different person. We owe you one.'

'It's probably best you don't know, Vic, but I'll try and make sure he doesn't break his neck. As for owing me, I'm sure we'll think of ways you can pay me back.'

A couple of weeks later Alec's phone went. It was Diego calling from the training ground. 'Hey man, the guys want to go racing,' he said.

'Have a day off, Diego. I thought we said you weren't going to let on to anyone.'

'They won't tell,' the player giggled, and passed the phone to one of the others.

'Alec,' came a familiar voice. It was Danny Duckham. 'I thought you were a mate. How come the rest of us aren't going driving? I just got me a new R8 and I need somewhere it can stretch it's legs.'

In the background the chorus of demands was growing and Alec knew he had little choice. 'All right, keep it down. You know what Vic would say. Look, I'll sort something out for next week, but keep it to yourselves, yeh. When's your day off?'

'Nice one, mate,' said Danny, and a cheer went up among the others. 'We're playing Sunday so see what you can do for Monday.'

'Leave it with me,' said Alec, knowing this would be just the start. He knew there were risks but the opportunity was too good to miss, so he pushed his doubts aside and googled 'driving experiences in the South East'.

When the day came, he sat up front with Diego at the head of a line of garishly coloured supercars heading up the M11. The disused airfield he had found outside Cambridge offered only spartan facilities but the adrenaline rush of going full throttle meant the trip was an instant hit. After that, the clamour for a proper trackday was irresistible and Alec was soon familiar with England's minor motor racing circuits. Third time out, players from other clubs started to muscle in and it became inevitable that a rainy day at Snetterton would start to lose its appeal. When a Grand Tour of mountain passes and F1 tracks was mentioned, Alec knew he was going to need help.

Top-flight footballers are surrounded by a retinue of agents, advisors, dubious friends and hangers on giving them questionable advice and new ideas for spaffing their cash. Alec felt he had a duty of care to his clients, but he knew others were a lot less scrupulous. He would have liked to find his own people to make the arrangements, but Garry, a hulking centre back, mentioned a guy he knew who knew a guy who could fix it up. The others piled in and before long things had slid out of his control.

Garry was holding a birthday party for his wife a few days later and had used the guy in question to make the arrangements. He had been talked into renting out Cliveden country house, former seat of the Aster family, for a Great Gatsby party. Garry had also been persuaded to throw more money at the occasion by hiring a Michelin starred chef and bringing in a DJ from Ibiza.

'Alec, it's going to be the perfect opportunity. Just come along, talk to my guy and you can get everything set up,' he said.

Alec tried to protest but he knew he was up against an irresistible force. And so, much against his better judgement, he found himself working with Marko Vasic.

Chapter 5

Alec returned from Marbella to a stormy reception. He had deliberately taken a later plane than the lads on the pretext that he needed to wrap things up with the hospital. Sophie was not an overly possessive type and would have known that his opportunity to call her was going to depend on what came up at the party. She was, however, less likely to overlook the scratches on his back which made it obvious just what had been keeping him busy, so he made sure to arrive home at a time when he knew she would be in bed.

The modest Enfield house which they had shared for the past three months was in darkness as his taxi drew up outside. Alec settled up with the driver and shut the car door quietly behind him. He took off his shoes on the doormat and padded silently upstairs. Sophie had left a light on beside the bed and with monumentally poor timing, she opened her eyes just as he was taking off his shirt. Not even the giant Toblerone he had brought back was going to be enough to prevent a domestic. For someone who had been asleep just moments before, she was impressively quick to go thermonuclear. Alec found himself dispatched to the spare room where he remained until after he heard the front door slam the next morning. When he did emerge, he found his favourite shirt cut carefully into strips and thrown onto the floor. A nice touch he felt, as he pulled on a robe and went downstairs. Not finding the case he had stowed carefully in the hall, he glanced out of the window to see it and its contents spread around the front garden lest he be in any doubt about how furious Sophie was. He was rapidly coming to the view that this relationship probably wasn't going to go the distance.

He wandered into the kitchen cautiously, unsure what else she might have in store, but everything seemed to be as he'd left it with dodgy laminated floor, mismatched door handles and uneven draw fronts. His playing career had ended before he had been in a position to put any serious money away, so compared to his mates, the property was small and shabby, but it was at least paid for and that would do for now. Alec made himself a pint of coffee and sat down with his laptop at the breakfast bar to check his emails. Seeing nothing that required his immediate attention, he drafted a note to Marko.

'I'm coming over to see you this afternoon. We need to get a few things straight.'

He re-read the message, thought better of it and crafted something more conciliatory knowing that asking for the meeting was itself an indication that things had not gone smoothly in Spain. Finishing his coffee, he showered and dressed carefully in a business like grey suit and open-necked shirt then headed for Enfield Town station.

London's mayor claims the city is a melting pot for people of all races and cultures, but the reality is a lumpy mix of individuals and communities who live parallel rather than connected lives. Anonymous within the city sprawl, immigrants do what they do everywhere else in the world and band together for familiarity, culture and support. Those from Serbia favour West London and a number of Serbian food stores, restaurants, churches and businesses are clustered in and around Fulham making it an obvious choice for Marko's operation. Access to the heart of his business was through a Victorian building which had started life as a traditional corner shop with rooms above. It had been variously a restaurant, a bar and an art gallery, but each enterprise had failed and there was now a blank wall where the shop door had been.

It took Alec ten minutes to walk from Parsons Green to the address on Munster Road and if there was any doubt whether he had reached his destination, the large black BMW parked on the corner confirmed he was in the right place. He approached the windowless side door, buzzed the entry phone and stood back knowing that he was being observed. After a few seconds, the door clicked, and he pushed his way inside. He had been here once before, several weeks ago, and not much had changed. To his right there was a small hallway with a threadbare carpet lit by a single bulb hanging from the ceiling. Each of the three rooms leading off the corridor were secured with Yale locks and there was a communal bathroom and galley kitchen at the end. Midway along there was a staircase giving access to what was likely to be an identical setup on the first floor. There were no signs of life although the stale smell of cooking mixed with the stink of an overflowing rubbish bin indicated human regular habitation. Alec assumed that Marko, along with his other business interests, had jumped on the buy-to-let bandwagon.

He went through a single door to his left and across a courtyard walled in on three sides by buildings and on the fourth by a high fence topped with anti-climb spikes. Another door led to a staff less reception with a vending machine which looked more like the waiting room for a Kwik-Fit. Ahead of him a door was open to an open plan office in which half a dozen guys in screened booths talked excitedly into headsets. Before he could identify the subject of their conversations, Marko himself was in the room ushering Alec upstairs to the floor above.

'You walked, Alec,' he said. 'You should have let me know. I'd have sent a driver.'

Marko led his guest across a large room where four large men were playing cards at a table in the corner. The air was thick with smoke and the smell of damp suits as the pair entered Marko's office though a door on the opposite wall. The room was lit by a fluorescent strip above a battered desk on which stood a single computer monitor. Behind the desk was a large black leather chair flanked on one side by a metal filing cabinet and on the other by an ancient safe with its door hanging open. The green-painted walls were smoke stained and grimy with lighter-coloured rectangles presumably a legacy of the previous occupant's taste in artwork. The floor was an irregular checkerboard of mismatched carpet tiles and, at the window, a dusty vertical blind hung unevenly adding to the room's general air of neglect.

'Sit down, Alec,' said Marko from behind the desk, gesturing towards a corner and the room's only other chair. 'I'm glad you've come. I wanted to congratulate you on the job you did in Spain.'

'Yes, well, that job is why I'm here...'

'Of course, my friend,' Marko interrupted. 'I know you weren't happy, but I heard from Blandine that you handled things perfectly, so I'm sure we can sort everything out. As you say, let's put our cards on the table.'

As he spoke, he reached down into the safe and re-surfaced holding a slim envelope which he pushed across the desk.

'It's for you in recognition of your help when our footballers were in trouble.'

When Marko had first been mentioned as a friend of one of the players, Alec assumed he was a fixer who would provide some logistical help with travel and accommodation while he organised the entertainment. Now, a few weeks on, the boot was very much on the other foot. Marko was in charge; the contents of the envelope simply confirmed the nature of their arrangement.

Marko had not been at Cliveden, but Alec had met Blandine and was charmed as well as impressed with how she handled herself. In addition to organising the party, she had arranged escorts for several of the players and guarded a discreet corner of the venue where a range of recreational drugs was available. The enthusiasm with which some of the guests indulged suggested to Alec that her services might indeed prove useful. She gave him the personal mobile number of her boss and Alec made contact a couple of days later. He mentioned the name of the footballer who'd passed on his details and was greeted like an old friend. By the time he made the trip to Fulham his fate was sealed.

His first visit had left him uncertain as to Marko's main business, but by the time of their next meeting it was abundantly clear that party planning was no more than an opportunity to push his main products, namely girls and drugs. The Serbian had dominated the relationship from the start. Dressed as now in a dark suit and black shirt open at the collar, he was a bulky, fit-looking man in his late 30s. Had had the blunt Slavic features of a bull terrier and the kind of face that makes mothers pull their children closer. Alec had met some impressive specimens in football and he knew plenty of guys who would easily have beaten Marko in a fair fight but, after dark, in a back alley, Alec knew who his money would be on. His words were friendly in near perfect English and Alec never heard him raise his voice, but his smile never reached his eyes and there was no doubt who called the shots from the very first overseas outing.

'I know what these boys want. You just leave the arrangements to me. Don't worry, Alec. There'll be a job for you, of course. In fact, you'll be an important part of the operation as you know the players. These boys can get a bit crazy, and I think they need someone with them who they'll listen to. We don't want our business to attract any unwelcome publicity, do we?'

The trip was set for two weeks after their initial meeting, which coincided with an international break, and Alec had no trouble attracting 12 players from among his own contacts and Diego's friends. The itinerary looked straight forward enough – lunch on a private jet during the short hop from Northolt to Nice, helicopter transfer to Monte Carlo, check-in at the Fairmont Hotel followed by drinks and an evening in a Casino. The next day would be spent driving round the historic Paul Ricard racing circuit near Marseille, then a team dinner, nightclub, hotel and home the morning after. Alec was going along in his new capacity as media manager although he wasn't sure he'd be called upon. Monaco was so protective of its position as the playground of the rich and famous that he wasn't anticipating any attention, welcome or otherwise.

Things started off well enough. Alec went out the day before and was on hand to greet the players when they arrived at Nice airport pausing to give them his 15-second media briefing.

'It goes without saying – but I'm going to say it anyway – that what goes on tour stays on tour so, as far as the outside world is concerned, we were never here. That means no social media posts please, and keep the passion in the party suite unless you want the world to know about it.'

They were shuttled to Monaco Heliport then spent the afternoon walking the F1 Grand Prix circuit and visiting Prince Albert's collection of rare vintage cars. It was only when Blandine welcomed them to the Fairmont Hotel that the boys perked up and Alec started to get an inkling of the kind of night it was going to be.

The next hour and a half were spent on the kind of personal grooming routine that would have put a supermodel to shame. Faces were exfoliated and moisturised, every hair on both head and body was obsessively manscaped and fingernails and toenails were buffed to a sheen. When they entered the party suite they were suited and booted, primped and pumped and ready for a big one.

The drugs had shocked him at first even after Garry's party. In his experience, players had many vices but drug taking was not particularly common especially in an era where testing was increasingly common. But it was when the girls arrived that the party really got started. Blandine had excelled herself with the catering and the group drank champagne by the magnum before heading off to one of Monte Carlo's famed casinos. Most of the players went straight for the roulette table with a girl on their arm no doubt channelling their inner James Bond. Between them they must have dropped at least €50k over three hours with bragging rights going to one of the West

London boys who was deemed the winner by dint of having come closest to breaking even.

At midnight, when they were tired of losing money, they swapped the casino for Jimmy'z, Monte Carlo's self-styled temple of clubbing. Alec had secured the VIP area and they ordered more champagne as they sashayed unsteadily towards the dancefloor. Like most footballers, they were massive lightweights when it came to alcohol and practically fell out of the club a couple of hours later weaving their way noisily along the Avenue Princess Grace back to the Fairmont. Once there, if he had expected couples to pair off discretely, Alec got a rude awakening.

His tenure in the Premier League had not been long enough for him to have witnessed first-hand the wilder excesses of some players, but Alec had heard the stories from those who had. Even so he was surprised when the group started getting naked in the large jacuzzi. Some, like Diego, hung back, but the others led the way eagerly and soon the water was full of writhing bodies. The shag fest progressed onto the sofas with the grunts of the boys matched by the moans of the girls as the room seemed to move in rhythm. The noise levels increased with some of the players practically roaring and banging their chests as they reached a climax. Once it was done, they started all over again but Alec made himself scarce; there were some things he just wasn't paid enough to look at. He glanced at Blandine, trying to look cool as he made his way out of the suite. She simply shrugged in typically Gallic fashion and blew him a kiss. In future he would be better prepared, but for now, he had to get out of there.

There were a few sheepish looks when the players emerged late the following morning particularly from Diego, but a couple of coffees later, the banter started to flow as they got themselves hyped up for the driving. Diego wiped the floor with the rest of them on the track where his years of karting put him entire laps ahead. But, by the time the helicopter came to collect them, the boys were well satisfied and already talking about next time. When that time came the itinerary took them racing at Le Mans and partying in Paris, and Alec needed to take his media management role rather more seriously. He arrived in the French capital two days before the main party and had his first experience of just how friendly Blandine could be. He spent two blissful afternoons receiving a personal education in the full spectrum of French erotic arts and evenings negotiating with nightclubs and paparazzi.

When the players arrived and the partying started, he knew his job and executed it without a single misstep. He knew what to expect when the group returned to the hotel at the end of the evening and made a discreet exit but not before noticing that Diego was not so hesitant this time around. By the third and fourth trips both Alec and Diego were well and truly into their groove. Until that night in Marbella.

'This isn't just about money, Marko' Alec said, picking up the envelope anyway. 'These guys are my clients and their faces could have been plastered all over every newspaper in Europe. They depend on me to stop that happening and you need to take your share of the responsibility. After all, you're taking a large enough cut of the money and without them you don't have a business.'

Marko was unruffled. 'I have many businesses, but the footballers interest me.'

'That's my point. Footballers interest everyone, and if you want to keep taking their cash, I'm telling you, you've got to deliver.'

Alec's raised voice had silenced the group next door and he became aware of a presence behind him. Marko raised his hand and the presence withdrew.

'Let me tell you what we're going to do,' he said. 'In fact, it's something I've been planning for a while. Before their training starts again, we're going to take your friends on a really special holiday. To

Las Vegas. And I'm coming too. Can you get a crowd together in four days' time?'

Alec was surprised. Ideas for the tours usually came from the players themselves and they'd been reluctant to suggest anything after what happened to Diego in Spain. He was also happy to call it quits after Spain, but he could see some of the lads going for Vegas given the chance. Whether they'd be all right with Marko tagging along, who could say.

'If you're serious, we need to get moving,' he said. 'Most of the players will need to be back with their clubs by the end of the month.'

'Yeah, no problem. Blandine's in the process of setting it all up at a hotel off the strip – she said you'd prefer it. We're calling in a favour at Las Vegas Motor Speedway to book it out for the day. All you need to do is make the calls and get yourself and the guys to the airport and there'll be £10,000 with your name on it when we get back.'

Alec was still hesitant, although he knew his job would be straight forward enough. He had worked with US media before and was confident he could handle things. The local snappers were kept busy by delinquent NFL players who regularly beat up their wives or smoked pot in public, and while Premier League stars were famous everywhere else in the world, most of them would pass unrecognised by most Americans. Once they had cleared immigration, no one would give them a second look.

'Why do you want to go?' he asked, his suspicions rising.

'As I told you, the footballers interest me.'

'You better know what you're letting yourself in for.'

'Ha, ha. That's funny,' Marko said, with a sneer. 'Listen, there's not much about these little trips that I don't know. Where do you think Blandine gets the drugs and the girls from? I'm sure I'll be able to take care of myself.'

Marko being able to take care of himself was the least of Alec's worries. He had always tried to put some distance between the players and his criminal operation. If they thought about him at all, most figured he was just a contact of some guy one of them knew rather than a shady East European pimp and drug dealer.

'I'm not sure you'd be welcome, you know. It's an exclusive club and they're pretty choosy about new members.'

'You let me worry about that.'

'Your call,' Alec shrugged, swayed by the prospect of an extra ten grand he hadn't banked on. 'I'm going to see one of the boys now. I'll sound him out and, if he's up for it, he'll probably persuade the others.'

'Ok, let me know tonight. Good to see you Alec,' said Marko.

He stood up and extended a large hand. Alec responded reflexively but the Serbian squeezed hard and pulled him uncomfortably close to his face.

'Enjoy spending your money.'

'Yeah, well. I earned it.'

Alec squirmed uncomfortably until Marko let him go a long two seconds later.

'Just call me.'

Alec retraced his steps past the card players who had restarted their game but glanced up at him with blank expressions. He hurried down the stairs and across the courtyard. He was out of the building and well down the street before he opened the envelope. Fifty-pound notes, twenty of them. He had sold himself cheap again but at least it would buy Sophie a decent peace offering.

Chapter 6

A glance at the popular press reveals so much about where footballers live that it is surprising more are not targeted by burglars or worse. The Manchester players inhabit the Cheshire triangle of Alderley Edge, Wilmslow and Prestbury, Liverpool's stars favour Formby and Woolton, but London's 200 plus Premier League players are a different matter.

When he was Chelsea manager, Jose Mourinho's insistence that his players lived within three miles Cobham inflated a property bubble which transformed the unassuming dormitory town into an exclusive millionaire's enclave. Players from the other London clubs live in up-market pockets like Totteridge and St Alban's close to their respective training grounds. But another group, the footballing royalty from Europe or beyond, go for the Capital's more exclusive neighbourhoods within striking distance of the bright lights of the West End. Diego was firmly in this camp and was living in a rented duplex penthouse apartment in St John's Wood, while his townhouse in Hampstead was being extensively and expensively remodelled.

Alec arrived at the front desk of the apartment building where fresh flowers half hid a surly concierge. The portly man in his sixties wore a black uniform and bristled with the kind of hostility typical of a former army NCO. If he had ever seen action at all, it would have been Falklands rather than Afghan and it was far from clear how much use he would be at preventing an actual intruder. Alec gave him the benefit of the doubt, however, and smiled in what he hoped was a disarming way receiving a blank stare for his trouble. He introduced himself and a call was duly made to the apartment above.

'You are not expected, Mr Munday, and Mr Rodrigues is unavailable.'

It was the first time Alec had heard anyone use Diego's family name and he felt himself rapidly losing patience with the obstructive flunky. He pulled out his mobile and called the player direct.

'Diego, it's me, Alec. Where are you man? I've got your old phone.'

'Hey Alec, good to hear you man. Are you at my apartment? I'm just coming back from the hospital. I'll be like five minutes or something.'

He clicked off and Alec turned back to the doorman. 'He's on his way.'

The gatekeeper gave the slightest shrug and his glacial expression rearranged itself without warmth. 'You're very welcome to wait in the lobby, sir.'

Within five minutes a white pimped out Range Rover swung round into the carriage drive at the front of the building and Diego appeared at the open window of the passenger seat. He was wearing a Moschino snapback, gold trimmed Armani shades, ripped t-shirt and a fist full of gold rings. He looked more like a well-paid extra at a Skepta gig than a footballer, but he smiled when he saw Alec and levered himself out of the car with the aid of a pair of crutches.

'Diego. Shit man, that looks serious.'

'Don't worry, don't worry, I'm gonna be fine. Is Robert giving you a hard time? Hey, Robert this is my good friend Alec. Next time just buzz him straight up, right?'

Robert smiled glassily as the pair made for the lift leaving Alec in no doubt that he should expect exactly the same kind of welcome on his next visit. They exited directly into Diego's apartment and right into what looked like a photoshoot for *OK!* complete with housekeeper, also in uniform, who was busy arranging a huge vase of flowers.

'This is kinda crazy, no? Look at this place. The maid comes with the package. This is Marta, but not *that* Marta,' he said indicating a stunningly gorgeous brunette sat on a chaise longue leafing through a pile of glossy magazines.

Alec's knowledge of Brazilian women's football was rudimentary at best, but he knew of Marta, the female Pelé and star of the national team, and found it hard to imagine the delicate girl in front of him ever kicking a football. She looked up revealing large, brown eyes and a perfect smile. Alec thought *this* Marta would do absolutely fine although his eye couldn't help but be drawn to the huge rock on her wedding finger.

The palatial penthouse apartment was like nothing Alec had ever seen. It was a masterpiece in glass and white marble and big enough to make its diminutive occupants look like children playing at keeping house. In the centre of the lower level was a spiral staircase in glass and chrome beyond which was a formal dining table also made of glass and set for 12 people. Behind the table a door led, Alec presumed, onto a kitchen although he was equally sure the young couple living here were not frequent visitors. At the other extreme of the room a wall housed a large polished steel bowl which was lit with an eternal flame despite it being 20degrees outside. Above the fire hung a theatre-sized TV and the space was completed by a dramatically curved white leather sofa which Diego now swung himself into from his crutches.

Alec took in his surroundings as the housekeeper set tea and iced water on the white marble side tables. His eye was drawn to the panoramic windows and a large terrace on three sides which housed an infinity pool and covered gym. There were views over Regent's Park and the Central London Mosque on one side with Lord's Cricket Ground and the unmistakable skyline of London's West End and The City on the others. He could only imagine what the monthly rent would be.

'This place is amazing. Did you just ask the estate agent for the biggest apartment in London?'

'No man, but you should see the bedroom. The bed is so big, we could have half of the team sleeping in there and I don't think I would even notice. And if we ever get tired of the pool outside we can do some lengths in the bath.'

Bringing the conversation to business Alec said: 'So, how have you been, mate? You got back from Marbs ok then, but what's the deal with your foot?'

'I'm good, man. They say I'm gonna be fine, but I don't think I'll be playing for a few weeks.'

'Did you tell the club?'

'I called Vic Vickers and told him I cut my foot. The club medics are speaking with Totò and my doctors at the London Clinic, so I think it's fine.'

'Did you tell Vic how it happened?'

'Yeah, I said I was off my face shagging hoes in a Spanish Jacuzzi and sliced it open on the razor used for cutting the coke. What do you think I am, stupid?'

They both laughed.

'Your English has improved,' said Alec glancing at Marta who continued to leaf through her magazines. He concluded that either the pair had an unusually open relationship, which seemed unlikely, or that she didn't understand a word. Just in case, he swerved any comeback about the fateful night and steered the conversation back to the foot.

'What are they telling you about the injury?'

'They say there is a little damage to the muscle, but it will all be ok in a while. Maybe not for the start of the season, but for sure by Christmas.'

'Christmas? Shit, man, what are you going to do?'

'What can I do? I'm swimming every day and the club physios are going to start work on me soon. But otherwise I'm going crazy in this apartment. Some of the guys came over yesterday but they're back for pre-season in a few days, so soon I'm going to be on my own.'

He looked dejected. After a couple of seasons in London he had made some friends outside the club, but he was going to have a lot of time on his hands. With his appetite for thrills and an instinct for trouble, the prospect of twelve weeks out of the game wasn't a good one.

'Well maybe I've got something that might interest you.'

Alec set out Marko's plan and the player's face lit up briefly then fell again.

'I'm not sure I can,' he said. 'It's been an expensive summer already.'

Alec was incredulous. 'What, Diego? Are you telling me you've got money troubles?'

'I know this all looks impressive,' he said, waving airily around the room. 'But I'm burning through cash like crazy. The guys in Brazil took most of my signing on fee and I'm still sending them half my wages. If I'm not playing, then I don't get any appearance money or bonuses and right now the sponsors are losing interest too.'

Although officially outlawed in football, third party ownership was still rife among the Latin American players. Promising teenage players are scouted by sharp-suited football agents who promise to take care of the youngsters' careers in exchange for a rich cut if they made it big on the world stage. At 13 or 14 it seems like the start of a dream but, scroll forward ten years, and they are trapped in a hugely expensive nightmare. The practice was outlawed in the Premier League and Ligue 1 in France in the early noughties after high profile cases involving Carlos Tevez and Javier Mascherano. With the exception of Russia, the rest of European football followed suit, and in the end, FIFA banned TPO completely, but that didn't mean under-the-table deals weren't still being done.

Diego's throwaway remark confirmed Alec's suspicion that the relationship between him and his agent went beyond simply football. As they talked, the player revealed that Totò had approached his family ten years ago promising to pull strings behind the scenes in return for a contract guaranteeing him the lion's share of the boy's future value. Despite evidence of Diego's prodigious talent, he justified the deal insisting it was his powers of persuasion and influence within Brazilian football which resulted in a contract with Corinthians and a call up to the National Team.

Later on, while Brazil was suffering a huge loss of prestige and national pride in their 1-7 defeat to Germany in the home World Cup of 2014, Totò was among an elite group of businessmen who hit the jackpot when the big European clubs came calling. If the Europeans suspected the transfer fees they paid were being channelled to shady commercial interests, they were prepared to turn a blind eye as long as the paperwork was in order and they got their man. In Diego's case that meant 80% of his fee went straight offshore to a holding company in Panama linked by a slender but unbreakable thread to the agent himself.

'Tough times, eh? said Alec. You just have to survive on £140k a week, right?'

'I told you, it's crazy, man. This place is costing me a fortune and the guys are charging me forty thousand a week for digging out the basement in Hampstead. Of course, I wanna go to Vegas, but I think this is maybe the wrong time. I don't know what I'm going to do here, though.'

From his years in the game and from writing his newspaper column Alec well understood that a footballer's life operates in a different reality from the rest of the world. Whenever he heard pundits talking about how hard a player has worked to get where he is, he always thought back to his own mum, a single parent holding down two jobs to put shoes on his feet. 'Hard' is a relative term. The routine changes a bit from one club and manager to another, but the reality for players can be pretty mundane. Training sessions are normally held on five mornings a week and last three or four hours. After lunch there will be some individual conditioning, a massage and maybe a yoga session but that still leaves a lot of time to fill. There are sometimes club duties with local children or similar and regular obligations to sponsors, but the biggest common factor is boredom.

Premier League players are such well-known faces that many retreat to gilded cages in their free time rather than running the gauntlet of selfie hunters or fans from rival teams. Some continue their studies, others become exceptionally good at FIFA, but gaming can only take up so much time. They can't comfort eat or indulge regularly in any quantity of alcohol, so it should come as no surprise that some develop serious gambling habits. In fact, it's about the only vice that they can indulge in without feeling the heat from the club or the media. And, carrying an injury, Diego was going to find life dangerously dull.

Ok, I'll let Marko know, but it's a shame.' Alec hesitated. 'If you could go, do you think there would be a group of guys up for it in the next few days?'

'You know what they're like, there's always a group of guys. And when the season starts again, they just don't get any time to travel like that.'

Alec was sympathetic to Diego's predicament and wanted to help out if he could. In the months to come he would look back on this moment and wonder what might have happened had he made a different choice, but hindsight is a wonderful thing.

'Ok, let me make the call and I'll see what I can sort out,' he said, and the future was decided.

He went out onto the terrace seeing the exclusive view of the London skyline in a slightly different light given the player's financial worries. He felt a nagging guilt at having been partially responsible for Diego's situation, so he decided to see how amenable Marko was prepared to be. After all, Diego was the hook they used to get quite a lot of the other players on board and if he could rope in a dozen or so at £30,000 a pop that would surely make a worthwhile venture. He prepared himself to try a bit of moral blackmail but, in the event, there was no need; Marko was more than prepared to help.

'Tell him I'll stake him if he can bring the other guys along,' he said. 'I'm sure he'll be successful enough at the tables in Vegas to pay me back.'

'Ok, if you're sure, I'll pass it on. He'll be made up.'

Alec hung up and shared the news with a visibly thrilled Diego and a rather less impressed Marta who hit the player with a barrage of rapid-fire Portuguese when he told her he was going away again. Even without last night's run in with Sophie, Alec knew enough about the universal language of relationships to judge that his continued presence was not going to help. He put the player's phone on a marble-topped console and called the lift. The last thing he heard was Diego calling after him, 'See you in Vegas, man.'

Meanwhile, in West London, Marko dialled a private number in Niš, Serbia's third-largest city, and had a brief one-sided conversation in his native language.

Chapter 7

The first thing DI Michaela Dagg saw was the outline of a police constable's helmet through the frosted glass door at the end of her bed. She took in her surroundings – pastel shaded paint on the walls, bed with a metal frame, vital signs monitor, transparent bags with tubes attached hanging from the stand beside her – then started a limited assessment of her physical shape. Her upper body seemed fine, but she had no movement below the waist. By the time the duty nurse came in to check on her she had some questions.

'Can I see my x-rays?'

'Ah, I see you're back with us, Michaela. That's good. Do you know you've been in an accident? You're at the Royal London Hospital and my name's Staff Nurse Suzie Sommers. You've been unconscious for four days so let's take things one step at a time. How is the pain?'

'I'd like to see my consultant. I clearly have some trauma to my legs or back. I want to know the extent of the injuries and discuss any proposed course of treatment.'

If the nurse was taken off guard, she didn't show it.

'There will be plenty of time for that when Mr Bhathia does his rounds in a couple of hours. For now, let's just see if you're able to drink something.'

Michaela consented to take a mouthful of lukewarm water then said:

'Can you ask the constable outside to come in?'

'You can have a couple of minutes with him, that's all.'

The nurse showed in a young policeman and Michaela waited until they were alone.

'What's your name, constable?'

'Harman, Ma'am. DCI Brice said to let him know when you woke up. Do you want me to radio in?'

'I need my phone.'

'That will be with your personal effects back at the unit, Ma'am. I could radio back and get someone to bring them over.'

She started to protest then closed her eyes with weary resignation. 'Ok, Harman. You do what you've been asked to, but I'm going to need a lot more cooperation if you and I are not going to fall out.'

She must have slept again because the next voice she heard belonged to a tall Asian man in a suit.

'Ms Dagg? My name is Oran Bhathia. I'm the orthopaedic consultant looking after you. I hear you've been asking about what's happened to you. We have kept you in an induced coma for the past 72 hours so things are going to seem fuzzy at first. Do you have any memory of your accident? You were hit by a car.'

'Umm, ok. I don't remember that at all but it would explain the lack of movement in my legs. I need to know how bad it is, and I'd appreciate it if you'd answer honestly.'

Bhathia went through the extent of her injuries as clearly and sympathetically as he could. Scans showed multiple leg and pelvis fractures, potential damage in the lower spine and lumbar region and extensive soft tissue injuries.

When he had finished Michaela said, 'So, what's your plan to get me walking again?'

'I'm sorry to have to tell you, but the next few months are going to be quite difficult for you. I have operated and pinned some of the fractures in your legs, but we still need to assess any nerve damage. At least one knee will require a reconstruction and there is a possibility the lower part of your back will need surgery also. There will be a recovery period then a physio will be working to help you build on what you've got in terms of mobility, but I am optimistic at this stage. The induced coma was precautionary and the good news is that there appears to be no injury to your brain but you have a long road ahead of you.'

'How long before I can get back to work?'

'Ms Dagg, you know I really can't speculate on a timeframe this early on, but we are looking at a period of months, maybe even a year of surgery, recovery and rehabilitation. A lot will depend on how your body responds. I'm sorry not to be able to be more specific but please rest assured that we will do whatever we can. As I said, I am optimistic.'

Michaela said nothing, and an oppressive silence filled the small room until it was broken by the consultant. 'We are going to get to know each other rather well in the next few weeks, so let's leave it there for now. I'll be round again tomorrow, and you can ask any questions when you've had chance to take things in.'

Michaela dozed again but came to at the sound of her boss, DCI Brice, speaking to Harman in the corridor outside. She checked that she was respectable as he knocked and entered.

'You're a sight for sore eyes.'

'Have you caught them yet?'

'I offered a £100 bet on those being your first words, but none of the unit would take my money.'

'So...?'

Brice sighed. 'Michaela...' then, reluctantly, 'We tracked the car through CCTV, found it burnt out just off the Western Avenue. It was reported stolen a week ago and wasn't picked up by any ANPR cameras, so we've got nothing to track it back to the driver or map its movements. I've got Carter and Kotecha working from the bank direction, but I'm not hopeful we'll ever make a strong enough link. Sorry.'

'Seems to be my day for 'sorry'. I'm going to need access to the Pepys Lyon case files and a computer. Has anyone processed the material picked up as a result of the raid yet?'

'Michaela,' he said gently. 'You're sounding like a bad TV cop. Bhathia filled me in soon after you were admitted. I think we both know you're not going near any case files for a while.'

She nodded quietly. 'Can't blame me for trying.'

'I want you back but only when you're fully ready. Meanwhile, do me a favour and cooperate. It will make life easier for everyone, you most of all.'

The next few weeks and months were as difficult as feared and Michaela was by no means an easy patient. Occasionally those around her showed their frustration but, for the most part, her bloody mindedness accelerated the recovery further and faster than anyone could have predicted. She left hospital in a wheelchair after six weeks and was walking short distances on crutches two weeks after that. Bhathia was pleased and said she was making a remarkable physical recovery but, as her body started to function again, her mental state worsened. At her first posting in Tottenham she was nick-named the Dementor for her ability to suck the hope out of any fellow officer who thought he'd chance his arm with her. Now the Dementor was back only, this time, the medical team took the brunt of it. Among her friends and colleagues no one was terribly disappointed when she refused visitors and shut herself away from the outside world. Everyone could see it wasn't a healthy situation but they took the view that, if she didn't want to be helped, then she wouldn't thank them for trying to push the point. Left in her private world, Michaela became obsessed with Serbian-backed international organised crime and the possibility that she would crack the criminal network that had put her in hospital. She spent hours hunched over her laptop, hardly sleeping or eating, barely aware if it was day or night. Despite the agonies of the early days having passed, she had also been left with a dangerous dependence on Tramadol.

By the time HR called to arrange meeting with Brice to discuss returning to duty, she was fragile and dangerously depressed. Almost exactly six months to the day since her hit and run, Brice looked across his desk to see DI Dagg walking stiffly, head down, through the unit's open-plan office. It had been weeks since anyone had seen her and her colleagues couldn't help but stare as she crossed the room and entered his glass-walled office. She slumped down into a chair opposite him looking red-eyed and dishevelled while he steepled his fingers in front of his face and tried to assess his broken officer. He gave himself a moment to think, then got up and shut his door. Sitting back behind the desk his wordless gaze returned to Michaela then he snapped to as if his mind was made up.

'I have a proposition for you.'

'I'm not sure I'm much use to you.'

'Hear me out. They want me to offer you a position at the training academy running a programme on financial crime. You're the best we've ever had and sharing your talents with a wider group of officers would make a big difference to our effectiveness in combating money laundering.'

'You know that would kill me.'

'Mmm, but, as you point out, in your current physical and mental state, I would have serious reservations about you returning to active duty.'

She flinched. It was one thing for her to quip that she wasn't much use, but to have it confirmed by her CO was hard to take.

'So, as I said, I have a proposition for you, and I hope you'll accept it. I've been looking at your personnel file. You took French and Criminology at university, yes? And I also understand that you're quite the linguist.'

'Where is this going sir?'

So, I've spoken to the Commissioner and recommended a posting to Interpol in Lyon. You would be joining their financial crime team.'

Brice stood up and walked over to the window surveying the road below through filthy glass. 'You should know that the boss is sceptical; doesn't think you're up to it. I have persuaded him that an outlet for your obsession with international crime networks would be as good a prescription for recovery as you're going to get. But looking at you, I wonder whether he's right.'

When he turned back to face her, Michaela Dagg was convulsed by sobs, crying properly for the first time since her accident.

'Michaela look, it could only be for a year or so and I really think you should consider...'

'I accept,' she said, cutting quickly across him.

Brice looked confused but pulled some tissues from a draw in his desk and gave her time to compose herself. It wasn't the first difficult conversation he'd had in this office.

'Thank you, Sir. It means more than you could ever know. Will that be all Sir? Only I'd like to say some goodbyes to the guys in the unit if that's ok.'

By the time she left the building an hour later she had laughed and cried some more, the honest camaraderie and affection of her colleagues coursing through her like a drug. She would miss them but was in no doubt that she was being offered a lifeline that she was determined to grab hold of.

Secondments to Interpol are usually seen as just deserts for those who have fouled up spectacularly at home. The organisation is institutionally dysfunctional comprising the misfits and screw-ups from the police forces of its 200 assorted member countries. They are overseen by a Secretariat which makes International Olympic Committee members look young and in touch. It lacks credibility and teeth, is pulled this way and that by its political masters, struggles to maintain a core purpose and, as a consequence, has to battle for every cent of its funding.

Michaela knew all of this but she didn't care. This was a chance for a new start, a route back to something like a normal life again. She was under no illusions about the work: it would be frustrating and the environment obsessed with bureaucratic administration, but she would have access to intelligence and could pursue her private obsessions unhindered. She also harboured a romantic attachment to the French city and a lingering affection for a lover dating back to her days as an exchange student there.

Brice wasn't prepared to countenance a return to work in the fragile state she was in, so an appointment was made with the Force's psychologist for a month's time. The target, and the prospect of a chance to turn the page on a dark time, gave Michaela the motivation she needed and she passed the assessment with room to spare. Another month later, she was installed in an apartment in the weak winter sunshine of France's second city and ready to take up a post in Interpol's Financial Crime Unit. Preparing for the move had done wonders for her mood; she had kicked the painkillers and even organised a going away party at which she and her girlfriends got uproariously pissed. Physically, too, she continued to make progress. She would never return to what she had been, but to the casual observer, a slight limp was the only outward indication of the injuries she had suffered.

France suited her and the flat she had bought in Shoreditch had rented easily, so leaving London had been remarkably easy. She would never have admitted it to her former colleagues, but her professional pride had also suffered a big dent in the collision with a large black BMW, and it was good to be able to leave the ghosts behind. Arriving at her new office for the first time, she felt physically and mentally ready to find out what life had in store once again.

The palatial Interpol Secretariat Headquarters could not be more different from the shabby buildings used by the CoLP in London. Sitting in a park on the banks of the river Rhône, the organisation occupies an imposing glass and steel structure which enjoys unique legal privileges similar to those of the Vatican. The 600 or so employed or seconded policemen and women work alongside a small army of fonctionaires who embody the very essence of French bureaucracy. Their official role is to provide administrative support, but it is a brave police officer who actually asks them to do anything meaningful in pursuit of their cause. Their strict adherence to office hours and insistence on a 90-minute lunchbreak were legendary and even Michaela's mastery of the language only got her so far.

Interpol units nominally investigate a wide range of international crimes spanning the illegal trade in chemical nerve agents and nuclear material to cybercrime and corruption. The reality, however, is that to supplement its otherwise meagre budget, the organisation has been forced to cast its net into the corporate world for financial support which tends to skew its priorities. It doesn't stray from crime fighting but, when a drug company is paying the bills, priorities have a habit of shifting away from frustrating the trade in illegal narcotics to preventing the import of counterfeit pharmaceuticals. The unit tracing the movement of illegal cigarettes is also disproportionately large and well-resourced by the major tobacco companies.

One of the more questionable partnerships Interpol has signed is with FIFA, football's world governing body, which has contributed a sum equivalent to a quarter of its official annual budget. For its money, FIFA receives the appearance of a great deal of useful activity against football match fixing around the world and by way of a by-product, a giant fig leaf covering the more dubious activities of its Executive Committee members.

Match fixing is linked umbilically to illegal gambling which is one of the favourite ways used by international crime syndicates to launder the proceeds of drug dealing, prostitution and their other activities. The connection with money laundering is how Interpol Officer Michaela Dagg found herself required to take a professional interest in the darker side of world football. However, if she thought she would be using her formidable skills to follow the money trail and issue Interpol's famous Red Notices for the arrest of match fixers, she was disappointed. The main output of the partnership with FIFA was a programme of education and training rolled out through football federations in over 150 countries. Michaela was joining a small team running match-fixing workshops at Europe's leading professional clubs. Her language ability meant she was sent to the farthest corners of Europe, but what would have been a dream job for many people was, in her view, the very definition of wasting police time.

Chapter 8

Vegas was a final fling for the footballers who would soon be back in harness at their clubs, and they were determined to enjoy it. Not even the unexplained appearance of Marko was enough to dampen the high spirits especially as he'd upgraded everyone from Business to First Class. The shrewd move had cemented Marko's position as host of the group and, as pack animals, the players fell into line behind him.

At the airport they made straight for the luxury lounge where they did what all international footballers do; traded stories of the various World Cups, Champions League trips and other international competitions they'd been part of. Most footballers are a lot less riotous than their rugby equivalents, so it was more pranks and practical jokes than drunken dwarf tossing. But the mood got a bit darker as some of the party shared their tales of mind games and other tactics they had seen deployed against their opponents.

Giancarlo, who had been everywhere in over a decade with the Italian national side, recalled one of his early Euro matches against Netherlands played in an old-school stadium in Tilburg. 'The Dutch were following us down the player's tunnel and one of our boys found the light switch. He caught our eye and flicked it off for a laugh. We started screaming and a few punches were thrown in the dark. By the time they got on the pitch they were really shaken up. It put them right off their game for at least ten minutes. They got their own back at half time, though. Their kit man superglued up our locker room door and we spent half of the break waiting in the corridor.'

'We had Portugal in our World Cup group,' said Ireland international Kevin, 'and one of our guys, I don't know how he did it, but he got a clone of their number eight's girlfriend's phone. He sent him a load of random text messages just to put him off his stroke. You know, stuff like 'your boots look like they're too big,' or 'perhaps give someone else the chance to take a free kick – they might score'. Don't know if it worked but I do know Portugal didn't get out of the group and the pair split up pretty soon after.'

Not to be outdone, Russian international Nikolai joined in. 'Mind games? Ha, you guys are amateurs. We had a chef with us who travelled with a bag of his own special ingredients. Do you remember, Giancarlo, when we sent pizza over to your team hotel? The Italian coaches sent it back with a message saying, 'your pizza is shit'. So, then we thought, why not try the Africans? Those guys will fucking eat anything,' he said roaring with laughter. 'We sent a special pizza to the Nigerian camp and just waited for the results, we weren't even playing them. That game where they just ran around like crazy guys, totally disorganised at the back. That was us! I don't know what was in it, but I'm telling you our chef has some very special ingredients.'

The tales of shithousery got taller and the laughter louder as the party made its way onto the plane and settled into the inflight hospitality. Nikolai tried to insist that they had the referees bought and paid for at the 2012 Euros until someone pointed out that they had wasted their money as they didn't get past the group stage.

'That's just how fucking shit we were,' he said, still roaring with laughter.

Around eleven hours later the players cleared security at McCarran International Airport. Alec was there to meet them with a fleet of limos waiting to whisk them to the hotel where Blandine had everything laid on. At Marko's request the off-strip hotel preferred by Alec had been abandoned in favour of rooms at one of the most iconic resorts in Las Vegas; The Venetian. It takes a lot to impress such a well-travelled group, but there was an audible whistle as the car doors opened and the boys spilled out into the Italian inspired, marble-colonnaded lobby.

The Venetian is famous worldwide for its luxury and service, but at Blandine's bidding they had really rolled out the welcome mat. A troupe of cheerleaders in tight lycra shorts and crop tops did a mini routine before grabbing the luggage and escorting the players to deluxe suites. Anticipating they would be ready for some pool action after the long flight, their hostess had booked out the hotel's exclusive Tao Beach where more cheerleaders were serving the drinks and promising a lot more besides. Alec had arranged access for the local paparazzi where the single players would pose for some casual shots with the girls before anything got messy. The deal meant some profile for the boys in a market where they might look to end their careers. It helped the snappers earn their corn and also provided some publicity for the hotel which, as usual, was hosting everyone gratis confident they would make their money back in the casino. Once everyone had what they wanted the paps left with a promise that the party would be left alone for the rest of the trip.

Diego had temporarily abandoned the crutches and was propping himself up between two of Nevada's finest each clutching a bottle of champagne. He looked pleased to see Alec who said, 'Hey, watch the glass mate.'

Diego managed a laugh. 'Don't worry, man; you don't catch me out like that again. I'm doing well don't you think. Docs say I'll should up to some light training by August. I'm going to miss the Asia pre-season tour but I should be back in the squad for the start of the season.'

Diego detached himself briefly from the two cheerleaders and took Alec aside.

'Hey man, thanks for sorting this out with Marko, you know, fronting up for the trip. I got a lot of people squeezing me for cash right now. He seems like a good guy.'

'Yeah, well, I wouldn't be so sure, but I guess he's as good as any of the guys you normally associate with.'

Diego laughed, conspiratorially and rejoined his new friends. Alec laughed along with him, but in truth, he was worried the player.

He'd been shocked to find out that he was so beholden to Totò yet spending money like he had it to burn. Alec felt a twinge of responsibility and was planning to have a word, but this was not the moment. That conversation would have to wait until they were back in London.

The pool party was soon well and truly started under the desert sunshine. Blandine pulled the strings in the background and Alec was relaxed and confident. Although they were celebrities in Europe, they were just a group of rich young men out for a good time in a country which preferred its footballers to wear shoulder pads and a helmet. He was tempted to join the boys in the pool but thought better of it as he glanced over at Marko. Sitting on a lounger in his trademark dark suit, he looked uncomfortable as Alec approached.

'What is this kid's stuff?' he chipped. 'They're like little boys chasing the girls in school.'

'You've got to understand these lads, Marko. They're athletes; everything they do is about showing off their physicality. Getting the girls' attention just proves to everyone what fine physical specimens they are.'

Looking at him, Alec felt sure the Serb was more familiar with brutality than physicality. Compared to the footballers Marko's movements were solid rather than graceful, but there was no doubting the possibility of explosive force, and he was getting impatient.

'Ok, ok, boys,' he announced. 'Have some fun but don't overdo it, eh. I gotta big evening planned for us. I'm going to wash up and I'll see you upstairs in the suite in two hours.'

As Marko left the poolside, the response from the players was predictably indifferent and he was soon forgotten. An hour later, however, a discreet nod from Blandine to the girls made sure the party moved on elsewhere. Once the boys were dressed and ready, the evening went true to form: team meal, plenty of champagne, a few lines of coke and then hit the casino.

With its sister hotel, The Palazzo, The Venetian has the biggest casino in Vegas. Its quarter of a million square feet extend over two vast levels, each the size of two football pitches, full of punters with faces lit up in neon colours by the mesmeric glow of a thousand slot machines. The background music is a symphony of robotic blips punctuated by rhythmic thuds which simulate quarters being paid out despite most machines being ticket only. Beyond the slots, right in the centre of the room, are the table games where tuxedo-sporting croupiers deal the cards and rake in piles of chips worth hundreds of thousands every hour. Forlorn punters talk in short staccato bursts asking for another card, sticking or folding joylessly. However, life for really high rollers is different again. For them, the High-Limit Salon is where the action is and Marko led from the front, steering the party into the one of the world's most exclusive casino experiences.

The atmosphere inside the room was more like an intimate London member's club than the bling of the hotel outside. It smelled completely different with a chemical haze simulating leather and wood piped imperceptibly through the air conditioning system. The décor matched the aroma with Chesterfield sofas strategically placed within the oak-panelled room. The carpet was deeply piled and the lighting subtle but insistent. A smiling waitress took orders for drinks and showed the party to green baize tables where games of poker, craps, roulette and blackjack were already up and running.

The players were expected, of course, and accounts had already been opened in their names. They fanned out around the room and soon the high-stakes action was in full swing. Marko laid a gentle hand on Diego's shoulder and encouraged him towards the roulette wheel where the table minimum was $500 a throw.

'Start slowly,' he said. 'Remember I'm staking you. Go for a dozen bet and you'll double your money every time.' The player followed his advice and was soon almost $16,000 up. 'You're a natural,' he said, but Diego wasn't listening. Small wins were fine but, with the coke still coursing through his system, he was looking for a bit more excitement. Leaving the players under Marko's watchful gaze for an hour or so, Alec joined Blandine back in the suite to go through arrangements for the following day. They kept it strictly business, finalising details of the trip to Las Vegas Motor Speedway home of NASCAR, Monster Trucks and drag racing. The track was ten miles north of Sin City and they had the run of the place for the day including the use of a dozen stock cars and access to a collection of supercars billed as 'the world's greatest'.

'I wish Marko hadn't got the boys all fired up about the NASCAR track,' said Alec. 'That circuit is a death trap even for the pros.'

Blandine was typically unimpressed. 'Just keep them alive and I'll do the rest when they get back.'

Alec's media duties were largely ceremonial, so he was going to be joining the rest at the track. Blandine had laid on an extra limo and some girls who would double up as highly persuasive minders as well as playmates, so they felt they had all bases covered.

Back in the casino the atmosphere was getting tense around the poker table where Diego was in a big-money stand-off with three other players. The stakes were set at $5000 a hand and all three were bluffing wildly. Marko looked on with interest as one by one each player revealed his character. Some picked up cards and tossed their chips down without a thought, apparently too rich or too stupid to worry whether they won or lost. They were there to be part of the team and would walk away as soon as the party got bored. Some were pros: cautious gamblers who played the odds and aimed to come out ahead at the end of the evening. Irish midfielder, Kevin Mooney was one of those.

Then there were the alpha males who viewed poker, as they did most other things in life, as a way to project their status and dominance. They bet big and aggressively using their charisma to carry off extravagant bluffs. They wouldn't give up until they won, and If they lost the sparks would fly. However, once they felt their manhood was secure, they too were happy to call it quits.

The final group were addicted to the rush that both winning and losing releases. They need the hit and constantly raise the stakes to get it. Psychologists would call them compulsive or addictive personalities. Marko just knew them as marks. To him they were soft targets who could be controlled by whoever turned the machine on or off. He could tell by their body language and the slightly frenzied look in their eyes that there were three marks in the group. Stevie Mac was the first one he identified. His compulsions had driven two marriages onto the rocks and would ultimately bring about an early end to his playing career.

The second was Nikolai who had already drunk enough vodka to lose what few inhibitions he had. He was losing but playing more and more quickly and raising the stakes with each hand.

The third was Diego.

Suddenly, as one, the alpha males reached a silent consensus that their dick swinging credentials would be better boosted in a club. The team players were happy to follow leaving the marks with a dilemma. Stevie was up substantially and keen to exploit his winning streak, Niko was just getting into his stride too, whereas Diego was nursing a $20 grand loss and desperate to play himself back into the game.

In the end the team dynamic won over the call of the cards and the group made a loud exit tossing hundred-dollar bills in the direction of the dealers. Marko watched them leave. He had what he wanted for now.

'See you in a while, boys,' he called after them as they made for the lobby.

Alec was alerted to the group's departure by the casino manager and he took the elevator down to meet them. The players were intent on tasting the full Las Vegas nightlight experience and soon linked up with the girls that Blandine had on standby. Out front she had a fleet of limos and the party was soon taking the short ride to XS at the Wynn Las Vegas. The club was one block north which was just enough time for another blow of coke before emptying out into the warm evening air ready to party. As they skipped the line and headed straight into the action, Alec gave Blandine a congratulatory nod. Things were going well. Inside Alec steered the group towards the VIP area where drinks were already lined up. He looked on as the players hit the dancefloor finding new ways to show off their athletic prowess despite having been up for 24 hours already.

As he always said: 'No one looks back on their life and wishes they got more sleep,' and this lot certainly wouldn't.

Alec took a limo and used a quiet hour to check out some other clubs for the next night. He had to think ahead, but in a place like Vegas it wasn't easy to guess what the flavour of the month was going to be. Part of his skill was to pre-arrange a club he thought the players would go for, then plant the name in one of their minds so it became their idea. Eight out of ten times it worked, and the group bought it, although how they imagined they were expected everywhere they went was beyond him.

By the time he returned to XS the group was all over the huge dance floor but the girls were good and at the appointed hour they rounded up their partners, corralling them into the waiting limos. Back at the Venetian Blandine had the party suite fully operational and Alec took his cue to make a discrete exit. An hour and a half later he had a call from hotel management: a group was riding the gondolas on the hotel's indoor canal singing at top of their voices. Security were well able to deal with all kinds of revellers but called anyway just to inform him as instructed. Alec was glad to get on the scene in the event of any unwanted cameras.

He heard the commotion before the lift doors opened but the situation was well under control. Although the hotel runs 24 hours a day, it was now 3.30 in the morning and the lobby was sparsely populated. A few zombie gamblers assumed the night was young enough for a couple more rolls of the dice, but otherwise there were no threats. The Venetian staff knew their jobs and the players were soon back in the party suite with most of them not even aware that they had had a brush with security.

Alec took a quick recce of the suite which was only around half full. He assumed the absentees had taken themselves and their girls back to their rooms. If they were lurking somewhere, Alec assumed he would be called again so he returned to bed. When the call did come it was from Marko. The clock on the stand beside the bed was showing 5.45 and Alec could hear there was a problem before he put it to his ear.

'I'm gonna kill that little fuck. He's fucking out of control. He's got no fucking idea how much trouble he's in.'

'Whoaaah, slow down Marko,' said Alec, reeling. 'What's the problem?'

'That little Brazilian fuckwit. He's the fucking problem. He owes me four hundred big ones and I'm gonna pull his fucking teeth out until I get it.'

Alec pieced the story together from Marko's expletive-laden rant. Apparently, Stevie, Niko and Diego had left the party suite but, rather than gondolas, the pair had gone back to the High-Limit Salon where they had spent the rest of the night at the tables. Hotel staff had called Marko just after 5.30 to check his credit and confirmed Diego's losses had topped $400k. Alec hung up to try and get to the player ahead of the out of control Serb. When his line of credit had been stopped Diego had gone back to his room where Alec found him still awake, the reality of his predicament starting to dawn.

'Alec, did you speak with Marko?'

'We need to go, now. Get your shit together and let's get to the airport. I'm going down to the lobby to get a limo. I'll call when you can come down. Once you leave the room don't stop for anyone.'

The first direct flight back to London was not until the afternoon but Alec got the player on an early United flight to LA. He would have a six-hour layover to contemplate his future, but at least he'd be out of Marko's way. The road to the airport went south from downtown Las Vegas, the opposite direction to the race track. Alec couldn't bring himself to speak: this was Diego's second DNF in two months and he didn't even want to speculate what it was going to cost him this time.

The limo pulled back into the Venetian an hour later and Alec braced himself to face the music with Marko. There was no sign of him in the lobby and no reply from his phone, so he picked up some coffee and went back to his room where he grabbed a few of hours sleep until race time. At midday he got up, showered and took the glass elevator to the rendezvous point ready to meet his fate. When he got there, Marko was already playing host to half the party and acting as if nothing had happened.

Alec stationed himself in a different limo from the Serbian who threw him a murderous stare as the cars started rolling out into the Mojave Desert.

Chapter 9

Back in London, Alec was happy to let the dust settle for a few weeks and get back to the normal routine of his *Guardian* column and media work with footballers and their clubs. Vegas had been a trip too far in many ways and, although he had tried to smooth things over at the time, Marko's presence and Diego's absence had meant a cloud hung over group. By the time they parted company at Heathrow the players were more than ready to be back home. Now with the season well underway, the only trip planned was an afternoon at Dunsfold Aerodrome which Alec hoped would reset expectations and keep future ventures more manageable.

He was also keen to put some distance between himself and Marko and not at all worried if he never worked with him and Blandine again. Knowing that his debt to the Serbian wasn't going to magically disappear, the one person he was keen to hear from was Diego. He had called a couple of times without success and was starting to worry. The player had dropped off the social media radar and Alec's only contact with him was via Sky Sport where he saw the occasional cutaway of a disconsolate face in the crowd. The pundits were reporting his return to the pitch was scheduled for the start of October and Alec knew he would be desperate to get playing if only to start earning his appearance money and bonuses again. A few weeks passed and Alec almost thought they might have lost touch for good, then out of the blue his phone went – it was Diego.

'Hey Alec, how's it going?' came his voice as if they'd been together only the night before.

'I'm good, mate. It's been a while. How have you been?'

'Where are you man? I could do with seeing you.'

He had tried to sound casual but there was obvious tension in his voice.

'I'm over in East London today, but I could be at yours around six. Are you still in the penthouse?'

'Ha, that place was great wasn't it. No, I've moved into the house in Hampstead.'

Diego gave him the address and hung up leaving Alec none the wiser as to what had prompted his call. He half wondered whether to call Vic Vickers at the club but thought better of it. There was no need to worry him without a good reason and there would be time enough for a conversation later on if it proved necessary.

Bang on six Alec pulled up outside the wrought iron gates of a vast property just north of Hampstead Heath. He buzzed the intercom, the gates swung open and he weaved gingerly between at least half a million pounds worth of cars. He approached the front door where Marta stood looking less than pleased to see him. She was dressed in a pool robe and little else and fixed Alec with a stare, then turned and led the way down to the recently excavated basement. They entered a cavernous living space which extended over the entire footprint of the house above and into the garden from where the evening light streamed in through a glass roof. One of the walls housed a giant blue-lit aquarium, full of exotic fish, which formed a perfect backdrop to the swimming pool which ran along it. Opposite the pool was the biggest TV set that Alec had ever seen, set into a glass console in front of an enormous Italian-style leather sofa.

The wooden-floored space under the glass roof had been kitted out as a gym with milled steel dumbbells and kettlebells stacked neatly on a mahogany rack, an ergonomically perfect Skillmill and a professional multi gym where the player was going through a half-hearted workout. His diminutive frame looked tiny next to the equipment, but he was clearly in much better shape than at their previous meeting. Diego greeted Alec with a big manhug and then, rather more demurely than the last time, found him some swimming trunks before getting into a steaming Jacuzzi.

Alec changed and took his place in the bubbling water. He decided to come straight to the point and said; 'So, what's the urgency Diego?'

The player's face fell, and he looked about as miserable as when Alec had first met him.

'I'm in trouble, man. Marko's got me by the balls.'

'Shit, why am I not surprised. Look, it's only money. Surely when you start playing again, you'll soon be able to start paying him back.'

'You don't get it. It's worse than that. He's given me a deal and, like they say, it's the kind of deal I can't refuse.'

'He's not the bloody Godfather. What does he want?'

'I'm back in the squad now and I'm going to be playing in the next couple of weeks as a substitute at first, but the manager says he'll start me as long as he knows I can play at least 60 minutes.'

'So, that's all good. You'll get your appearance money and Marko will soon be history.'

There was a long pause before the player finally said, 'He wants me to fix games.'

Once the words were out the room started to spin. The jacuzzi kept bubbling and the music kept playing on the room's sound system, but Alec couldn't hear any of it. He opened his mouth a couple of times to respond but he was too stunned to speak. He looked at the player, seeing him suddenly in a completely different light. He saw the desperation in his face. The Brazilian had everything in the world that anyone could want, fame, fortune, the team and the adoration of his fans, but at this moment he was the loneliest man alive.

'Diego, man. What the fuck? What do you mean, like score in your own net or what?'

'No, not like that. I think just the occasional miss kick, you know, put the ball wide when I'm through on goal, that kind of thing. It doesn't mean we have to lose. I just have to do something he can bet on.'

'Fuck, no man, you can't do that. Apart from getting you sacked from the club and banned from the game, that would mean going against your every instinct and reflex. People would see straight away that something was wrong.'

'You know, it's much easier to miss the target than to hit it. I miss all the time; everyone does. No one will ever guess.'

'But what if someone found out? The other players would kill you; you'd be finished. Tell Marko he'll get his money. If you haven't got it, you could borrow it easily. I tell you what, I'll call him and talk to him.'

'It's no good, Alec. He doesn't want the money. He says I can keep it, but he needs me to do him a few favours in return.'

'You just have to say no. You can't get into fixing games. I know he's a menacing bastard, but he's not actually going to hurt you. It wouldn't be worth it for him.'

'Me, no, but he knows where I live. Don't say anything, but he's already threatened to have someone throw acid at Marta. If I do what he wants, I can keep the money and no one gets hurt. But if I don't, then those around me are in real danger.'

The seriousness of the player's problem was starting to dawn on Alec but he kept talking. 'There's got to be a way out. We can figure something out, surely. What about your guys in Brazil? Isn't there someone you know who can put the frighteners on Marko?'

'Believe me, I've thought about it, but Brazil is a long way from London and, anyway, if the guys back home got to know, I'd probably be in as much danger from them as I am from Marko.'

The sound of the bubbling music went unchallenged once again as the two men weighed up both the situation and its implications. In the end, Alec said: 'It sounds like you've already decided what you're going to do, so why are you telling me?'

Diego shrugged miserably, his body language telling the truth of what he really felt. 'I'm scared. As I get closer to playing again, I just hate the thought of what I've got to do. I've never been so desperate not to be fit again, but I know if I don't play, the situation will just get worse.'

Alec went quiet again then he said: 'There is something we could do and it might even work. We need to find a way of letting the club and the League know what's going on without giving you away. If people at the top of the game thought there was fixing in the Premier League, they'd be all over it.'

The player raised his head for the first time in almost half an hour.

'Can you do that?'

'No, I can't, but the author of Direct From The Dressing Room could.'

Chapter 10

Alec Munday sat down at his laptop as soon as he got home. On the drive from Hampstead he'd been turning over in his mind how to give enough away of the player's dilemma without compromising him completely. Then there was the question of making sure that whatever the Premier League authorities did to protect the game would not backfire on the him or expose either of them to Marko's thugs.

The first thing he wrote was a note to the sports editor at *The Guardian* letting him know what was coming.

'I want coverage in the main paper,' he said, 'or at least a headline in the sports section.'

He ended with a promise that the column would be delivered in the morning and said he wanted to talk about the kind of coverage they could get. Then he poured himself a drink and started to write.

As the writer of Direct From The Dressing Room I've brought you the genuine voices of hundreds of footballers over the years. Some have been entertaining, some have been frustrating and others are just the product of the bizarre life involved in playing for a Premier League team. |As the writer, I set myself just two rules: first, I keep everyone's identity secret and second, I always tried to tell the truth or as close as I can get to it, so I hope you'll trust me when I say this is the most difficult and important column I've ever written.

Some of you are going to be outraged by what you're about to read. Others, some in the game itself, will wish I hadn't told this story at all. But, I've got to put it out there as a friend of mine, a Premier League footballer, is in trouble. He's trapped by match fixers who are forcing him to throw games so they can win big bets on the outcome.

How he got into this position is not really what matters, but it won't surprise you to learn that he's a gambler himself. He found himself briefly owing money to some people who turned out to be match fixers working for a criminal gang. He couldn't pay them back as quickly as they wanted and they called in his debts by insisting that he fix matches for them.

Regular readers will know that we've talked about gambling and footballers before and the explosive combination of shed loads of money, too much free time and a competitive mentality that is part of any successful athlete. My friend is young and exceptionally wealthy by any standard you can think of. He's away from home and he has been injured which has disrupted his regular routine of training and matches. I've spoken to him and he is ready to admit that he has been really stupid. But, nothing he's done means he deserves to be trapped by match fixers who are threatening to attack his family if he doesn't do what they want.

He breathed a massive sigh of relief when he paid back all his debts thinking that would get him off the hook. But it's not enough. The guys controlling him won't let go saying to him literally, "you're done when we tell you you're done". They know that if his actions were ever made public, his career would be over, so he's over a barrel if he wants to keep playing.

Now I know some of you will be thinking, 'why doesn't he just come clean?' It's a good question. But these are some of the most evil characters you could ever have the misfortune of running in to. And they're not the bosses. They work for the kind of international criminals that use violence and even murder without a second thought.

My friend isn't being physically threatened, of course: they need him fit to keep playing and keep fixing. But there is the constant threat of violence to those around him, his family and friends. Imagine living with the fear that you could come home, and your wife or girlfriend has been beaten up and it's your fault. So, he keeps doing what he's told and that's killing him.

Fixing football is totally different from taking performance-enhancing drugs. I'm not making excuses for them, but the dopers do it to win so that's just like an extension of what they've done all their lives. They've already sacrificed blood, sweat and tears chasing that dream, and they're so focused they would do almost anything to win. They've tried so many training regimes, diets and coaches that it's really hard to know when taking an extra cocktail of nutrients or infusion of blood crosses the line into doping.

Like I say, I'm not defending them, but I can at least understand how drug cheats end up going down that path.

Fixing is different. My friend is being forced to lose, to deliberately miskick in front of goal or to give away a foul. His team is suffering as a result and, as any team player will tell you, knowing that you are letting your colleagues down eats away at you inside. His reputation as a player is taking a hit too and that will cost him financially. He was once one of the top stars in world football but suddenly he looks ordinary and off the pace and soon none of the top teams will want to sign him.

But worse than all of that is the psychological impact. Every time he gives in to the fixers and agrees to do it again he feels worthless, a loser and another part of him dies. It's costing him his health, his relation-ships and his sanity. He is desperate. He needs help and he doesn't know who he can trust with his family's safety and the future of his career.

He can't talk to his club, but it would be possible for him to have an anonymous conversation off the record so that something could be done to help him. Premier League bosses and club management I'm pleading with you to make this happen and set up a whistle-blower's hotline that is totally anonymous. If you can satisfy me that your system is secure, then I will bring this player in from the cold.

Don't think this doesn't affect you if you're towards the top of the table. The fixers aren't stupid and they know how far they can go before anyone gets suspicious. You'll never identify him from results or any spe-cific incident either because he's completely paranoid about covering his tracks.

Don't leave it until it's too late. Contact Direct From The Dressing Room through this newspaper and together we can help this player and play a massive part in keeping our game clean.

He read his copy over twice to check it did justice to the story, hit send on the email and closed his computer feeling he'd done a decent night's work.

The next morning was Thursday and he woke early, but the expected string of excited emails was conspicuously absent from his inbox. By 9.30 he'd had the normal thanks from his sub editor but nothing more.

He called into *The Guardian's* sports desk and asked for the editor but got nowhere. Apparently, there had been an incident the night before involving one of United's more combustible players in a Manchester night club and everyone was busy working all the angles on the story. Alec left an urgent message and moved on.

He tried a contact who worked on Match of the Day for the BBC and offered them an exclusive interview. The contact had sounded very enthusiastic about getting something into the magazine slot in the middle of the programme the day after the column was going to appear. Alec knew not to put all his eggs in one basket, so he called ITV, Sky and BT offering the same thing, hinting strongly that the BBC was already interested.

He did the rounds of the Saturday and Sunday papers but drew blanks wherever he called. Thursday was a notoriously busy day, so he wasn't too surprised. He could have done with more time to set things up, but he was convinced that, in the end, the interest would be there for such a big story.

He spent the rest of the day phoning round the various club fanzines, blogs and social media accounts but struggled to get them to take the match-fixing story seriously. They were all interested in getting a scoop on the player himself and rifled questions at Alec supporting or disproving their guesses as to his identity. He got a few mentions and promises to link to the story on social media the following day, but the reality was they were all too focused on their own clubs to think about the bigger picture.

By the end of the day, all he had to show for his attempts at working the dark arts of PR was another note from his sub-editor with a slightly amended version of his piece for publication.

The Guardian ran the column in full for which, in retrospect, he was grateful. Alec copied the link from its website and hit the social media networks scheduling a series of Twitter updates via the Direct From The Dressing Room account throughout the day.

He sent the link to the big sports broadcasters and got on the phone a few minutes later. He never did speak to anyone from Sky but did manage a conversation with his contact from Match of the Day, who sounded very sheepish.

'Alec, we're in a real spot with this one. We called a few of the clubs to try and stand up your story and they flatly denied there's any match fixing going on: all we've got is your anonymous source. The editor was going to try and include it as a talking point for Gary and Jermaine, but in the end, it was killed by the DoS. He's going into bat for the Beeb next month in the latest round of rights negotiations. You know what the Premier League's like; we just can't risk a massive hike in fees or, worse, losing Match of the Day completely.'

The voice tailed off and the penny dropped for Alec. He should have known of course, but he was too wrapped up in Diego's story. If anyone even hinted that the EPL product was less than a thrill a minute they found themselves out in the cold. Suggesting it was fixed was tantamount to picking a fight with the most powerful commercial sports juggernaut outside the US. Looked at from that perspective, there was no way Sky or any of the Murdoch press was going to run the story and BT Sport was still too new in the game to rock the boat on their own. The best he could hope for was that *The Observer* and some of the foreign media outlets would pick it up, but their lack of currency among football fans would hardly apply the kind of pressure he needed on the clubs or the League.

Alec sat at his desk staring at the screen on his laptop. He had to admit his plan had utterly failed and worse, he had effectively alerted Marko to the fact that Diego was talking. The best he could hope for now was that his rearranging of the facts of the story had muddied the waters enough for Marko not to make the link, but he wasn't hopeful.

Reluctantly he picked up his phone and made one more call of the day.

Chapter 11

Media training workshops were Alec's bread and butter, so it was not unusual to find himself on a grey Thursday afternoon in early September pulling into Everton's training ground, Finch Farm in Halewood, known to the fans as the School of Science. While crosstown rivals, Liverpool, enjoy a state-of-the art complex with extensive gym, full medical facility and a luxury suite of conference rooms and offices, Everton's first team keep their feet on the ground with something rather more functional; a collection of shed-like buildings which they share with their youth academy. Alec was unconcerned, however, as it was the youth team he was here to see. He unloaded his stash of soft porn and headed for the conference room to give his standard message to the players. He had just finished attaching the last of the posters of topless girls to the walls when the door opened, and an attractive uniformed policewoman walked in. Alec was slightly abashed but breezed through any embarrassment assuming, rightly, that she had seen worse.

'I'm Alec,' he said, 'Media training.'

'Senior Agent Dagg, Interpol' came the reply. 'It would appear we have a timing conflict as I'm due to give match-fixing training to the youth team in here now. Still, I can see you're all set. I'll just observe if you don't mind and follow on after you.'

'It's down to the club, I guess, but a police presence isn't really the atmosphere we're aiming for. I try and put the players at ease, get them as comfortable as possible, if you know what I mean.' He gave his most charming smile, but the response was formal if not downright frosty.

'As you like,' she said. 'I'll go first but I'd appreciate it if you'd cover up your, err, visual aids.'

Alec shrugged and started packing hi poster away. 'Interpol,' he paused, his brain making the obvious connections. 'Match fixing? I didn't know there was a problem in the Premier League.'

Michaela observed him expressionlessly as if weighing up whether to get into this particular conversation or not. Then reluctantly she said: 'There has never been a prosecution for match fixing in the Premier League and part of my job is to keep it that way.'

'So, you've got the dubious privilege of trying to get the attention of a room full of bored teenage footballers. Not the most exciting part of your job, I'm guessing. Do you mind if I sit in?'

Now it was her turn to shrug. 'Why not. At least one person will be paying attention.'

The players filed into the room, most wearing headphones, as Senior Agent Dagg flipped open her laptop, hooked it up to the comms leads and beamed a powerpoint onto the projector which declared, 'Match Fixing – don't even think about it!'.

Everton's Player Liaison Officer introduced the 'speaker with an extremely important message' and she was off. Twenty minutes later the players filed out again with at least half having never removed their Beats.

Alec caught Dagg's eye. 'You could throw in a few more laughs next time,' he tried.

'Maybe I should try your posters,' she replied, ruefully but with a smile. 'To be honest, it's a box ticking exercise. Interpol has a contract with FIFA and my police time is spent traveling from one European club to the next so they can say they're taking a zero-tolerance approach to match fixing. The clubs are obliged to give me the time otherwise I'd probably never speak to a single player.'

'Where's your next stop?' Alec asked, reattaching his posters to the wall.

'I'm on what I think they call the red side of Liverpool tomorrow morning then it's the two Manchester clubs in the afternoon.'

Alec turned the smile back on. 'I'm staying here tonight too,' he said. 'Perhaps it needn't be such a wasted evening after all.'

Her face returned to the look she had earlier, weighing up the options, but then she seemed to give in. 'I'm at the Hilton,' she said. 'You can give me a call there when you're done, and I'll see how I'm fixed. I may get a better offer.'

'Ok, but can I ask for someone other than Senior Agent Dagg?'

'Michaela,' she called over her shoulder as she left.

Alec watched from the conference room window as she walked to a rented Ford Focus in the car park. She took off her jacket and revealed a pressed white shirt which, while buttoned up to the top, still flattered her figure. He had never thought of himself as having a thing for women in uniform, but he was enjoying the view.

He had just rehung his posters as the players came back in and this time their attention was rather less divided. He already knew one or two of them from previous visits and there was soon a good buzz in the room. At the end, a couple of the players took him aside for some one-to-one advice. He was always happy to oblige as, while they might be young, some of them would be the stars of the future. For their part, the players knew there was money to be made from social media and Alec had a reputation as someone who could make it happen.

During the conversations he casually established their interest in motor racing under the guise of getting to know their wider interests in sport. It couldn't hurt to line up a bit of future business and they nearly bit his arm off at the chance to race supercars. Before he left, they exchanged numbers and Alec promised to be in touch just as soon as they'd passed their driving tests.

As he drove into the centre of the city to his hotel (Holiday Inn rather than Hilton) his thoughts turned to Diego's predicament. Nothing the policewoman had said in her presentation was remotely relevant to the real-life pressure he was under to fix games. Maybe her

talk was helpful to the younger players who could avoid getting into trouble in the first place, but on the basis of what he'd heard, Alec
could say with absolute certainty that no one caught in the match fixers' trap would ever turn to Interpol for help.

Liverpool's culinary scene was improving all the time and Alec
confirmed a table at Veeno, his favourite Italian, before calling
Michaela. She sounded distracted on the phone but agreed a time to
meet before hanging up abruptly. He changed out of his skinny suit
into jeans and a fresh white shirt then spent the next hour walking
through the old Albert Docks talking on his mobile. First, he called
Sophie who he knew would have just got home from her day working as a GP's receptionist. They hadn't parted on great terms that
morning and the conversation was transactional rather than affec-
tionate.

'How was his day?'

'Fine, and hers?'

'Ok. Evening plans?'

'No just a quiet one.'

'Tomorrow?'

'Newcastle in the morning, lunch on the road, Leicester in the
afternoon and back around seven.'

He knew he should treat her better, but he also wondered sometimes what it was that kept them together at all. The only regret he
felt about having slept with Blandine was over getting caught and
who knew how the evening would pan out with the Senior Agent
Dagg? He promised Sophie he would take her out for a meal when
he got back then got off the phone as soon as he could without setting up another row. The rest of the time he spoke to Diego and got
an update on his situation. They were both still disappointed that
the Direct From The Dressing Room piece hadn't yielded a better
result but Alec promised he wasn't going to give up trying to help
his friend. He ended the call within sight of the restaurant where he

was surprised to see his date was already seated. Out of uniform she looked great, dressed simply in a plain cream silk shirt open two buttons at the neck above tight blue jeans. Alec took it as a sign that she had made an effort on his account, but any hope that his luck was soon dispelled.

If their dinner had been for an episode of First Dates both participants would have reported a complete lack of chemistry and that it was highly unlikely they would chose to meet again. Things didn't start well when he attempted a kiss only to be parried awkwardly by her extended hand. He shook it gamely and tried his usual disarming smile but her reaction was glacial. He tried to lighten the mood with behind the scenes tales of misbehaving footballers to realise quickly that not only was she not the slightest bit interested in football, but her recent exposure to players had coloured her view of the entire game. When he tried to turn the conversation towards match fixing, she clammed up even more until he was beginning to wish he was having that quiet evening in his hotel. Eventually he decided to at least see if he could get some professional advice so that the evening wouldn't be a complete waste. He took a deep breath and popped the question.

'I must confess I asked you out with a bit of an ulterior motive. Do you think that Interpol would be interested if I had information about a current match fixing scam going on in the Premier League?'

'I'm listening,' she said, narrowing her eyes.

Briefly, and without revealing any of the more incriminating details, Alec outlined Diego's predicament.

'So I'm clear,' Michaela responded, 'your boy has got himself into debt to some very bad people, he's being lent on to repay money he doesn't have, he's willingly agreed to interfere in the outcome of Premier League football matches. And you're telling me why?'

'I just thought you might want to go beyond simply parroting crap to footballers and get involved with the actual criminals,' Alec shot back.

'He should have gone to his club before he fixed the first time. They might not have got the police involved but they would have done something to make the situation go away. After all, even $400,000 is barely a dent in the weekly wage bill for a club that big. As it stands though, he's best to go to the Met Police, fall on their mercy and hope they're feeling generous.'

A frosty silence descended over the pair before Michaela relented.

'Ok, just say I was interested, what can you tell me about the criminals he's tied up with?'

'Serbian,' Alec said, aware he was in danger of blowing apart his motor touring business. 'Marko Vasic is based out of an office in West London, but I'm sure he's working for someone bigger back home.'

Her body language changed. She leaned forward slightly, her face revealing a fraction more engagement. 'Keep talking,' she said.

'I've only been there twice but I've worked with him on and off since the beginning of the year organising driving trips for the players. I do the cars and the media protection and he lays on the sex, drugs and rock 'n' roll.

'We'll gloss over for the moment that you're admitting an association with a known drug dealer and looking at possible jail time for procuring the services of prostitutes. Tell me more about the office.'

'Interpol doesn't have any jurisdiction here,' he reminded her, but continued hesitantly.

'The place looks like an old shopfront, now bricked up and turned into flats. Marko's office is out the back across a yard sealed off from the outside world, so unless you knew it was there you'd never suspect it existed. He's got a reception on the ground floor and his office is at the end of the corridor upstairs. There were four or five heavies in one of the rooms speaking what sounded like Russian. But apart from that, there was nothing out of the ordinary. There was no phone or computer on his desk, just a big floor safe behind it. I've only ever contacted him via mobile and I reckon everything's done like that.'

Michaela thought for a moment, mapping out the scene in her mind. 'It must have been a big reception for there to be two offices upstairs.'

'Ah no, you're right. There was another room downstairs full of Brits on phones. They looked like wideboy salesmen sitting at computer screens with headsets on. I only saw them for a second before Marko came down to get me.'

'What about in the flats? Did you see anyone or anything there that could be interesting?'

'No, both times they were very quiet. I didn't see anything except a bunch of doors.'

'What time of day was it when you visited?' asked the policewoman, interested now.

'Morning, both times.'

She paused as if making a decision then in the end she said: 'Of course, I can't be certain but it's possible that what you saw is a classic small-time East European gang operation. Prostitutes in the flats at the front. Asleep, obviously, as it's morning. Out back, Mr Vasic and his associates could be up to anything, but it's the downstairs activity that interests me. If I were to guess, I'd say it was a boiler room operation.'

'Sorry, you've lost me.'

'It's like a call centre but, instead of trying to get your WiFi connected, they sell you fake investments and other scams. When I was in the City of London Police, we saw more and more of it with some people being taken for tens of thousands of pounds.'

She paused again then, as if against her better judgement. 'So, here's the thing,' she said. 'Serbia is of particular interest to Interpol and to me personally for reasons that don't concern you. We are keen to disrupt the networks of organised crime which take their orders from the country's gangland bosses giving them tentacles all around Europe especially in London. As you say, Interpol doesn't have any jurisdiction here or anywhere else so, contrary to what they show in films, I can't parachute in a team of international crime busters and arrest them. The only real power we have is to issue red notices to national police forces advising them that one of their citizens or residents is suspected of having connections to transnational crime. We share intelligence at a country level but it's up to the locals to follow up with arrests and to comply with extradition requests. Unless there's an embarrassing level of evidence that a crime has been committed by one of their own, Serbian police will simply ignore the advice. In fact, at one point they were facilitating cross-border travel to encourage their criminals to operate outside the country rather than at home. They don't do that anymore, as far as we know, but the relationships are still very cosy. Whether they are on the payroll or just frightened, the police are highly motivated to protect their local mafia boss. Having said all that, your cell, if that's what it is, sounds like it would be of interest to police here and it could help fill in another gap in Interpol's knowledge. I'll speak to a contact at the Met, see if Vasic is on their radar and get someone to take a look if not. Ok?'

'I'd be grateful,' said Alec. 'Let's swap numbers in case there are any updates.'

'Here's my card. It's got my mobile on it. Give me a call in a couple of weeks if you want and I'll see what there is to report, but don't get your hopes up. I'd strongly advise you to encourage your client to tell his club or go to the police and preferably both before he gets sucked in so deep he can't get out.'

Alec picked up the tab for the meal without complaint from Michaela but she declined his offer to walk her back to her hotel, preferring to leave on her own. Outside it was a pleasant evening and he made a detour along the waterfront talking to Diego as he went. He gave the player the benefit of his newly acquired information.

'She's concerned about you, I'm concerned about you,' he said. 'As it stands, the worst you're looking at is a ticking off from the club. Speak to them, mate, before it's too late. Meanwhile, I'm following up two leads that submitted comments on *The Guardian* website. They're an odd pair: an Irish academic called Declan something and a sport security organisation based in Qatar. I'll keep you posted if there's any news.'

There was a pause then Diego said: 'I've decided I'm going to talk to Totò. He always helps me, and he will know what to do.'

Alec bit his lip. 'Your call, mate but keep in touch. Let me know how it goes and if there's anything I can do.'

Chapter 12

Alec was at his desk at home on a drab Monday morning trying to give some personality to the Twitter and Instagram accounts of Darren, a goalkeeper with a club in the Midlands. He was an honest and genuine lad and he'd been with the club since he was 14, but if brains were semtex, he wouldn't have enough to blow his headguard off. He would need more than his current plodding stream of earnest posts about his diet if he was going to tap into the commercial potential of social media.

Alec was just contemplating how he might set the player up as one of the contestants on Celebrity Masterchef when the email came through.

Dear Mr Munday,

My client, Mr Rodrigues, is conducting a review of his suppliers and advisors and requests that you join him for a meeting at the Dorchester Hotel, Park Lane, at 2pm on Wednesday, November 22nd.

We trust this will be convenient and await your confirmation.
Cuprimentos,
Salvador (Totò) Diaz
Perfect10 Player Representation

It had been nearly a month since Alec had heard anything from the Brazilian, not that this was unusual. His retainer was clear on deliverables and Alec had kept up his end of the deal. He had watched some of the games Diego had played in and could detect nothing amiss. In fact, with his injury behind him he was back to the dazzling form of last season. His club were benefiting with a rise up the table that put them in contention for a top-4 finish if not the title itself.

Alec sent a one-line reply to the email and 48 hours later was directed by staff at the London hotel into an anteroom that looked like the set of The Apprentice. A group of young executives, mainly men, variously kitted out in sharp suits, city pinstripes, yacht casual and expensive hipster were eying each other up, suspiciously.

Sensing that there might be an opportunity, one of the shinier suited boys introduced himself to the room as Spencer, client relationship manager with an exclusive London car dealership. The ice broken, the others chipped in and soon everyone was talking freely. Over the subsequent two hours Alec was given business cards by an international property agent, a private wealth manager, Learjet leasing agent, yacht broker, Panamanian law firm, offshore tax accountant, interior designer, personal shopper and a florist.

Spencer, still the most voluble, was happy to boast of the business he had done with Diego.

'Yeah well, we took the piss a bit on the chop-in for his Aston Martin but I'd had a crap month. Anyway, I worked through the weekend to source a Ferrari Portofino for him and get it shipped from Monaco but, as I always say, that kind of service is what our football clients are paying for.'

Other members of the group were more circumspect but Alec received quiet assurances of the utmost discretion from both the lawyer and the tax accountant. The private wealth manager spoke in the lazy drawl of an Eton education and rumbled Alec as an oik as soon as he opened his mouth. The rest swapped cards and promised Alec he would be handsomely rewarded if he introduced them to his clients.

As the clock in the room ticked towards four pm, a set of double doors at the end of the room swung open and Diego walked in flanked by three men. They wore dark suits, white shirts and sober-looking ties and looked unsmilingly around the group. One, clearly the leader of the delegation, introduced himself.

'Good afternoon everyone and thank you for coming. My name
is Totò Diaz, I am Mr Rodrigues agent. I am sorry if we have kept
you waiting but I trust you have been well looked after. The purpose
of this afternoon is to help Mr Rodrigues to review some parts of
his life and the quality and cost of the services he has been receiving
from those of you who have been advising him.

'We will be inviting each of you in turn to make representations
to us following which you will be advised of the nature of any continuing relationship. My colleagues will distribute a list giving you the
order of the meetings. As you will appreciate, this process may take
some time and I would like to ask for your patience. Mr Rodrigues
would be grateful if you would follow the order on the list and, if
there is anything you need while you are waiting, please feel free to
ask the hotel staff.'

Having delivered this short statement and overseen the distribu-
tion of a single-sided sheet of paper, the player, the agent and their
associates withdrew behind the double doors taking up places on the
opposite side of a large boardroom table.

The mood in the room outside was now distinctly more appre-
hensive: even Spencer the car salesman was lost for words. Alec saw
that he was towards the end of the list and decided to take himself off
for an hour's walk in Hyde Park. As he left the room, he sent a quick
text to Diego, 'Bet you'd rather be karting.'

He returned at five to find the anteroom practically empty with
only the interior designer and the personal shopper left.

'Wow, that didn't take long. I thought I was going to be here all
evening.'

'I haven't seen so much blood on the carpet, darling, since I
dressed the room for the Beckham's Halloween party,' said the interior designer theatrically.

'Did everyone get fired?'

'It seems Mr Rodrigues has no further use for his Learjet and his order for a 68ft Sunseeker has been cancelled,' said the personal shopper, 'and Spencer has to pay back 10% of the profits he took from the last four deals as the price for keeping Diego's future business.'

'You should have heard the language, darling. That florist does a better hissy fit than Rebecca Vardy. The dodgy lawyer and the tax guy stormed off so who knows what their fate was, and the banker left soon after saying, "there goes my bonus".'

At that moment, the estate agent emerged from the boardroom looking flushed and spilling a pile of property brochures. Alec bent down to help her retrieve them.

'Don't worry,' she said. 'Turns out I'm not going to need them today after all. Anyway, you're up next. Break a leg'

Alec entered the boardroom without knocking, winked at Diego and sat down. Totò had a slim folder open in front of him which he was reviewing.

'Thank you for making time to see us today, Mr Munday, and thank you for your text. Mr Rodrigues has changed his mobile phone so won't be receiving messages from you in future.'

Alec ignored the inference. 'Totò, good to finally meet you. I think last time we spoke I was in the back of an ambulance bailing your client, err, Mr Rodrigues, out of a potentially career-ending predicament.'

'We are aware of who you are and what you have done, Mr Munday. I am advised that you have been more than adequately compensated and I am here to tell you that Mr Rodrigues has no further need of your services.'

'And I am here to tell you that none of us would be here telling each other anything if I hadn't dug Diego out of the shit.'

'Your point is understood Mr Munday but, as I have said, you have been well remunerated and I should also add that we are aware of the hand you had in creating the shit from which Mr Rodrigues required extraction.'

'Cut the crap Totò. You're just a jumped-up bull-shitter who got lucky,' Alec shot back, deciding that, if he was going to go down, he'd rather go down in flames. 'If you think Diego needs any help getting himself in the shit then you don't know your client as well as you think you do. By all means dispense with my services but let me give you some free advice. Mr Rodrigues here attracts trouble like shit attracts flies. Sooner or later you're going to need me or someone as good as me to hush things up if you're going to keep your cash cow still producing.'

'Again, we appreciate your feedback Mr Munday. We are taking certain steps to give Mr Rodrigues the kind of support he needs to avoid becoming the object of any journalistic interest, but we know of your reputation and where to find you should the situation change.'

Alec rolled the dice one more time and asked, 'Diego, how's Marko?'

Diego opened his mouth, but Totò interrupted:

'That particular situation has been successfully resolved. Goodbye, Mr Munday.'

Alec left the Dorchester and wandered north up Park Lane, a jumble of thoughts running through his mind. He was delighted for Diego if it was true that Marko really had been put out of commission and was pleased for the player that his agent recognised, albeit belatedly, that he needed better people around him. He doubted that life would be happy for his friend, however, and wondered how long it would be before he gave his new minders the slip. Meanwhile, what about Marko? Totò didn't seem the violent type, but he presumably had connections with those who were. Violence, or at least the very realistic threat of it, would certainly have been required to persuade the Serbian to release his grip on the player.

Idly, Alec googled 'gang wars Fulham' on his phone but came up with nothing relevant. He dug a bit deeper on Twitter and found reference to a fire on Munster Road three nights ago. Perhaps. And if Marko really was out of the way, maybe there was an opportunity for Alec himself to create a new enterprise to entertain his wilder footballing clients.

He entered the tube from Marble Arch intending to travel east then north back to Enfield, but at the last moment, he changed his mind and switched to the westbound line towards Fulham instead. He was curious to find out just how 'resolved' the Marko situation was. When he got there he found that there had indeed been a fire but it was in a house at least 150 yards before Marko's office. Alec approached his destination cautiously. There were no cars outside and no lights on in the interior, but it was after six pm so the office may simply have shut up shop for the night. As he rounded the corner he saw a tell-tale To Let sign attached to the side wall. Maybe Marko was more resolved than he had thought possible.

Alec made a mental note of the agent marketing the vacant property with the aim of calling the following day to find out a forwarding address. On a whim he buzzed the office entry phone and knocked the door of the apartments. Both went unanswered. Finally, he tried the houses on either side and the only remaining shop in the street on the pretext that he was returning a wallet lost by their recently departed neighbours.

The occupiers were not unfriendly but the residents of Fulham, like many in similar areas, had become so used to people moving into and out of their neighbourhood that they had stopped noticing. The most he got was that the previous occupants were quiet and 'kept themselves to themselves' although there had been some police cars outside a few weeks ago.

Alec retraced his steps to the tube station putting a call in to Michaela Dagg along the way.

'It seems our Serbian outfit has relocated. Would that be any-thing to do with you?' he asked.

'Don't know anything about it, but heat from the local uniform may have persuaded them they would have more operating freedom elsewhere.'

'The Met investigated Marko then. What did they find?'

'It was all pretty much as I predicted. They made a couple of ar-rests but I'm not sure that any charges are pending. Day-to-day op-erations are usually well covered with a veneer of respectability. It's only when things go wrong that they break cover and reveal what's really going on underneath. I'll see whether my contacts have any up-dates but don't hold your breath. How's your boy?'

'He's not my boy any more: I've been fired. His arsehole of an agent is trying to get control of his finances. Understandable, I know, but he has no idea just how exposed his prize asset is. Diego is like a moth to a flame. He did say the situation with Marko was resolved though.'

'Really? I'm not going to ask, but all I would say is that the re-prieve may only be temporary. From what I know, Marko's team were small fry, but he swam with some very big fish back home and you really wouldn't want to mess with those guys.'

Alec hung up and disappeared into the tube network and out of range. He emerged forty minutes later and heard his phone ping. He glanced at the screen to see a single letter 'D' sent from an un-known mobile number. He added the number to his contacts with-out replying. The media man returned home to a dark and empty house. Sophie would not have been home at this time anyway, but the fact that she had moved out a week earlier made it seem that much darker and emptier. Inside it was still strewn with traces of her and, turning on the lights, Alec experienced the familiar mixed feel-ings of relief and regret. Today wasn't up there as one of his best and he could have done with the company this evening. He would make sure to connect with her again if only to offer to return her stuff. Losing Diego as a client wouldn't put much of a dent in his finances, but nonetheless he hated getting sacked and objected in particular to being lumped together with the bunch of parasites he'd met at the Dorchester. Reflexively he checked out the Brazilian's social media and reviewed the blizzard of clumsy posts and status updates endorsing a disparate range of brands. Clearly Totò was working his magic for his client.

'Just using my ManLux miracle volumizer for hair that is ready to go the full 90 minutes.'

'Thanks to Bolland and Scarett for my libido boosting ginseng. Feeling hot and ready to go the full 90 minutes.'

'I'm backing the Opal, a new luxury apartment complex in Delhi, because quality is not an option.'

It was more than enough to give product endorsement a bad name. Alec shut down the laptop his mood darkening as his phone buzzed. It was Michaela Dagg.

'I thought you'd like to know that the local nick in Fulham is conducting a murder investigation dating from around the time in question,' she reported. 'Eye witnesses reported a car being sprayed with bullets from two shooters riding pillion on motorbikes. The bodies of four large males were recovered and evidence at the scene confirmed they were Serbian nationals.'

'Was Marko one of the victims?'

'I have requested the IDs but, from your description of him, I suspect he got away. This group looked like the hired muscle but either way your boy seems like he's mixing with some rather interesting acquaintances.'

'What are you going to do with the information?'

'Believe me, if I thought it would help, I'd be fingering Diego to the investigating officer. However, I wouldn't be telling him anything he doesn't already know by suggesting it was a professional hit carried out on the instructions of someone with a grievance. I've mentioned that I believe there could be a Brazilian connection which may get them a bit further. But by then I'm sure the agent will be back in Brazil or wherever so the most I can do is put an Interpol flag against him and his company. It'll slow him down a bit at border control in future, but that's about it. As for Diego, you'd better hope that his path doesn't cross with Marko's anytime soon, or ever.'

'I feel I should say thanks but I'm not sure why.'

'Don't thank me Alec. The world isn't going to miss a few East European gangsters, but as I see it, your boy deserves whatever he gets from here on. And just a word of warning. Like mobsters the world over, these guys aren't the forgiving type: revenge is normally quick and brutal and takes out the whole crew. I'd be staying well away if I were you. See you around.'

Chapter 13

'Wait before you post that message! Last time I checked The Sun newspaper had around 1.5 million Twitter followers and the Daily Mail just over two million. Most of you have got four or five times that number so if you post that message you might as well hire a fleet of planes and put it on a banner behind them. Think: are you happy to have your message plastered over all the front pages? If not, swallow hard, calm down and hit delete.'

It was five days later, and Alec had just delivered his punchline to a reluctant group of players at a Midlands club when his phone started vibrating. He glanced down and at the name on the screen, dismissed the class quickly then took a deep breath and answered the call.

'Marko, long time, no speak.'

'Shut the fuck up. I need Diego's mobile number.'

'Can't give it to you, Marko. His agent has made him change his phone and cut all his old mates adrift.'

'You've got one hour to get it or his stupid bitch of a wife is dead, and don't think I'm joking.'

The line went dead leaving Alec's head spinning. He knew that getting Marko off his player's back was never going to be as easy as Totò made out, but he hadn't expected anything like this. He scrolled through his contacts and paused over 'D' before hitting the call button. The line rang twice then he was listening to dead air again.

He started to write a text message, but Diego sent him one before he had chance to finish tapping out the words.

'Call you in 20 minutes.'

'This is life or death!' Alec wrote back.

He used the next few minutes to sign off with the club management. He was waiting in the carpark when his phone went off.

'Alec, how've you been man. Sorry about Totò...'

'Diego, listen, I'm not calling for a chat. Where's Marta?'

'She's on holiday with her girlfriends in Greece. Why?'

'When did you last speak to her? Who knows she's there?'

'Alec, man. What's this about? I spoke to her yesterday evening. She's good.'

'Right, listen. I just got off the phone with Marko. Remember him?'

'What? Fuck! That's not possible. Totò told me he wasn't going to make any more trouble.'

'Well I can tell you it wasn't a ghost and he sounded seriously pissed off. He told me that if I didn't get him your new number within the hour, then Marta's life was in danger. I'm pretty sure he's serious. Sorry, man.'

'Puta que pariu. Que diabos devo fazer?

The phone went dead again. Alec was getting used to the experience and waited for the player to call him back again. Seven minutes later he was starting to get concerned. It was nearly half an hour since Marko's call, and he hadn't sounded in the mood to extend his deadline. Eventually Diego called.

'I called Marta's phone and one of her girlfriends answered. Some guys pulled up in a car with blacked out windows while they were walking outside the hotel. They grabbed her and forced her inside and drove off. The hotel called the police and they are talking to the girls now. How did they even know where she was?'

'At a guess, I'd say they were monitoring her social media. Did she post any selfies?'

'Filho da puta. Alec, what am I going to do?'

Alec let the player rant in Portuguese for a few seconds while he tried to think. How far was Serbia from Greece? Could one of the most poorly funded police forces in Europe be persuaded to set up road blocks?

'Ok look, Diego, we're running out of time. The only thing we can do right now is just call him back. If I call him with your number he's just going to get straight onto you so you're going to have to do it yourself.'

'No, man, I can't talk to him. You've got to sort it.'

'What do you think I'm going to do? You need to get the police involved. This is bigger than anything we can handle ourselves.'

'No police, no police!'

'Diego, think. The police are already on the scene. You need to call the girls back and talk to the police. Tell them who she is and that you suspect she's been kidnapped and is being taken to Serbia. Ask them to set up road blocks and make sure you offer them a big reward for their trouble. Meanwhile, I'll see if I can buy some time. I could try and tell Marko you're on a plane which doesn't land for a while but it's a massive risk.'

'Do it, Alec. He's only taken Marta so he can get to me; he's not going to hurt her.'

'You just killed four of his guys. I don't think you can rely on anything like logic in this situation.'

The player let out a deep and desperate moan. 'I swear, Alec. I never knew Totò was going to kill anyone. Oh, Marta. O que eu fiz?'

'Diego, we've got around 20 minutes until the hour's up. Let's use it to achieve as much as we can. You need to call the hotel back and speak to the police like I said. Can you do that?

The player said he would although Alec had his doubts.

'I'm going to call Marko in exactly 15 minutes from now. I'll try and string him along but we can't risk Marta's life. You need to get ready for him to call you. Make sure you're off the phone and get yourself somewhere quiet with a good phone reception. Get some paper and a pen and be ready to make notes. Better still, find some way to record the call. Is there anyone with you? Can you get another iPhone? Put him on speaker and use voice memos to record the conversation.'

Alec could hear from his breathing that the Brazilian was starting to panic.

'Diego, nothing bad is actually going to happen on the call, ok. He's going to make threats and a lot of noise and it will be scary but at the end you just need to be very clear what he's asking you to do next. I'm going to hang up now so get onto the Greek police and get things moving at that end. I'll call Marko in a quarter of an hour, so you can expect a call in twenty minutes tops. I'll get straight on the road and be with you in a couple of hours. We'll see where we are then, ok?'

He hung up. Exactly fifteen minutes later took a deep breath and called Marko. The call sounded like it was connecting overseas but was answered on the second ring.

'Ok, give me the number.'

'Yeah, Marko, I've managed to connect with Diego but he's not in a good way. Maybe it's better if you and I...'

'Just give me the fucking number, you prick. The clock is still ticking.'

Alec had little choice but to hand over the information and the line went dead as soon as the number was exchanged. He spent a few minutes rearranging his schedule for the following day, checked out of the hotel and got on the road back to London.

Once he was moving he put a call through to Michaela who wasn't exactly overjoyed to be talking again so soon.

'I told you, I think he deserves whatever's coming. He's never going to get any sympathy from me,' was her harsh assessment.

'Yeah, I know, but think about Marta. She's all alone out there and God knows what they're planning to do with her. You know what these people are capable of.'

He hit a nerve. Alec may not have realised it but she knew only too well what happens to people who stand in the way of Serbian criminals.

'If you could just meet with us later, find out what Marko wants and help Diego see sense about what he should do next.'

'You're putting me in a very compromising situation, Alec. You want me to meet with someone who has had four guys killed...'

'He denies any knowledge of that, in fact he was completely shocked. As far as Diego is concerned, his hands are clean.'

'You have a very odd definition of clean hands. You do know I'm still a police officer, right? If your client says anything at all that links him to those murders or any other crimes, I will have no choice but to hand that information over.'

'Understood. Look, he's no angel, for sure, but he's not a killer. Once you meet him, you'll see there is no harm in him. He's made some mistakes, that's all. Surely he deserves a chance to put them right.'

In the end she admitted that she was in London and reluctantly agreed to meet at Diego's house in Hampstead. She hung up leaving Alec alone with his thoughts. He assumed there would be an update from the luckless player but his phone was silent for the entirety of the drive back to London. He turned the problem over in his mind but however he looked at it, he concluded that the chances of getting Marta back were slim. Maybe Michaela would have some ideas. The longer he drove the more despondent he grew: whatever Marko wanted it wasn't going to be good and he couldn't see any way out for the player or his wife. Marta would be terrified and she didn't seem like she was strong enough to deal with being taken hostage. That would put huge pressure on Diego meaning he would be left with no choice but to agree to whatever Marko demanded. If he tried to stand up to the thug, alert his club or go to the police there was a massive risk that Marta would simply be killed.

By the time he pulled up outside the gates of the Hampstead property his imagination had been working overtime. Alec was a natural schemer but this time he was stumped. He parked his BMW and waited until a Toyota Prius glided up a few minutes later. Michaela emerged from one of the back doors, Alec buzzed the house and they were let into the drive.

The door was open but there was no sign of Diego. The pair found him in the basement looking even smaller than usual, alone in the massive room. Alec made the introductions.

Michaela greeted him gently in Portuguese. 'Olá, Diego. Como vai você? Desculpa por ouvir sobre os seus problemas.'

Alec thought Diego would be suspicious of Michaela but, if anything, he seemed relieved. The two chatted fluently in his mother tongue before Alec interrupted.

'For my benefit, do you mind if we switch to English? Diego, can you update us?'

The visitors sat in silence as the player relayed details of what he knew. The snatch had taken place over six hours ago as the girls were returning from a shopping trip. They had tried to fight but were taken by surprise and had no chance of stopping Marta's kidnappers. The hotel had called the police who arrived on the scene a few minutes later. They had Marta's phone but couldn't open it to get Diego's number, so it was more than three hours before his offer of a reward came through. That was also the first time the police knew of any Serbian connection – they had been working on the assumption that it was a local operation. Although they were keen to earn a reward, they had been honest and admitted that road blocks would almost certainly be a waste of time. The girls had been staying at the luxury Eagles Palace resort in Halkidiki and the Macedonian border was only just 90 minutes away.

Despite news reports of crossing points being closed between the two countries, European passport holders could cross easily into

Macedonia and from there on to Serbia with only a perfunctory glance at their paperwork. The call from Marko to Alec had been from a vehicle which at the time was almost certainly across the border and out of reach of Greek officials. Once the police established that it was unlikely the kidnappers were still in the country, they quickly lost interest. There would be a report and someone higher up might make diplomatic representations to Macedonia but that was it.

'What about Marko?' asked Alec. 'What did he say?'

Diego glanced at Michaela then continued. 'It was terrible, man. He put Marta on and she was crying and asking me what was going on. Then he said that if I wanted to see her alive again, I had to do exactly what he said. He wants me to fix matches but it's much worse than before. I've gotta get other players to do it too to make a much bigger operation. He said he wants to own the Premier League and he would kill Marta if he doesn't get what he wants.'

'I have to start with the midweek game on Wednesday night as, like, a present he can take to his boss. I should get a yellow card at the end of the first half otherwise he's going to kill her. If I do it, I can speak to her later that evening and after that he's going to give me more instructions. That's all he said. He just cut the call.'

There was silence in the room as Alec and Michaela digested Diego's position before Alec spoke.

'So, Michaela what are we looking at?'

She thought for a long time before answering. 'Look, Diego, I'm sorry about your situation and especially for Marta. Let's perhaps try and think things through. The first thing to say, I suppose, is that my assessment of the threat is that it's serious. Serbia is not the gangster hell that it was under Slobodan Milosevic, but in a way it's worse. Criminals have become organised into a series of effective mafia enterprises. They are strong, politically well-protected and they run large operations. The supply of weapons is still plentiful, and they have a habit of using them without much provocation. I'm sorry to have to tell you Diego, but Marta's life is in real danger and there is no local cavalry that is going to be riding to her rescue anytime soon.'

The player nodded in recognition.

'I did a bit of digging earlier today and can offer you one piece of information which may turn out to be important. When the Met arrested Marko they examined his mobile phone. Most of his connections in Serbia were not in the capital but in a smaller city called Niš. It's around 180 miles south east of Belgrade and close to the border of Macedonia which they would have driven through from Greece. So, I'd say that makes it much more likely that Niš is where the gang's headquarters are. My professional judgement is that's where Marta is and that's good news.'

Diego and Alec looked confused but Michaela went on to explain.

'To give you some background, the chaos of the 90s and early 00s meant that mafia-style organised crime was quite slow to take off in Belgrade. No one stayed alive long enough to get organised, but in Niš the situation was more stable. After the Balkan wars ended the city was effectively controlled by two brothers, Lech and Arkan Belovic, both paramilitaries and bitter rivals. You may have heard the name Arkan but that was actually the real name of Željko Ražnatović, a notorious warlord around in the '80s. This Arkan is a dumb thug who ruled his part of the city at the point of a gun but, Criminal feuds being what they are, two became one in 2008 when Lech's gang wiped out his brother's in a move which was suspected to have had the support of local politicians.

'Arkan Belovic survived but had no choice but to join his brother's operation now renamed the Belovic Clan. Since then the city has been run as what Interpol would call a Joint Criminal Enterprise. The Clan effectively controls Niš as a mafia state but from the outside you wouldn't be able to tell them apart from a regular company. They have lots of completely legitimate businesses, they pay tax and play a big part in the social life of the city doing things like owning and financing the local football club.

'Their main business is international trucking but that is just a front for the usual criminal activities: drug dealing, prostitution, extortion and human trafficking. They are suspected of having links with criminal gangs in Asia and Latin America but locally, officials and police are well looked after. They let them go about their business largely unchecked as long as there is peace on the streets. Crime levels in the city are low as police are quick to tackle any potential rivals who threaten to disrupt the status quo. So there's very little violence and in general, everyone's happy.'

Diego kept blinking and nodding but it was clear he was taking in very little. Alec was left to try and interpret what the Interpol officer had said.

'Ok, so we're dealing with a seriously powerful gang of organised criminals but they're not as trigger happy as their cousins in Belgrade?'

'Correct,' came the response. 'Without pointing fingers, someone connected to Diego arranged the assassination of four gang members. If you were dealing with Belgrade, they would hunt you down and take their revenge in blood. Lech Belovic is different: he has made a great deal of money and now he's more like a businessman than a gangster. He has engineered it so the Clan has complete freedom to operate. They are not at risk of showing weakness to a rival gang and could be prepared to at least consider whether there is a way then can take advantage of this situation financially. It may not feel like it, but Diego, Marta got lucky.'

Chapter 14

The pair left the footballer's mansion and reconvened in Alec's car. Diego had been completely vacant by the end of their conversation so they had fixed him something to eat from the sparse contents of his fridge then put him to bed.

1400 miles away his wife was preparing to face her first night as a hostage. Her cell was a room in a nondescript block of apartments with peeling paint and wire reinforced glass in its only window. The dim light of a single low-wattage bulb illuminated a wooden chair and an iron-framed bed on which a single blanket lay in a pile on the thin mattress. On the floor was a threadbare carpet which might once have been orange but was now muddy brown with a large stain. Apart from these few items the smell of damp masked by stale layers of cheap perfume was the only thing that filled the room. The apartment outside was equally ill equipped and what furniture it did contain looked like unwanted donations to a homeless shelter. A tiny kitchen had a cracked sink and a freestanding gas cooker of a type long since removed from all but the poorest homes in England. Inspection of the single cupboard could be done from the hall outside as it had no doors. It did contain a few mismatched plates, cups and some basic pans and the draw beneath it held some spoons and a fork. There were no knives. Alternate patches of grease and mould on the walls and ceiling added to the air of decay.

After hours on the road squeezed between two large men Marta had been handed over to a middle-aged woman who simply looked her up and down, shrugged and led her away without a word. She had been offered some dried sausage and a hunk of black bread which were still on the floor beside the bed. The woman had given her no instructions or warnings, simply left her alone in the apartment locking the door behind her. Marta had the run of the place but was trapped as surely as if she was handcuffed to the lukewarm radiator in the corner. She had lost her bag in the snatch so had no phone, purse or passport. The only clothes she had were the thin dress she was wearing and, as she stretched up to get a glimpse of the world outside, she saw it had started to rain.

She lay down and wept silently, the panic of earlier in the day overtaken by uncomprehending desperation. When the tears eventually stopped she looked at the ceiling for hours trying to think of anything which might help her make sense of what was happening. Eventually, when nothing came, she fell into a light and restless sleep.

Back in Hampstead Alec sat at the wheel of his car without speaking. Michaela waited quietly for a while then shuffled in her seat making a slight cough.

'Sorry,' he said, jolted back to reality. 'I'm just trying to get my head around all of this. Look, I don't live too far from here. Would you come back to my place?'

He didn't quite know why he'd asked and she didn't know quite why she accepted but they were soon weaving their way through Hampstead and on past a still bustling Golders Green and Finchley towards Enfield.

'That was impressive knowledge back there about the ins and outs of the Serbian mafia,' said Alec. 'Some kind of specialist subject?'

'I was investigating a Serbian connection when I was at the City of London Police and organised crime in Serbia became a bit of an obsession. Not that any of that's going to help Marta. As I said back there, the local police aren't going to be of any help and trying to navigate the diplomatic route through the Brazilian embassy in Belgrade isn't going to work either. Apart from anything else, we don't actually have any evidence and it would probably just make her situation worse. It's ironic really; I'm probably one of the world's leading experts on crime in a country beyond the reach of the international criminal justice system.'

'What do you think of her chances?'

'She is fortunate not to be in Belgrade but they've got to be 50:50 at best. The way these things usually work out the longer she's held the less chance she has, but it's hard to know what kind of a game Marko is playing. He may think Lech Belovic will see some advantage in having control over a Premier League footballer but I'm willing to bet that a high-profile celebrity kidnapping takes the Clan way out of its comfort zone. My biggest fear for her right now is that she tries to escape while they're still really jumpy. If they can all settle down until after the midweek game is over, there's a chance she'll survive. After that I really don't know. Her best hope is that someone can give them a reason to let her go and quickly.'

'Diego doesn't have anyone to turn to for help, though. I don't know if he's fixed games already but you could see in his face that he's going to take that yellow card on Wednesday. He could come clean with his club but, however sympathetic they might be, they can't accept him interfering in the results of games. He can't go to the police as they would make the link to the London killings and, as you said, they wouldn't really be able to do anything to help Marta anyway. His agent seems to have contacts who are prepared to take the law into their own hands, but he'd need a small army to stand any kind of chance in Serbia itself. At the moment, I'd say we're all he's got.'

They were silent for long time then, as they crossed over into Tottenham, Michaela said, 'This used to be my old patch.'

'Really?' said Alec. I'm surprised. I mean, I guess I don't really know anything about you.'

They were grateful to have something else to talk about and Michaela gave up some of her reticence as she recalled her time at Tottenham Nick with surprising warmth. The tension of the day and the immediate concern for the player and his wife seemed to recede slightly as the slow crawl of the North Circular gave way to the leafier streets of Enfield.

As they entered Alec's house Michaela took in the scene with a well-trained eye. 'So, where is Mrs Munday this evening?' she asked. 'I mean, I guess I don't really know anything about you either. And yet here I am, alone in your house with clear evidence I'm not the first female companion you've entertained here.'

They both laughed and Alec blushed covering his embarrassment smoothly by picking out a bottle of white Burgundy from the fridge.

'Senior Agent Dagg, I'm sure you are well able to take care of yourself if it came to it. Her name was Sophie and we weren't married. She moved out two weeks ago, I just haven't got around to getting rid of the evidence. I wasn't exactly expecting an inspection this evening. Are you hungry? We could get a takeaway if you fancy it. There's a decent curry house locally that delivers.'

Alec made the call before she returned to the same line of questioning.

'Are you still in touch, with Sophie, I mean?'

'She's ghosted me on Facebook which I'd say means probably not. She was quite right, though; I was a bit of a shit.'

'Maybe she just wanted more than you had to give at this point.'

'What, like exclusivity you mean?'

'Oh, I see, that kind of shit.'

He spread his arms: 'My life is an open book, but I wouldn't exactly say the same about you.'

'What do you want to know?' she asked. 'I can't promise I'll answer, but you can always ask.'

'Ok, how come you speak Portuguese?'

'I had a Portuguese boyfriend when I was at uni. A brief fling but long enough to pick up a decent enough grasp of the language.'

'You see, you're full of surprises. How many languages do you speak?'

'At the last count, nine quite fluently with a few others that I can get by in.'

'That's a lot of boyfriends.'

'I'm a linguist; it's one of the things I do, although getting friendly with a native speaker makes it a lot more interesting. Learning a language is about more than finding equivalent words and phrases to those you use at home; it's about the cultural reference points, the history and politics that go with it. You'll always be a foreigner unless you dive into the things that lie beneath the words and, if you do, you'll always get on with the locals no matter how badly you speak their language.'

'Is that how you got interested in Serbia, some kind of language project? When we met in Liverpool you said there was a personal reason why you were interested.'

'No, that was something different, although I do speak Russian which is quite close to Serbian, so I'm sure I'd be able to make myself understood there.'

She paused then continued slowly. 'I told you I was investigating a Serbian-backed bank in The City. We were just closing in on the operation when I was knocked down in a hit and run. There was never any proof who did it, but it had all the hallmarks of a planned attack by those connected with the bank. It took me six months to get anything like fit again and becoming an expert on crime in the country was the only thing that kept me from going completely insane. I'm still not going to be running a marathon anytime soon, but I'd dearly love to see justice for those who tried to kill me. I took the Interpol job partly for a change of scene and a new start, but also to be able to tap into their archives.'

Michaela fell silent giving Alec time to examine her face. He could see the pain of the memory in her eyes but was also struck by their beauty. 'Sorry,' he said. 'I thought I was starting with the easy questions to put you at ease before getting personal. It must have been a difficult time.'

'The worst, but you were a footballer; you must know what it's like to get injured.'

'I'm not sure my experience really compares. I was a promising youngster, worked my way up through the youth system at my club then got a professional contract and spent two seasons in the reserves. They did the usual thing and loaned me out for a couple of years then brought me back to train with the first team and the manager started picking me as a sub. I made a few second-half appearances but my one and only first-team start was in the early rounds of the FA cup against a League One side. I was a bit too cheeky with my opposite number in defence and the referee gave him the benefit of the doubt once too often. One thing led to another, I got completely clattered and ended up being stretchered off the field with a busted knee and ankle.

'The medics did what they could, I had a top sports surgeon who operated on the cruciate ligament, but with the ankle too it was always going to be a long shot. I went from a young hopeful to washed up might-have-been overnight and it took a hell of a long time to get over it. The club were really good; I had the best physio and rehab money could buy but there was no way back into the game for me. The mental part was the worst. After the operations I had nine months when I was told, basically, I couldn't move and those were dark times. Every sportsman knows their career isn't going to last for ever but mine was over before it even started. That was the worst part, knowing that I had got so close then having the dream snatched away right at the moment the finish line was in sight. I had invested everything in becoming a footballer so it felt like suddenly I had nothing in my life at all. I suppose I kind of lost my identity.'

The silence that followed was broken by the sound of the doorbell. Alec was quick to get up and busied himself spreading the various aluminium cartons on the breakfast bar. She topped up their wine glasses and asked, 'What happened to the other player? The way you described it, it sounds like he should have been charged with assault.'

'I was in so much pain that I wasn't really aware at the time, but they said afterwards that the game just carried on. I was told I could press charges but I've never really held it against the other guy. He was being outplayed and he just did the only thing he could to stop me. He was very apologetic afterwards; came and saw me in the hospital which couldn't have been easy. No, it's the referee that I blame. The crowd was going crazy and he could see that the situation was in danger of erupting yet he made no attempt to intervene. When the tackle came in he didn't even give a yellow card. I know who he is and I thought for a long time that I'd like to get even with him but, as I say, it was a long time ago.'

'What do you miss most about football?'

'Definitely the team,' he said, without a hesitation. 'I still see it every day. You know, I go into a club and I can tell straight away if the team is working or not and I'm rarely wrong. If the team dynamic's not there you can see it in the results. Sometimes a really special player can make up for the rest but mostly everything just starts to misfire. The goalie can't keep hold of the ball, the defenders look like they've never played together before and the strikers can't buy a goal. But when the team's working it's like those birds that make patterns in a great swarm.'

'Starlings?'

'Yeah, how do they do that? It's like they're one living organism not a collection of individual birds and that's what the team's like when it's working. Everyone knows their job but you get carried along by some sort of higher energy. You're unstoppable and it's the best feeling in the world. Of course, I miss the money too. Well, not really the money itself; I miss not having to think about money. You know, that carefree feeling that whatever things cost, there's always going to be enough.'

'Not a feeling I've ever experienced to be honest. No one goes into the police to get rich.'

'Maybe not, but you have team camaraderie, you do a job that everyone actually needs, and you have the status that goes with that.'

'Stop, I'm going all misty eyed. Let's just say there are good days and bad days.'

'You really notice what kind of a life you've got when you're forced to stop and change direction. When I had to give up being a footballer people's attitude to me completely changed. Not the players; they just moved on with their teams, but people that you meet. Before I'd say I was a footballer and there was always a connection. The blokes would either shake your hand or buy you a drink and, of course, they'd have an opinion on our current form or tactics. And the girls would fall over themselves to get up close and personal. Now I'm just another bloke making his way.'

'I'm sure your ego will survive you leaving the ranks of the immortals.'

Despite the circumstances of their evening they sparred good humouredly for a couple more hours, the conversation wandering from sport to relationships, hopes and ambitions until Michaela shifted in her seat and coughed slightly. Alec recognised the gesture from earlier in the evening.

'Ah, yes, sorry,' he said, awkwardly. 'We could talk all night, but I'm sure you have somewhere official you need to be in the morning.'

'Alec, look, this has been nice,' she said, ignoring him. 'Now would you take me to bed please?'

If he was surprised, he tried not to show it. He took her wine glass and put it aside before leading her upstairs to the bedroom desperately trying to think as he did so when he last changed the sheets.

They kissed gently at first then with more urgency. As he undid her blouse Alec realised that since that disastrous evening in Liverpool, he hadn't really seen Officer Dagg as anything except a policewoman. Maybe he had been too ready to accept her brittle exterior, or maybe this evening she had unbuttoned emotionally a while before he unbuttoned her physically.

If he was in danger of over thinking the situation, Michaela was the opposite. She seemed to lose herself in their love making, moving like a dancer taking her lead from his touch. Her eyes were closed but her hands guided his as he undressed her and explored her body. She straddled him on the bed offering up her breasts to his waiting mouth as she took him inside her. She rode him slowly and deeply then more insistently and the two moved as one as they reached a shuddering climax.

They lay quietly in each other's arms with Alec turning over the events of the day in his mind. Eventually the thoughts overwhelmed him and he slept.

The next morning Michaela woke early and as Alec started to stir, she said, 'I've had an idea.'

He blinked and rubbed his eyes blearily. She was sat on the side of the bed in one of his shirts with her tousled hair pushed up in a grip. From where Alec lay, she looked great.

'Of course you have,' he said. 'That's why I brought you home and can I say that was one of the best ideas I've had in a while.'

'I'm serious. I think there's a way that might help us with Diego.'

'Alright,' he said noting the turnaround from 'your boy' to 'us'. 'Let me get some coffee on and you can tell me about it.'

Her idea turned out to be a person; Toby Ashburton, a former banker and contact from her time in the City.

'He used to be a futures trader,' she explained, although Alec wasn't really any the wiser. 'Now he runs a spread betting company. He's a very bright guy and I'm sure he'd have some ideas. I'm certain money is the key that's going to unlock this whole thing and Toby is exceptionally good at making it. Let me call him. We might be even able to get together today.'

'Don't you have to be somewhere saving footballers from match fixing.'

'Oh, didn't I tell you, Interpol dropped that contract with FIFA. Bit too toxic for us at the moment so I'm on leave for a month. I was at a loose end so came to London to check up on my old flat and catch up with friends. You've got me for the next three weeks if you want me.'

Chapter 15

A call to Hugo Ashburton's office established that he was out of the country until Thursday so they booked an appointment for Friday morning. Alec looked at his watch and said, 'I reckon Diego will have gone to training even if it's only to take his mind off what's happening with Marta. I'm going to suggest I meet up with him later to keep him company. I don't suppose he'll have told anyone else what's going on. That does leave us with a few hours to kill though.'

He reached out to Michaela and slipped his hand under her shirt pulling her towards him. 'I can think of plenty of ways to fill the time,' he said, trying hard to sound playful rather than creepy.

She wriggled free although she did dazzle him with a smile. 'Not so fast, tiger. I've got things to do. I'm going to pay some house calls on my old City Police colleagues.'

She showered quickly putting yesterday's clothes back on but applying her eye makeup with care. 'I'll be back,' she said, which wiped any trace of disappointment from his face.

He gave her a spare key and watched as she departed in an Uber leaving the house to revert to its usual library-like state. Out of deference to Michaela he went room-to-room collecting Sophie's things and boxing them up carefully although he made no attempt to contact his ex to arrange to deliver them. He used the next few hours to do some research of his own with the germ of an idea starting to take shape. He drew up a short list of players he knew well enough to talk to and who could be trusted. Then he did a trawl of their social media posts to try and establish any patterns. He already knew some of their habits and this filled out a fuller picture. He reviewed the list and then broadened it out to friends of friends; other players he could access and whose reputations he was already familiar with. He did a similar social media review and within three hours was pretty satisfied with the result. The players in his team would never win anyone's Fantasy League, but he was sure each of them, given the right circumstances, would rally round and help a fellow professional.

Alec looked at his watch. Diego was likely to be eating lunch before a session with the physio so he picked up the phone and made the call. The noise in the background was the usual lively team banter but Diego was happy enough to break off from the group. Footballers are well practiced at whiling away their spare time and Alec suggested the usual afternoon of hanging out by the PlayStation.

'I'd rather go karting,' came the reply, which suited Alec and they agreed to meet up an hour or so later.

Diego was as focused and competitive as ever during the afternoon at the track. Alec marvelled at his ability to compartmentalise; to put distractions to one side and perform as an athlete whatever else was going on in his life. He came away with a new track record but any sense of elation had worn off almost before they parked up for the last time. They drove back to the player's house in silence. Marta hadn't been mentioned once but her shadow hung over them. Alec knew the prospect of a quiet night alone would be tough for Diego and he fully expected to be spending the evening with his friend. As it turned out he was dismissed on the doorstep.

'I'm going to do my usual pre-match evening routine,' said Diego. 'But it would be great if you could come back tomorrow evening for when I speak to Marko. I'm already feeling sick about that but I need to know that Marta's ok.'

Alec agreed and left the player to his preparation. Diego was as superstitious as every other footballer and Alec could only begin to imagine the full range of rituals and nervous ticks he would be performing tonight. Any obsessive tendencies would also be magnified ahead of a game where he not only had to perform for the manager, the team and the fans, but also for a remote gangster holding a gun to his wife's head. Unknown to Alec the player was relying more on divine intervention and planned to spend the evening in a Brazilian church in Seven Sisters. In any event, Alec was no longer required and he pointed his car in the direction of Enfield.

The first thing he saw as he opened his front door was a medium-sized suitcase in the hallway. Michaela had clearly made good on her promise to return and it looked like she was planning to be around for a while at least. As he entered the house he was hit by the heady smell of what he hoped was dinner. Onions and garlic, and probably wine too, as well as the deep savoury aroma of something meaty. It was a while since the kitchen had been used for anything like home cooking and he entered it with a smile on his face.

'Make yourself at home, why don't you' he laughed.

'Don't get any ideas of domestic bliss,' she said nonetheless moving her body against his as he embraced her from behind, kissing her neck. 'You have to remember that I'm used to the high gastronomic standards Lyon's chefs and I really couldn't stomach another takeaway. Anyway, I see Sophie's moved out.'

'She's in a box in the garage actually.'

'You know how to treat a lady, don't you?'

She had on a pair of jeans and a pale blue cotton shirt and this time made no protest as he moved his hands from her waist up to her breasts. She did draw the line at the buttons, however, and pushed him away to find some wine.

'Have you got any decent red?' she asked.

'Lyon, that's Rhone territory isn't it? I'm pretty sure I can offer you a bottle of Châteauneuf du Pape.'

'Mmm that's a bit further south, but you're less of a Neanderthal than I gave you credit for.'

'It may interest you to know that most footballers know plenty about the finer things in life: it's the simple pleasures they're not always so clued up on. Anyway, were your City Police mates able to provide anything useful?'

'I got what I thought I would; confirmation of the links between the City of London and organised crime in Niš and, as there's only one crime outfit based there, I'm still assuming we're looking at Marko's bosses' international activities. There's nothing close to proof of course but my colleagues estimate that around £30 million has washed through various accounts over the last year. That's quite a step up from where they were 12 months ago lending weight to my theory that they've made links with organised crime in Asia and maybe Latin America. It's not a complete or detailed picture but it provides some useful scale in terms of what Diego's up against. What have you been doing?'

'I took him karting to take his mind off things,' he said, as he uncorked the bottle with a reassuring plop and poured two half glasses. 'He's amazing, you know. To see him on the track you wouldn't think he had a care in the world. The only thing that existed for him was the car and the obstacles in front of him. There was a group of the usual boy racers who'd got the afternoon off but he left them for dead.'

Alec let the conversation take a natural pause wondering at the turn his luck had taken as she moved smoothly from the fridge to the hob. 'To be honest, I wasn't really sure you'd come back this evening. I was half expecting the 'last night was a mistake' text message.'

She turned and looked him straight in the eye. 'I think long and hard before inviting anyone to take me to bed. It's a long time since I've made a mistake like that and I'm rather looking to you to convince me I've made the right call.'

'So, what changed between our first meeting in Liverpool and yesterday?'

'Don't over think things, Alec. I just wasn't having a good time in Liverpool. I'd had nearly three weeks of being ignored by stupid footballers, I was wasting a huge amount of my time and living out of a suitcase. It was a million miles away from the reasons I signed up for the police and I think I probably took it out on you. So, Sorry, ok?'

'No need to apologise. I can see how trying to lecture players would get anybody down. Why did you join the force, then? The more I get to know you the less like a policewoman you seem.'

'Then we both have our prejudices don't we. You don't seem at all like most of the footballers I've met.'

'I think I'm probably quite typical of the breed although less extreme than some I could mention. In general we all suffer from arrested development to some degree but, it's like any walk of life, you get a lot of decent guys and a few idiots. I'm still struggling to imagine you as a copper walking the beat and dealing with the lowlifes of Tottenham.'

'Yes well, you better believe it and I can tell you I learned some pretty useful skills along the way. I think I got my interest in the police from my parents. My mum's a head teacher and has always seen it as her job to make sure everyone keeps to the rules. My dad's a bit of an action man. He's an engineer, very practical but with a strong social conscience; a bit of a have-a-go hero who would always get involved rather than look the other way. I guess I take after both of them.

They chatted as she cooked then Alec took the food through to a formal dining room which he felt it deserved.

'God, did you and Sophie actually eat in here?' she asked looking around at the red striped Regency wallpaper and dark mahogany table, chairs and matching display cabinets.

'Just the once but it was her idea that we should be hosting dinner parties all the time.'

'Tell you what, if you light the fire in the lounge, we'll eat there on our knees.'

He did as he was asked feeling slightly stupid but happier than he had been in the company of a woman for a while. Dinner on knees turned into love making on the sofa then the floor which was his chance to show a bit more initiative. She tried to dominate again but he flipped her over and pinned her wrists to the rug. She writhed and fought but eventually gave up and became a willing partner urging him on as he took revenge on her for the night before.

'You bastard, that was rape,' she breathed heavily as they finally pulled apart.

'Liar.'

'Ok, I concede I'd struggle to get a conviction. So, now let's go upstairs and do it my way.'

The following morning they both slept late then woke and did it all over again. Eventually Alec looked at the bedside clock muttered 'shit' under his breath and grabbed a robe. It was a busy midweek evening with over half of the EPL clubs in action and he spent the next hour in his office posting various social media messages on behalf of his clients.

'On the bus to Manchester, great to have the fans behind us. Hope we can do you proud.'

'Drinking a Monster energy drink cuz I want to go full out for this game. Really pumped to get a result.'

'Looking for a big win tonight and need the support from the stands. With you we are strong.'

'Really lookin' forward to da game. It's a must-win and we're all up for it'

Did the hyphen and the apostrophes give the game away, given his client could barely string two words together in a post-match interview? Probably. The final version was dumbed down even further.

When he emerged Michaela was gone. She had left a note on the breakfast bar saying 'see you at Diego's,' but, other than that, he was on his own. He tried to focus on his column but struggled for inspiration. There was no lack of material but, as he had discovered, very little that anyone at the paper would consider printing. In the end he managed to knock out 1000 words about football boots including his own version of the apocryphal story of the Fergie, Goldenballs and a stray Adidas Predator. He signed off with: 'Next time you accuse a footballer of having his brains in his boots you can take comfort from the fact that they're protected by the most intelligent part of his kit.'

It wasn't exactly Pulitzer material but it would fill the gap and might even open the door to some work for the apparel firm in question at some point. With his deadline met and his clients otherwise engaged, Alec hit the gym before returning to make a post-workout meal and settle down in front of the TV to watch Diego's game.

As someone who knew what was going on in the player's life he was on heightened alert for the slightest sign of tension, but everything looked as it should be as the Brazilian made his way down the player's tunnel. He took his place on the field and within seconds was dictating play. The team played a high pressing game and Diego had a goal and an assist within 30 minutes of kickoff. Then, with just three minutes to go before half time, an apparently wayward challenge earned him the yellow card he needed. The move was so perfectly timed that Alec had to wait for the replay before he would believe it. He watched it three times on rewind and concluded that he would defy anyone to call it as a fix. The Sky commentary team were certainly none the wiser and there was not even a suggestion that Diego had taken one for the team. As far as they were concerned it was just one of those non-events that happen on any given matchday.

The second half was uneventful; his team went on to win comfortably so, in the player's mind, there could be no question that the move had affected the outcome. However inconsequential it had been on the match result, Diego's foul caused ripples which spread far beyond the stadium although there were probably only four people in the world who knew about it.

From the comfort of his sofa Alec had genuine mixed feelings. What he had witnessed could never be justified. If it became known what he had done, the player would be ostracised by the football community and buried under an avalanche of invective from the pundits, if for no other reason than that they had been made fools of. For them it was black and white. Fixing was a cynical calculation which could cost a side the game and there was something very wrong with a player who could ever set out to give less than 100%. That said, watching Diego's fix was like watching an artist at work. He didn't break his stride and his move was precisely calibrated to bring his opposite number down without injury drawing a yellow card rather than a red. As with everything else on the pitch, Diego was a perfectionist. What he had done took a remarkable amount of skill and who could really argue that a yellow card mattered more than the life of his wife?

Alec spent another hour adding to the post-match social media torrent on behalf of his clients with soundbites ranging from variants of "we were robbed" to the usual platitudes about fan support being crucial. Sometimes during these moments he wondered whether his life had any meaning at all, but then he thought of Diego and went through the motions he knew he had to before setting off for Hampstead.

Chapter 16

Alec's arrival coincided neatly with Michaela's but they found the house in darkness. They buzzed the gate and, receiving no reply, settled into Alec's car to wait.

'I'm worried about what Marko's going to ask him to do now,' said Alec. 'That yellow card was a nice touch, but it is relatively easy for a player to do and it didn't have any impact on the result of the game. What he can't do is get a yellow in every match. His trademark talent is his ability to keep the ball and stay out of trouble: he's just not the kind of player who picks up cards and pretty soon it's going to start looking suspicious.'

'I'm sorry, but you'll have to excuse me if I focus on the bigger picture here. His wife is being held hostage by East European gangsters, her life is in serious danger and right now we don't have any plan to get her back. Looked at in that light the fact that his silky skills might attract a bit of media comment here or there doesn't really seem too relevant.'

Neither of them spoke again until, five minutes later, the automatic gates opened and Diego's Bentley Continental swept into the drive. Alec followed him in.

'Sorry. The boss has a rule that whoever picks up a yellow has to clean up the changing room when the team has left,' the player said miserably, all his spark left on the field of play.

'Like life isn't shit enough already, mate. Good game tonight, though. You were brilliant and no one would ever suspect that yellow card. It just looked like a normal part of the game. So, what time are you supposed to be speaking with Marko?'

They followed the forlorn footballer through his oversized entrance and down into the basement below. Mention of Marko had brought Diego sharply back to reality. He visibly crumpled and Alec saw him for what he was; a desperate young man struggling to keep his life together.

'He knows when the game is and he said he would call two hours after the final whistle, so that should be in like 20 minutes.'

'Ok, so I've been thinking. We know he wants you to create a network of players to fix Premier League games, but I think we have to persuade him that you are not in a position to do that and to let me get in on the act. I've already drawn up a list of possible players who could be approached. If we can spread it around it reduces the risk to any single individual, and it should be easy enough to give him some bankers to bet on. If I approach the players myself I can protect your identity and theirs, so there should be no chance of anyone getting to know the entire network. You know what it's like if there's a bunch of guys involved; someone's going to talk and, this way, I'm the only one with the full picture. When he calls, put him on speaker and we can both talk to him. Don't mention Michaela, though. He doesn't need to know that there are police involved however unofficially.'

Diego shrugged but his body language seemed a bit more positive. As he went into the kitchen to get some drinks Michaela turned to Alec with a furious look on her face. 'Are you out of your mind?' she said, in a fierce stage whisper. 'As it stands you've got a mate whose wife is in trouble but you're talking about setting up an entire criminal operation. If you're actually going to follow through with this plan, then I'd better leave now.'

'What do you mean? I can't just leave him in the shit.'

'Listen to what you're saying. You're putting yourself at the top of a match-fixing pyramid extending right through the entire Premier League. Not only would you personally be guilty of committing a criminal offence, but you'd be aiding and abetting a whole bunch of others to do the same. And even if you managed to evade the League and the Police and pull off the fixing part, you'd be getting in up to your neck with some violent and dangerous criminals with no guarantee you're even helping Marta. And all for no personal gain.'

'Yes, for no personal gain. That's the most important bit. Look, I'll admit it's early days but I think I'm onto something and, if my plan comes off, there won't be any laws or legs broken. I do need you to trust me though. I need your help.'

'You've got some persuading to do,' she hissed as Diego returned with some cokes and a plate of sandwiches which had obviously been prepared by his housekeeper earlier in the day. The three ate in silence as they waited for the call to come through.

It was late in the evening in Serbia and Marko was garrulous and animated when he called.

'Ha, ha, Diego. You did good today and my associates were impressed. We made some money and I have a good feeling that our project might work out for everyone.'

He didn't object to Alec being on the call but soon got down to business. 'So, when are the next games, guys? What have you got for me?'

Alec answered: 'Marko, look we've been talking about this network idea. Diego's just not going to be able to get a group of players together.'

'You better start thinking how you're gonna do it then, because this little girl here is running out of time.'

'Yes, so we have been thinking and our idea is that I approach players and set up the fixes. That way I can make it something that's going to work long term. But we do need to have Marta back in England.'

'Oh, you think. What you need doesn't mean jack shit to me. I'm not even *talking* about letting her go until your network starts delivering.'

'Look, it's not going to happen overnight, Marko but we will try to give you something each round of matches.'

'I don't care what matches. It can be FA Cup, Champions League or whatever. I want at least five things that are guaranteed to happen each week.'

'I'm going to need money though. No player is going to fix games for no reason. I need you to give me access to cash.'

'What the fuck…? You want me to give you money? You must think I'm fucking crazy. Your friend there can front up whatever cash you need. The way these thing work, you pay ahead of the fix, so as soon as they take the money you've got them. Then you keep turning the screw. If your network is as good as you say it will be, you'll make enough money betting on your own to keep it going without any help from me. In fact, you'll even make a nice profit.'

The possibility of personally betting on fixed matches had already occurred to Alec, but he avoided all eye contact with Michaela and tried to focus on the main objective. 'So, if we can set you up five guaranteed events a week, Marta gets to come home, right?'

'You just set it up and we'll talk about it.'

'You've got to do better than that, Marko.'

'Fuck you. I don't gotta do nothing. Now, do you wanna talk to this bitch or not?'

'Yes, let me speak to Marta,' came Diego's frightened voice.

She was put on the line, her voice quiet but echoing around the couple's basement. She spoke Portuguese, which Marko seemed unconcerned about. Alec observed the player's face minutely as the conversation unfolded. After a minute or so he frowned, then frowned again as Michaela suddenly jumped up and grabbed a pen. She wrote down a sequence of numbers then showed it to Diego who reacted immediately.

To a linguist his next few sentences would have sounded odd but it had the desired effect.

'So are *zero, seven, one, seven,* they treating you well enough?'

'Yes.'

'Are the people *six, two,* you, *four, five,* are living with are ok?'

'Yes.'

'*Three, four,* try not to worry, *six,* this is all going to be over soon, ok?'

'Ok.'

The conversation then continued as before until Marko's voice boomed around the room once again. 'Ok, that's enough. Let me know what the next events are and remember, my patience is not gonna last long. I need something at the weekend or this bitch will start to feel the pain.'

There was a muffled sound of a women's voice before the line went dead leaving Diego, Alec and Michaela in silence again.

She spoke first. 'So, I think we can establish a few things from that call, some good, some not so good. Alec, you won't have understood, but it sounds like she's being held with some other girls being trafficked to the West, which is quite lucky. At this stage they're normally well looked after: they think they're going to a new life in the UK or wherever, and their traffickers need to keep them healthy so they don't lose value too fast. The fact that she's got access to a mobile phone and had the presence of mind to share the number is also positive; it suggests she's not panicking.

'So, the good news, Diego, is I think she's doing ok and she's with people that are looking after her. We also have a better sense of the risks she faces now. It's just a judgement, but it seems unlikely to me that they will simply kill her however, they do have a ready-made route in place to traffic her on to somewhere else if they need to. That would be a real problem as we'd have no idea where she was so it's vital that you speak with her as often as possible just to make sure she's still in the same place. Don't use that number too freely, though. That first call is going to be a risk. Just ping her a message sometime later in the evening and she'll come back to you if she can.'

Diego nodded but seemed happier feeling that her situation was at least stable.

'I also thought Marko's first comment was revealing,' she continued. 'I'm reading between the lines here, but I think he is reporting directly to someone he's scared of and he was under quite a lot of pressure to deliver tonight. The whole organisation is taking a risk by kidnapping the wife of an international celebrity and I suspect both their lives would have been in danger had the fix not worked today. The language of the call was also interesting. Maybe she's persuaded him that she doesn't speak English but the fact that Marta was allowed to speak freely in a language Marko can't possibly understand tells me he's feeling more sure of himself. He's confident that nothing she can say will help her or us to secure her freedom without his say so. So, from where we're sitting, I'm more certain than ever that they're in Niš at the heart of the Belovic Clan, and that the biggest threat to them both is from the gang itself.

'He seemed way too happy with the money he made from the first fix which means it probably wasn't about the money itself but pressure from the Clan. I think he's on borrowed time after screwing up in London and he's working hard to get himself back in favour. His reaction tonight suggests they've cut him some slack, but it doesn't mean he's fully won them over. Remember, they have to launder their money anyway, so betting on fixed sport isn't really different from business as usual. If I'm right about Lech Belovic and he's now more of a businessman than a gangster, then he just wants to make the most money with the least amount of risk. Marta is a big risk for them so he's not going to want her around for too long. The best chance we have is if we can find something that's going to change the game for them financially, then I think Marko will negotiate Marta's release himself.'

'What if we don't?' came Diego's frightened voice again.

Michaela put on a confident expression. 'I think we're ok for a week or so, as long as Marko feels progress is being made. They are used to having women around effectively as prisoners, they've looked after her ok so far and they've made a bit of money, but the threat to Marta will keep growing as time goes on. We need to find a way to bring things to a head sooner rather than later, but that's down to whatever Alec has in mind,' she said, throwing him a sideways glance.

'Yeah well, I told you I'm working on a plan, Diego, but whatever I come up with, we're still going to need you to perform as well. When's your next game?'

'The boss seems happy at the moment, so I guess I'll be playing again at the weekend.'

'I've been thinking about the fixes: you can't just keep giving away yellow cards. At some point you'll get suspended and, anyway, it's going to look suspicious. Can you get the boss to try you out on the wing? That way we can do something around putting the ball out for a throw in or a corner.'

'Maybe. I'll work on him in training. Who else are you going to approach? Anyone from the club?'

'It's better you don't know, mate, but I will say that it's no one you're playing with.'

Their conversation was interrupted by the buzz of Diego's phone. It was Vic Vickers.

'I have to take this,' he said moving into an anteroom that doubled as his office. He was back a couple of minutes later but as he sat down it was Alec's turn to receive a call; Vickers again.

'Hi Vic, how's it going? I thought you guys would be out celebrating. That was some performance this evening.'

'Yeah, the boys are having a good run at the moment. Look, sorry to call so late Alec, but the reason for my call, I'm worried about Diego again. He picked up a yellow tonight and the boss did his usual thing of getting him to clean the dressing room, you know, all just a gentle nudge to keep him grounded and remind everyone that no one's bigger than the club. But he looked so miserable. I was going to have a word, but he just drove off on his own 20 minutes later. Have you seen him recently?'

'We get together from time to time. What do you think the problem is? Do you want me to get in touch with him?'

'If you could Alec, that might be helpful. I can't put my finger on anything specific, but he's clammed up tighter than a duck's what-sit. I'd like to help him if I can, but I can't even start if he doesn't let me in on what's happening. You know I wouldn't normally ask, but if you have a chance to catch up with him, I'd really appreciate it.'

'I'll see what I can do, Vic, and let you know.'

'Thanks Alec. Anyway, how's life treating you? How's that girl-friend of yours? Sophie wasn't it?'

Vickers had the kind of voice which invited confessions and an amazing memory for names and faces; it was part of what made him so effective as the club's player liaison. Five minutes on the phone with him and most young men were spilling their darkest secrets, but Alec was determined not to be caught open kimono. 'I'm pret-ty good, mate,' he said. 'Listen I'm actually not too far from Diego's place. Maybe I'll drop round and see what I can find out. I'll buzz you back tomorrow if I can shed any light on his domestic arrange-ments.'

Diego had wandered off with the empty plates leaving Alec with Michaela. 'I don't know how long he's going to be able to keep this thing secret from the club. They are all about the team and, if he doesn't play along, questions are going to be asked by the manager. The January transfer window is only a few weeks away and he would be a prize asset for any of the top teams in Europe.'

When Diego came back Alec tried to lighten the mood. 'Do you fancy some FIFA or we could shoot some pool?'

The player shook his head miserably. 'I can't think about anything except Marta right now. The only time I can switch off is when I'm playing and even then, with the fixing, it's getting in my brain.'

Michaela shuffled and cleared her throat. 'Well, you've spoken to Marta and you know she's ok tonight. She's a strong one and she's got that mobile number too, so you know she's thinking and functioning well. She just needs you to stay positive for her.'

He nodded. 'Look, I know I have to thank you guys. I don't know what I'd do without you. I'm sorry to be so much trouble.'

We're mates, Diego,' said Alec. Then, glancing at the policewoman, 'We're not about to leave you on your own, are we? As Michaela said, you've spoken with Marta and she's ok for now. The fix worked and we have the start of a plan to get us through the next few days. I'd call that a good evening's work mate, so I suggest we make a move. I'll call you tomorrow but we do need to find a way to keep the club off your back.'

Chapter 17

Outside, Michaela said: 'I have somewhere else I need to be tonight. I'm going to take an Uber.'

Alec shrugged, trying not to look disappointed. 'I was hoping I'd have a chance to work through my idea with you.'

She didn't respond, working the app on her phone.

He tried again. 'Look, err thanks for coming tonight. You were really helpful on the call with Marko and, when he thinks it through, I think Diego will feel a bit more positive too.'

Again, no response.

'Will I see you at Hugo's office on Friday then?'

'Listen, Alec, I like you,' she said finally, her voice quiet and controlled, 'and I feel sorry for your friend, but I am a police officer. My career has been dedicated to upholding the rule of law whether that's on the streets of Tottenham or in the backrooms of City banks.'

She was starting to get into her stride. 'I've only known you for five minutes and I can count at least six major and several more minor crimes that you're in some way connected with including murder, supply of class A drugs, prostitution and kidnapping. You may not have done anything criminal yourself, although I'm becoming less sure of that by the minute, but at best you're knowingly getting into a zone that's shadowy and getting darker, and I am not going to follow you.'

Alec hung his head. 'You're right, and I wouldn't even ask if it were just a couple of stupid footballers in trouble. But Marta's life is at stake. It's too late for Diego to go to his club and you know that the police can't do anything. You agreed that we're all he's got and I can't just walk away and leave him. I know my plan is full of holes but it's a lot more likely to work if we do it together. You talked about the reasons you went into the police, but surely saving lives and taking down the bad guys is what it's all about? And I promise I will never put you in a position where you're covering up criminal activity...'

'It's late and I have somewhere I need to be. The only thing I can promise is that I'll think about it and be in touch before the meeting with Hugo.'

They waited until her car arrived then kissed awkwardly and he watched as she disappeared into the night. Alec didn't have time to consider Michaela's change of heart as, barely had he left Hampstead, when his phone buzzed and a number he recognised flashed up on his display: it was Andy Grubber, Daily Mail sports correspondent.

'Hello Grubber. Haven't heard from you in a while. How's tricks?'

'Yeah, I'm good mate, I'm good. Yourself? Have you got a minute?'

'Fire away.'

Listen, you do media for Diego don't you? I've heard a whisper that he's in some kind of trouble and I wondered if you might know anything about it.'

Alec's mind was racing. That was bloody quick, he'd been counting on keeping the story quiet for a couple of weeks at least. As he saw it, he had three choices: deny everything, come clean and swear the journo to secrecy, or throw him a bone and hope it would be enough. A denial would just mean Grubber kept on digging and giving him the story would drop a bombshell in the middle of their plan, such as it was. He needed to know more about who was talking and what the story was before he could decide how big a bone to throw.

'I know he hasn't found it easy coming back from injury, but what have you heard?'

There was a pause whilst Grubber made a similar calculation, then, 'So, the story I've heard is that he's run up some massive gambling debts and someone's putting the frighteners on him to get their money back.'

Ok, this was bad, but it could be worse. 'Do you know how much Diego earns every week?'

'I think most people reckon it's around £180k.'

'Well most people don't know the half of it. The club pays him £230k, his image rights are worth another £40k a week and personal endorsements add up to around nine million a year,' Alec said, knowing he was giving the journo his story. 'There's no gambling debt in the world that he couldn't pay off, but who's saying different?'

'Steven McBrien. Told me he'd been with Diego in Las Vegas and he'd blown half a mil' at the blackjack table.'

Stevie Mac. He was on Alec's hit list of players and now his was the first number he would call in the morning. 'It sounds unlikely, mate. I don't even think they even know each other. Did he say how come they were in Vegas together?'

'No. It seemed like he knew he'd said too much and he clammed up. So, you don't know anything about it?'

'No, I don't, mate. I mean thinking about it, I wouldn't completely rule it out. But I'll say this, even if Diego did lose half a million dollars, he'd earn it back within a fortnight. I can't see anyone needing to put any real heat on him. He'd just pay them off.'

'Stevie said you couldn't believe everything you heard about footballer's money and he cited Diego as an example.'

'Well, Stevie's not the brightest, is he? He was probably just deflecting attention away from his own situation. You know he's only still in the game 'cos he's got money problems of his own.'

'Yeah maybe', Grubber mused. 'but I can smell something and I've learned to trust my nose. My instinct tells me there was something more on his mind than that, and claiming he was sat right next to him in Vegas goes a bit further than deflection, don't you think? If you do hear anything, though, let me know first, right.'

The call ended with Alec cursing the nerve of the journalist. It would be a cold day in hell before Alec ever decided to talk to him first. Still he felt reasonably confident the story wouldn't be in the papers the next morning and resolved to call all the Vegas squad first thing. There could be a moment when a media storm might be useful but, with Marta still a hostage, it was way too much of a risk. For now he needed to make sure no one was going to talk to Grubber or anyone else.

At the same moment as Alec was planning his conversation with Stevie Mac, Marta was getting out of a small white car and climbing the stairs to the apartment, her minder alongside her. Her hopes had soared when the woman had come to get her an hour or so earlier. They had driven for less than ten minutes before arriving at a modern football stadium where Marta had been taken into an office suite. Inside she could hear Marko's voice talking loudly with some other men including the two who had snatched her off the street in Greece. He switched to English when he saw her, punching a number into his phone.

Once the call started she barely registered what was being said as she was so determined to pass on the mobile number if she got a chance. When Marko handed her the phone she took the risk of speaking Portuguese but had barely got the number out before he grabbed the phone again and ended the call. He turned his back and went back into the office leaving the two women with nothing to do but go back to the apartment. Marta tried to take in more of her surroundings on the return trip but it was dark and within a few minutes the journey was over.

Alec started calling early the next day before the players had left for training. Everyone got the same message: there was a journo sniffing around trying to get details of their driving holidays and, if they were approached, to keep shtum if they didn't want the clubs to crack down. With the players squared away for now, his thoughts turned to Michaela and how he was going to get her back onside. In the end he decided on the direct approach and made the call.

'Alec, I'm still not sure I should be talking to you at all.'

'Really? I was hoping you'd have come around after having the night to sleep on it.'

'Yes, well keep hoping. I said I'd think about it and the more I think about it, the more I'm convinced it's a stupid, dangerous and criminal idea.'

'Look, only time will tell whether it's stupid or dangerous, but I can tell you it's not criminal, at least I don't think it is. I really need to talk it through with you, though. Can we meet for lunch somewhere? There's a place for journalists that I like to go to in Paddington called the Frontline Club. Would you meet me there?'

'Isn't that a warzone reporters' hangout.'

'I know, it's a bit of a cliché but the food's good. Does one o'clock work?'

'You're not going to give up, are you?' she said, but allowed herself to be persuaded nonetheless.

By the time one o'clock came around Alec had been in the club for half an hour. He had also relaxed his no lunchtime drinking rule and was well into a large gin and tonic as Michaela walked in. She took in the grainy black and white photos of major 20th Century conflicts and the grizzled hacks at the bar and shook her head at Alec.

'You were right about it being a cliché,' she said, but kissed him warmly on the lips and he caught a whiff of perfume. 'Is this where you get all your scoops?'

'I think the last scoop in this place was during the cold war, but it's anonymous enough and conspiratorial conversation is actively encouraged. I thought you'd like it.'

He kept up the chat as they looked over the menu and ordered, keen to put off the moment where they had to talk business.

Michaela saw that he was playing for time so, with the waiter dispatched, she interrupted his running commentary and put her hand on his.

'Sorry I was a bit harsh last night. I don't actually think you're a criminal, but you've got tendencies and I'm not going to be around if you go over to the dark side. So here's what I'll do. I'll listen while you tell me the plan and I'll give you my considered opinion, and make my decision based on that.'

Alec took a deep breath then said, 'It's really very simply. I just set up a few fixes until Marko releases Marta then we all sack the whole thing off. As Diego's finding out with match fixing, once you start it's almost impossible to stop. The people behind it have all the power, they can tell the club, they can threaten you or your family and basically, you're caught. But if I'm the one controlling the fixes, we can stop anytime. Marko won't have a direct link to the players so he can't get at them and the network just dissolves when Marta's back safely.'

'But that's still a criminal network in direct contravention of the Gambling Act. You're bribing to players to fix games so someone else can cheat at gambling.'

'Ah, that's the clever part. I'm not going to give money to the players; they are going to do it for free to help out another player. No cash will change hands so no payments, no bank records, no paper trail and no one can ever accuse the players of taking money to fix a game. They decide what minor action they can deliver in the next game and simply get on with it with no come back.'

'Ok, so I can see what you're trying to do, and I hate to burst your bubble, but it's not going to work. Aside from the fact that it's still illegal and you've got to persuade a whole bunch of players to do something deeply uncomfortable. For no money. What is going to put pressure on Marko and the Belovic Clan to release Marta?'

'That's where the second part of the plan comes in. We get the network up and running and show them it's making money, then we say we're going to pull the plug unless they release Marta. Not only that but we threaten to go public which would blow the whole thing apart and at that point Marta becomes a liability for Marko. Assuming, as you said, that the Belovic Clan are already uncomfortable with holding an international celebrity's wife, they are only going to go along with Marko's scheme as long as it's making them money. So, if that tap is turned off, that puts the pressure right back on Marko. I think he'll do the deal to get Marta released on the basis that it's the only way he can keep being useful.'

He paused, waiting to see the effect of his words on Michaela who was going through the details of his plan in her mind. In the end she said, 'I think you're making all this up as you go along, but let's try and pick the bones out. As I see it, you've got four things to worry about. First, it is still illegal. Second, you've got to persuade the players not only to take part in fixing, but risk ruining their names and reputations. Third, the sums of money are going to have to be huge: you're going to have to offer the Clan a real game changer that's interesting enough for them to be bothered. And fourth, you're going to have to give Marko some leverage over you personally so that he's confident you'll keep going with the network once Marta is released. Otherwise it's lose-lose for him and who knows how he'll react.'

'Ok, this is great. See, I knew you'd be fantastic at this stuff and obviously I am making this up on the hoof, but let's think about your issues. On your legal point, we're talking a minor technical infringement for a few days, a fortnight at most. The person doing the gambling is outside the country and I would make sure there was no connection or paper trail. No one's going to get hurt and I won't involve you in any of the details, so you won't be covering anything up. The worst you'll be doing is turning a blind eye and, with Marta's life at stake, I hope that's something you'll be prepared to do.

Then on the players, the media thing is not an issue. They live their lives in the glare of publicity and even if there was a media storm it would be lots of rumours but no proof. They'd just shrug it off and the clubs would close ranks. No, my biggest worry is whether they'll actually deliver in the heat of a game. With nothing real at stake for them off the field, will they even remember to do what they promised on it? What I'm thinking is I give them a hint of Marta's situation to show them what's at stake then hold out the prospect of a free road trip when it's over and hope it's enough to focus their minds.

'I agree with you about the money but I'm hoping your banker friend will provide the answer to that. I did a bit of digging on him and his company and I reckon he may be good for a lot more than just advice. I want to hear it from him to make sure I've understood things right but, if I have, he could be the one to make a difference. Which leaves your leverage point and that's still a work in progress. I was hoping Marko would see a chance to keep the money tap open as the only way he'd be able to get back in favour at home, but I see what you mean. Obviously I can't give him an actual hold over me, but he's going to need to think he's got my balls in a vice otherwise he's going to make a grab for them anyway. Perhaps that's something we can work on together, that is, if you're still on the team?'

'I'm sorry, but the jury is still out on that one. I will come to the meeting with Hugo though, listen to what he says, and we'll take it from there. Meanwhile, I'm here, so what are our plans for the rest of the afternoon?'

In all honesty Alec hadn't expected lunch to go so well, so he crossed his fingers under the table and said, 'I thought we'd go back and hit the gym near my place. You know, workout, sauna then you can make us something back at the house and it's Netflix and chill.'

'Oh, is that what you thought?' she said, but followed him out of the door anyway.

Chapter 18

The world of office interiors was a foreign one to Alec. He imagined a former banker would sit on a leather chair in an oak-panelled room so was surprised when the satnav led them into the alien landscape of the Queen Elizabeth Olympic Park. They drove past the twisted legacy of the Orbit tower into the semi-deserted London 2012 theme park before pulling up outside the former Olympic press centre. Now rebranded 'Plexal', it was, according to the illuminated signs in the main reception, "an innovation community and the most connected workspace in the world." Finding Hugo Ashburton's NumbersGame company proved beyond the powers of the digital concierge so Alec and Michaela went old school and called his office number. As they waited in the glass and steel greenhouse they watched bearded hipsters with Macbooks balanced on their knees holding impromptu meetings on furniture that looked like it had been rejected by a primary school. Everywhere Alec looked there were earnest individuals deep in conversation but no sign of anyone actually making any money.

'This place couldn't be more Google if it tried,' he said. 'It's like Silicon Valley has been picked up and dumped in an east London carpark.'

'Companies like this are supposed to be the future.'

'I can't actually see any companies, just some liggers pretending to work in the gig economy.'

'Isn't it marvellous?' came a booming voice from behind them, 'and just a short hop from Westfield East.'

They turned to meet a large tousle-headed figure in a check shirt barely big enough to contain his substantial belly, tucked into a pair of scruffy jeans.

'Ah Hugo,' said Michaela and threw her arms around him. 'It's great to see you. You look like your new life suits you way too well.'

'New shirts required, ma'am,' he replied, in a mock military tone. 'And this must be the redoubtable Mr Munday.'

He grabbed Alec's hand in both of his and shook it vigorously. 'Come on up to my office. It's the only concession to my former life. I'm a bit too old to do meetings on a sodding bean bag.'

He led them along a corridor the length of an airport terminal then up in a lift to a corner office on the third floor.

'Sit down, sit down, and tell me your troubles. You sounded very mysterious on the phone, Mickey.'

Alec took a few minutes to bring Hugo up to speed with Diego's situation and the reason for their visit. 'So Michaela thought you might be able to help,' he concluded.

'Fuck me, Mickey. Kidnap, East European gangs, match fixing? Things are really hotting up at Interpol.'

'It's worse than that: this is strictly freelance.'

'That's bad. Look, with what you've told me so far, I think I can guess why you're here, but perhaps it would help if I explained how we work.'

'That would be useful,' said Alec. 'I think you'll fit into the picture somewhere, I'm just not sure where.'

'Well, it will be a pleasure to give my elevator pitch an outing for your benefit,' Hugo said, with relish. He stood up to command his audience: this was clearly something he'd been working on for a while. 'NumbersGame offers an algorithmic betting service based on the trading technology I used when I was in the employ of one of Britain's finest financial institutions. For bookies we monitor exposure in real time and enable them to cover their risk with hedges or wagers in the opposite direction. For sophisticated punters, though, we use High Frequency Trading technology and Smart Order Tracking to find bets that meet the parameters we give the system. We exploit information gaps between markets to spot the kind of arbitrage opportunities which City traders use to make their money. We can automate the entire wager process and even incorporate a stop-loss position for clients who want to limit their risk.

'As I'm sure you're aware, the differences between trading and betting are remarkably few but I believe my company is the first to actually follow through and use a trading system to manage bets. When I left the bank I must confess I helped myself to an exact replica of their proprietary trading platform; the crown jewels, at least they were as far as I was concerned. I've been working with some coders in Hungary and we've added a few bells and whistles to turn it into a betting system that's unmatched anywhere in the world. Without getting into the weeds, NumbersGame can place or lay bets faster than any human and on hundreds of markets around the world. We harness it to the kind of distributed botnet used by hackers to do that thousands of times in rapid succession whilst remaining completely anonymous.'

'And if the outcome of the bets is already known before they are placed,' Alec chipped in, 'then the opportunity to make money is practically limitless. I'm beginning to see why Michaela thought you could be helpful.'

'We've got a bright one here, Mickey. Now Alec, I understand your problem lies with the English Premier League so allow me to fill you in with a few facts that may help. There is at least $20 billion bet around the world on every single round of EPL matches. That's obviously the appeal: plenty of covering fire for your unscrupulous punter. The challenge is that it is stubbornly tricky to infiltrate. Turns out it's hard to persuade someone who's being paid upwards of £100,000 a week that it's worth taking the risking for a quick fix. Most people can be bought for the right price but top-flight footballers are already extremely rich and have no need of the one thing match fixers have; brown envelopes full of a few thousand quid.'

Alec could come up with a whole list of exceptions to Hugo's rule but he kept his thoughts to himself as the banker continued.

'To provide extra protection the League, UEFA and FIFA use fraud detection systems which track betting patterns around the world in real time. Anything unusual and the market is suspended. Like most burglar alarms the systems are not unbeatable, but they do enough to encourage your average felon to move on to where the pickings are easier if not richer. In reality, you're much more likely to find match fixing in smaller leagues and countries where regulation is looser. You'll be familiar with expressions suggesting some punters will bet on two flies crawling up a wall. The footballing equivalent is the Danish regional Under 15s league and you'd be amazed how many Chinese punters there are at one in the morning completely glued to a dodgy video feed from Aarhus.'

Hugo paused and looked at his audience checking they were still engaged before going on. 'Correct me, but as I understand Diego's case, we're looking at someone who has a stranglehold on the player and is intent on using it to create a network of other players who can be tempted into fixing games or at least certain events within them. So far, so bad. However, their next challenge should not be underestimated. Large bets, or a high volume of smaller bets on a specific and unlikely outcome quickly arouse suspicion in regulated markets so it's hard to make big money even if you're betting on a sure thing. A good 80% of all bets are in illegal markets that most European punters can't access, but even if they could, they'd stick out like a sore thumb if they went on a big winning streak. The markets would simply close to overseas bets or, more likely, not pay out at all. But that is where NumbersGame comes in. We are experts in the betting markets and master practitioners in flying below the radar. We can access thousands of bookmakers around the world where we place bets which fall just below the threshold that triggers the warning signals. We also help punters avoid attention using nominee accounts in multiple jurisdictions. By playing a longer game we can deliver solid returns and gradually go for bigger and bigger wins.'

Alec wasn't sure he followed completely, but the last sentence set off alarm bells. 'When you say, "playing a longer game," how long are we talking? We don't have much time to work with.'

'You have to realise that the market for the kind of eclectic bets you're talking about is considerably smaller than for what one might call plain vanilla wagers. The kind of bets you're talking about – a corner in the first five minutes or for player X to miss a penalty – those are possible of course, but the market is a lot thinner and high volumes or large wagers would quickly be picked up by the fraud detection systems. If, say, 50 £1million bets were placed on a specific sending off it would instantly trigger the systems. Having said that, there is a sweet spot well before that point where we can operate very profitably.'

'So, not a licence to print money but still possible to make a decent return?' asked Alec.

'Correct. With our expertise, of course. But it depends what you're comparing it to.'

'The backdrop to this is the reason why organised crime syndicates get into sports betting in the first place,' Michaela interjected. 'They use gambling to launder money and they see betting losses as the price they have to pay for making the proceeds of their crimes appear to have been legitimately obtained. They employ smart guys to beat the bookies and are obviously highly motivated to fix, but still they absorb between 10% and 30% of losses. It would be a big win for them just to reach breakeven.'

'Depending on the amounts involved that should be easy then,' said Hugo. 'We would typically advise customers to target a position just one or two percentage points above breakeven. That may not sound much but, if you're making 2% every time, you can pretty much treble your stake over the course of a year. The difference with these chaps is they are betting on things they know will happen, so we should be able to create a portfolio of bets that will deliver a higher return every time without arousing too much suspicion.'

Hugo started tapping away on an oversized desk calculator. 'As you raise the target return the number of offers goes down and the size of bets reduces but 20% could be achievable. If we could deliver even 10% per week they'd be looking at a return of 4000% over the course of the season. How sustainable that is over the long term depends on the overall sums involved, but if we kept it to, say, half a mil' per round of matches, it should be doable.'

'What are we talking about in actual money?' asked Alec, the light starting to dawn in his eyes.

'Think of it like compound interest. If they add back their winnings each week and there weren't too many lost bets, we would turn £500,000 into around £22 million over a single season. To pull off a big heist is possible but it would leave players around the world very suspicious and unlikely to play again without taking precautions. Your best bet, no pun intended, is to take a steady as she goes approach rather than get greedy. The luckier you seem, the less time you'll have before the markets slam shut. If you start generating huge returns against highly unlikely events, then someone's going to smell a rat.'

'Ok, but that sounds like the game changer we're looking for,' said Alec, his face and body language giving off the kind of buying signals that Hugo had been exploiting for many years.

'It could be but I should say, though, that you are both rather assuming NumbersGame would be prepared to go along with your proposition,' Hugo said, acting coy. 'I'd have to think long and hard before getting involved in something that's both highly illegal and involves doing business with some very dubious and dangerous characters.'

'Hugo, I love you dearly,' Michaela sighed, 'but you know and I know that you'd sell both your children into slavery if you thought it would make you enough money. From what my sources tell me, punters haven't exactly been flocking to your new venture and you've already told us you're not going to be welcome back at the bank, so let's not pretend you're going to go all Mother Theresa on us.

'Once a policeman, always a fucking policeman, eh?'

'You're too kind but I do have one more question for you. We're looking at a strictly time-limited proposal of big money and big bets for just a few weeks, maybe just two or three. Does the maths still stack up to deliver the kind of winnings we need?'

'Mmm, I'd need to run some models, but my instinct says 'no',' said Hugo. 'We might be able to push it to a million quid per round of games but, if anything, we should look to lower the return profile to reduce the risk of being caught. Doubling down on both implies some large positions and you're not dealing with normal counterparties. If the bookies in regulated jurisdictions think the market is rigged, they just shut down pending an investigation. In the grey markets you simply lose your money. Couldn't we get longer to work with? The season's not over until June.'

'We're not talking about going into the match fixing business long term, just doing enough to get Marta back,' said Michaela.

'And anyway,' Alec jumped in, 'as the season gets towards the sharp end no one's going to be thinking about anything except results. It's one thing to get up to a bit of mischief in the dark days of January and February but after that the pressure ramps up on players and managers, and the legendary 110% effort kicks in big time.'

The room went silent for a minute before Hugo started again more cautiously. 'Maybe we're looking at this the wrong way around. My fault probably, the banker in me talking. Let's take a three-week working time horizon. How would it be if we used the first two weeks building up to the big one in week three? A good spread of bets from accounts based all over the world would go completely unnoticed allowing us to go with regulated markets. In that final week we place thousands of bets, maybe even more, so that even if one or two are challenged, the majority will be paid out. We couldn't repeat it for a long time but that could get you a prize that's big enough to buy our heroine's freedom. What do you think?'

'It's all about presentation.' said Alec. 'These people are no fools. We'll need to show some numbers, but it sounds like we should be able to work up some sort of proposal which Marko can sell to his bosses, If, as we suspect, he's desperate to rehabilitate himself, then I think he'll be keen to do the deal. What do you get out of it, Hugo?'

'My terms are very modest, dear boy: I take a standard 1% of the stake or 5% of winnings. Most of my clients see the benefit of working with someone with skin in the game, as it were, so I suggest you build that into any proposal.'

'5% will net you a small fortune if our plan is anything like successful, *dear boy*,' snipped Alec.

'The operative word in that sentence is 'if', and as you point out, the fortune would be very small.'

'Before we start dividing up any imaginary spoils, boys,' interrupted Michaela, 'can I ask how we move this into the real world starting with the stake money. They're not about to wire money into your bank, Hugo.'

'You're the expert Mickey, but I'd say a nominee account in the British Virgin Islands. Basically, anywhere outside the reach of the main jurisdictions which can make and receive payments.'

'And how are we going to persuade them to trust you with the keys to the safe?'

'That's something I can't help you with, I'm afraid. Rest assured, though, I can be ready at a moment's notice, so when you've got your Serbian chums on the hook just let me know.'

The visitors attracted little attention as they walked back through Google Stratford East and out into the windswept park.

'Mickey?' asked Alec.

'I learned to be a bit of a chameleon when I worked in finance. If the posh boys needed a nickname to call me by, I was happy to oblige as long as they gave me what I wanted. Don't get any ideas, though: I hate it.'

'I saw a different side of you in there. A real smooth operator.'

'There's a lot of bullshit in the City, but, underneath it all, it's a ruthlessly successful money-making machine and Hugo was a real player. If you can find a way to make it work, I have no doubt that he'll be able to deliver.'

Chapter 19

Early that same November morning, Marta had woken up to the sound of excited chatter. In London it was 13degrees and drizzling, but in Eastern Serbia it was hovering just above zeroand had been snowing on and off for days. The apartment where the girls were being kept was draughty but, with 12 of them now sharing the space, no one was cold. When Marta arrived she had been on her own but, as each day passed, she was joined by others until they were sharing four to a bedroom with four more on the floor in the small lounge and all using the single bathroom. One or two of the girls were Serbian but the rest were from further east. Using broken English or Russian they shared basic details of their journeys from Albania, Romania, Azerbaijan and even Vietnam. During the day they huddled around a small TV, smoking and chatting in the limited common language they shared. The older woman who was their minder came in mid-morning with a supermarket bag of basic supplies. The girls took turns preparing whatever they could from the limited ingredients and the highlight of the day was a communal meal after which those with mobile phones would connect with friends and family.

This morning the routine was different. There were men in the girls' apartment, bags were being packed with provisions and a few precious belongings, and the atmosphere was one of excitement: this was a moment the girls had been waiting for. The older woman supervised the evacuation and within fifteen minutes the young women were filing out in silence through a rear entrance onto a quiet side street and into a white panel van. Excitement soon gave way to boredom as the van jolted its way through suburban streets then onto the highway. A couple of hours later, the vehicle slowed and came to a stop. The smell of diesel filled the interior but the doors remained closed and the girls knew better than to draw attention to their presence while they were at a service station. Once the van was underway again they banged on the front panel and shouted. There was no response but twenty minutes later they slowed again and pulled off the smooth road onto what felt like a rough track. The van's suspension creaked in protest and its passengers were thrown around like dolls in the back until finally the engine went dead. This time the doors swung open to reveal a clearing surrounded by woodland. The girls blinked in the daylight as they emerged stiffly, stretching their limbs. It was soon clear the only kind of relief they were going to get was in the woods but most were too desperate to care. They stopped long enough to have a cigarette then the men handed out hunks of black bread and dried sausage before herding everyone back into the van retracing their passage across the dirt track and back onto the highway. The next time they stopped, after another few hours, the driver and his mate opened the doors and spoke to the girls roughly in Serbian. There was going to be a wait and they were to keep quiet. The doors would be left ajar but if they needed to get out, they had to do so individually and walk directly away from the van.

A thousand miles away, Alec and Michaela were in his BMW peering through spray on London's orbital motorway. They were chewing over what they had learned from the meeting with Hugo and Alec's thoughts had already turned to plans for a loved-up evening when an alert pinged on Michaela's phone. She spent the next five minutes tapping on the small screen, then looked up. 'How far are we from Luton airport?' she demanded.

'About half an hour. Why?'

'Ok, could you drop me there?'

'What's this about, Michaela? I was looking forward to getting your advice on what I should say to my network of players.'

'You were only looking forward to one thing and it had nothing to do with my advice. I'll explain when I get back, hopefully tomorrow, but if we're lucky, there's a chance I may be able to make all this go away.'

They went north off the M25 and onto the M1 driving in silence with Michaela tapping away all the while on her phone. She wasn't going to be drawn into giving away any more information and practically ran from the car as soon as he pulled up outside the airport. Alec watched her go then shrugged, exited the passenger drop-off zone and headed for home. Her perfume hung in the air and he wondered whether they would actually have anything in common if Diego's situation hadn't thrown them together.

By the time he reached his front door it was just before 5pm, the ideal time to catch players at a loose end. He spent a few minutes working through the implications of what he'd learned at Numbers-Game and revising his target list of players accordingly. Most of what Hugo had said about algorithmic trading and target yields had gone straight over his head but he had heard something which was music to his ears. To actually guarantee the result of a football match a fix-er needs goalkeepers to leak goals, strikers who refuse to score and referees who change games in his favour. In the Premier League with its dozens of cameras and eagle-eyed media pundits the environment is an extremely hostile one, so if they did it regularly, they'd stand as much chance of evading detection as an Australian cricketer with bright yellow sandpaper.

With Hugo's system, though, it seemed possible to generate the kind of returns that would deliver for the Serbians without arousing suspicion, putting any players at risk or affecting the outcome of the games in any material way. If NumbersGame could find deep enough markets that would pay out on small in-game events, then life was going to be a whole lot easier. More to the point, if Hugo was right, it was unlikely that Marko could make significant money without the kind of system they were offering which put pressure on him to accept their offer. Just one hurdle remained: he needed to persuade the players to go along with his scheme without any financial reward and Stevie Mac was top of his list. He had revealed his true colours at the roulette table and Alec was confident he could be recruited.

'Stevie, mate. How's it going?'

'You again, Alec. The wife's going to get suspicious that there's something between us.'

'Hasn't she left you yet?'

'Very good, you wanker. Now what do you want? Are you just calling to remind me to keep my mouth shut or are we going on another one of our little jaunts again?'

'We are indeed, mate, and the next one's a freebie. I just need to ask you a couple of favours in the meantime.'

Without naming the player, Alec outlined Diego's problem.

'Count me in, mate,' Stevie said without hesitation. 'But you know 30k's the going rate for a yellow at this level.'

'There's no money in it, Stevie. It's for your own protection. If the bad guys think they've got you then they'll never let up. Without a money trail it's impossible to prove anything so when we say it stops, it stops. If my plan works out it will only be a couple of times and, when it's over, we are going on the road trip of a lifetime.'

'That's a big claim, Alec, but I'll hold you to it. Now, what do you want me to do?'

'I'm asking all the boys the same thing: just look ahead to your next game and give me something to bet on. It could be a card, if you don't think it will hurt, or a corner or a free kick. You have to give me a time window when it's going to happen, like you're going to kick the ball out in the first five minutes or give away two corners in the final quarter, then just WhatsApp me the details. I'll remind you on the morning of the game, then just delete the messages and no one's any the wiser.'

'That's no problem, mate. I pick up a card every other game so that should be easy.'

'It has to be unpredictable enough for these guys to get a bet on, so have a think and let me know, right? And whatever you do, seriously, don't tell anyone; not the wife and definitely not Grubber. It's essential that no one else knows so they can never point the finger at you, do you understand?'

'Yeah, all right, Alec. I get the picture. Now fuck off and sort out that road trip.'

Alec smiled to himself as he hung up. Stevie was an idiot, but he was 100% solid. This plan might just work after all. He called the next player on his list: Nikolai, another veteran of the Vegas trip. The Russian was surprisingly reluctant to get involved, not that he had any moral qualms.

'You know, Alec, I find I just can't concentrate on a thing like this if there's no money in it. In the moment, I might just forget what I've agreed to.'

'Nikolai, you greedy bastard. I know you're on 130k a week. What could I possibly give you that would make a difference?'

The player thought about it for a moment then asked: 'Will that shlyukha be organising the girls for our next party? You know, the French blonde who was in Vegas.'

The question took Alec by surprise. He hadn't given any thought to the details but could see the appeal. He certainly didn't have connections who could arrange the kind of sex and drugs and rock'n'roll that the guys were expecting. 'Err, yeah, why not? Blandine is part of the team.'

'Blandine, yes. Blandine, I want her.'

'Fuck me, Nikolai, you're sick man.'

'Call me what you like; that's my price.'

'Look, I'll see what I can do but no promises.'

'I do this, you owe me, man, so you get me Blandine or it's no deal.'

'You can dream about her, you filthy fuck, if it helps you concentrate on what you're doing for me.'

'Ha, ha, I will, but I want her at the end,' he said, insistently.

Alec ended the call knowing that Blandine would never, ever agree to be part of the trade. He would work out how to manage the Russian when the time came, but for now he had another recruit. It was slow work but by nine in the evening he had three more players signed up as well as Diego, Stevie and Nikolai. He would need more options to cover squad rotations and injuries but Marko would have his five events to bet on for this round at least.

He looked down the list again. Everyone looked solid with the possible exception of Kevin Mooney, the Northern Ireland international who had been the only one to come home with a profit from the Vegas trip. He had been way too curious about the ins and outs of the betting and how it was going to work. At first Alec had been happy to talk about NumbersGame but he started to regret it as the conversation went on. Kevin was a smart guy and fancied himself as a bit of a wheeler dealer. He also had a big gambling habit which was why he made it onto the list in the first place. Kevin had pushed hard to know who else was involved and for details of the various fixes they were going to pull, so it was pretty obvious what was going through his mind. Alec knew the enterprise would only hold solid for a few games but Mooney could be the one to bring it crashing down. He made two decisions: one, don't recruit any more hardened gamblers, and two, call Hugo and warn him off taking on a new client. He wasn't sure how far the banker's scruples would hold and the prospect of a wealthy new punter would be tempting.

Alec pulled together the notes of his various calls and put everything into a simple spreadsheet. He created a system of abbreviations for the players and their actions so that even if his laptop was compromised there would be nothing to hint at the kind of operation he was running. Separately, on a single sheet of paper, he kept a list of the players' WhatsApp contact details and the date and time of their next games. He would rewrite the list each round destroying any evidence from the previous one. Michaela had already told him she didn't want to know who was involved and what they were doing, so this was strictly personal.

As he was contemplating his next move, Michaela's Whizz Air flight was touching down in Budapest, the Hungarian capital and she was soon in a police car speeding the one hundred miles to the border between Hungary and Serbia. She had used her Interpol connections to put a trace on the mobile number that Marta had given them and received assurances from contacts in countries along any likely route that she would be alerted if they picked it up. The Serbians had not been cooperative but the text she had received was from a contact in the Rendőrség, the Hungarian police force, telling her the mobile had just popped up on the Telenor mobile network. Triangulating with three cells had shown the phone was just a few metres from the border crossing at Szeged. It hadn't moved for several hours and Michaela was gambling that the driver was waiting for nightfall before attempting to cross. The local police had jumped at the chance to make some headway with people trafficking and met her from the airport.

The border town was the frontline in Hungary's vigorous attempts to turn the tide of refugees, economic migrants and young people, mainly, but not exclusively, girls being trafficked for sex work in Western Europe. If they made it over the border, the Schengen Agreement meant they could travel freely throughout the continent until they faced the natural barrier of the Channel in Northern France so EU governments were looking on keenly. Non-EU citizens faced the possibility of identity checks and a vehicle search, but as the local time ticked around to 1.07am, a white panel van with German plates emerged from its hiding place in woods beyond a makeshift refugee camp and joined the road approaching the frontier post. It drove up the EU lane where the driver held up two German passports assuming they would be waived through unhindered.

A few metres away Michaela's phone pinged again: the target was moving. She alerted her Rendőrség escort and observed from the police car as the van was waived towards a covered area for inspection. The driver made a vain attempt to hand over a bribe but the officers had their instructions. Routinely armed, they unclipped the straps on their holsters and stood with hands hovering over their pistols as the driver reluctantly opened his door and got out. He looked for an exit but found none and had no choice but to open the rear doors and reveal his cargo. He and his companion were promptly arrested and taken away for questioning, while the girls were shepherded into a portacabin used as an office and temporary transit lounge by immigration officers.

With the driver and his mate out of the picture, Michaela emerged to get a first sight of the girls. Her heart sank as she observed the bedraggled group through a one-way mirror: there was no one who could possibly be confused with a petite, Brazilian beauty. She handed a telephone number to one of the immigration officers and asked her to text it. As the message was sent, one girl in the group reached reflexively for her bag.

Chapter 20

Before he finished his first coffee the next morning Alec had received three messages from his footballers detailing what they planned to do in their weekend games. He chased the other two who came back promptly, then he carefully inputted abbreviated details into his spreadsheet. The players weren't very creative and he could tell some of them were going to need his help, but, for a first round, it was good enough.

His fixes lined up, Alec took a deep breath and called Marko.

'Why are you calling me? Just send over the details and fuck off.'

'Marko, you of all people should know we don't want anything that could make a paper trail. I'll read out what I've got and you can make a note, get your bets on and there'll be no incriminating evidence.'

The Serbian grudgingly agreed and a couple of minutes later the information had been exchanged.

'Now, what about Marta? When can Diego come and pick her up?'

'I'm in no hurry. The bitch is fine, and she's in a place where no one's gonna come and get her. I need to see this network of yours in action before anything's gonna change but you can tell Diego to call me at eight tonight, and maybe I'll let him speak to her.'

Alec bit his tongue, knowing he needed to keep the Serbian onside. 'So, what's the plan now, Marko?' he asked affably. 'How are you going to find someone to accept big enough bets to make any serious money? As a punter, you know, it's not easy to get a lot of money on a dead cert, particularly if you keep winning big.'

'You worry about your business and I'll take care of mine. We've got guys placing bets all the time. This is a large-scale operation.'

'I just wondered whether you could use any help, that's all. There's someone I know who could be very useful to you.'

'Why do you want to help me?' said Marko, immediately suspicious.

'Well, look at it from my point of view. Obviously I want to get Marta back. That's my first priority and I reckon you're going to need to win big to give her up. But I'm also thinking about the longer term. I've gone to a lot of trouble putting this network together and I've got some ideas that could make us all a lot of money.'

'You always were a fucking snake, Alec. What was all that shit about responsibility to your clients, eh? Where's that all gone? You're just a fixer, screwing them over.'

'Then we've got plenty in common,' Alec shot back, keeping up the bravado. 'I'll tell you what, this weekend you get your guys to do it your way and I'll get my mate to do his thing, then on Monday we'll compare winnings. Yours should be much bigger than mine, as I haven't got any real money behind me, but I should be able to make enough to show you that the system will work.'

The call ended with Marko still cruelly mocking Alec's apparent change of heart, but there was no doubt he was interested.

Alec's next call was to Hugo Ashburton.

'Ah good morning Mr Munday. How may I be of assistance?'

'Our fish is on the hook but he's going to need a convincer before we can reel him in. I've got five events that I know are going to happen in the Premier League this weekend and I need a demonstration of how we can make money. I can put up £10,000, so what can you do?'

'You probably realise this already but you're asking for something rather different from what we're offering your Serbian pal. We are assuming he has a large amount of money which he would like to invest yielding positive but unspectacular returns at minimal risk. Excuse me if this sounds demeaning but you, I think, are looking to turn quite a small amount of money into a large pile in one hit. Correct?'

'Correct.'

'If we had longer to play with, I would recommend some sort of leveraged spread bet and, of course, if you didn't know the outcome of the events you were looking to bet on, we would use leverage through matched betting to make your stake work much harder for you...'

'Hugo, I don't need the sales pitch. I just need you to take my ten grand and turn it into enough money to make Marko sit up and take notice.'

'Yes, of course. We'll target all the online operators and use the system to open a large number of completely untraceable accounts and spread your £10,000 between them. That way, with a combination of introductory bets and offers, we should be able to get your pot up to around £40,000. Then if, say, the odds of each one of your events happening is 4:1, then we make £160,000 in your first round of bets plus your stake. After that it gets a bit more tricky. In theory we should be able to reinvest that amount on the next incident at 4:1 making £800k, and so on, yielding a possible total return of over £100 million. The reality, however, is rather different. Even if the bookmakers paid out immediately it would take a few hours for money to appear back in your account so we'll be restricted to using the accounts we've already got open. Then we won't get anything like the full amount on another four events without arousing suspicion and it will get harder the further we go. But, all things being equal, I think we should be able to make a profit of around one-and-a-half a million by Sunday evening. Does that sound like the sort of thing which will impress Johnny Serbian?'

'What's to stop Marko simply doing a similar thing?'

Hugo bristled. 'Alec, I'm not sure you quite appreciate what NumbersGame is offering you. First, I'm putting at your disposal several dozen bank accounts, then we're exploiting the characteristics of the web to give us the cover of complete anonymity. It will appear as if we're operating from hundreds of locations around the world and we're using those in different combinations to create up to 1000 small-scale betting accounts. Even if your man has that kind of capability, which I strongly doubt, he would then be up against the power of the technology set up to detect fraud and shut down suspicious accounts. With NumbersGame we automatically place dozens of bets in amounts that go undetected by the bookmakers whilst simultaneously tracking what is being picked up by the Premier League and UEFA's systems. Without that sort of intelligence he is likely to lose his money entirely whether he knows the outcome of an event or not. I don't know how much he has to play with but if I were a betting man, which incidentally I'm not, I'd wager your profits from this weekend will comfortably outweigh Marko's come Monday morning and you'll get paid out into the bargain.'

'Thanks Hugo. I didn't mean to doubt you but, as you can probably tell, I'm new to this game.'

'Yes, well, I must confess that complexity is one of the barriers which prevents me persuading more people to take advantage of the NumbersGame system, so it never does one any harm to practice dumbing it down for the masses. Now, are we a go for this weekend? It will take me a couple of hours to get everything set up and I assume your first game will be starting around lunchtime.'

Alec gave him the green light and read out the list of events he had prearranged.

The banker was clearly delighted. 'Excellent, I'll get to work,' he said. 'I'll text you details of the bank account to send the money to then just leave the rest to me. In your case I'll need to insist on the 5% of your winnings option in terms of my fee but I'm sure now that you can see it will be money well spent.'

'If you deliver anything like the numbers you've talked about then I'll be happy to give you 5% of the profits, but only if you swear on pain of death that you won't let Michaela in on our arrangement.'

'Agreed and quite understood, dear boy. She has never been terribly accommodating around the greyer areas of the law.'

'And I'll tell you now, you'll not be able to get anything like 5% from the Serbians if they do go ahead.'

'I rather suspected as much but as it's all guaranteed, one will just have to suck it up, as they say. Oh, while you're on, I had a call earlier from a Mr Kevin Mooney, a footballer I believe. He claims to be an acquaintance of yours and said he was interested in some betting action.'

'Well, if he calls again, I hope you'll tell him that he is strictly forbidden under FA rules from betting on his sport. He'd be risking a lengthy ban from playing as well as committing a criminal offence.'

'He was quite insistent...'

'Hugo, I've got another call coming through. Text me those bank details then we'll talk later and it's a 'no' to Kevin Mooney.'

Alec hung up and saw it was Michaela on the line. 'Ah, the international woman of mystery. Where are you?'

'I've just landed back at Luton. Can you come and get me?'

'I'm on my way. You sound fed up. Are you ok?'

'I've had better nights. I'll tell you all about it when you get here. Don't be long.'

He saw her almost as soon as he arrived at the airport, in the same place he'd left her 19 hours earlier.

'Blimey, you're a sight for sore eyes.'

'I really need a shower and a change of clothes so you'll have to excuse the smell. Where I've been wasn't exactly the Ritz Carlton.'

'Come on then, where was it?'

'That mobile number Marta gave us, I had it tracked and I got an alert yesterday afternoon that it was on the move. It had been traced to the Hungarian border so I flew to Budapest and got a ride with Hungarian police to try and intercept what I hoped would be a group containing Marta herself.'

'I spoke to Marko an hour ago and he agreed that Diego could speak to her later, so I'm guessing you came up short.'

'If I had her I'd have brought her home, but sadly no. The Hungarian police stopped a van containing 11 girls being trafficked to Western Europe. The driver and co-driver were arrested and the girls taken to safety, but Marta wasn't among them. I've spent most of the night with an Albanian girl called Fetije whose mobile Marta was using. I got what I could out of her but it wasn't the breakthrough I'd hoped for.'

'But is Marta ok, though? Have you got any news to give Diego?'

'As of early yesterday morning she was fine, but Fetije was clearly worried about her. Communication wasn't easy; Albanian is not a language like any others I know. Initially she was very suspicious – from her perspective I was taking away her dream of a new life in Germany – but in the end, she provided some information which may be useful. They had all been living in a two-bed apartment in a block in the town but she either couldn't or wouldn't tell me exactly where. She said she only saw the block at night so couldn't give me anything by way of a description other than that it was like all the others. She thought they could have been on the third floor and didn't recall any movement or footsteps above. Outside there were no particularly distinct sounds; no sirens, just light traffic, but there was a bell quite close by, like a church clock, which sounded the quarter hours.

'Marta and another girl were there when she arrived and they spent four days together with new girls arriving every day. They had no language in common except for a few words of English but she did say that Marta was different from the others. Everyone else seemed excited about their adventure but she was miserable all the time. Fetije thought she might be homesick. Physically she was ok but she wasn't really eating and seemed permanently cold. One of the other girls lent her a coat, which she wore all the time, but she had to give that back when they all left. They were overseen by an older woman called Branka who spoke Serbian to the girls and came to the apartment every morning with food. She was in her forties, medium height and slim build with dyed black hair which Fetije described as a bit wild, like a gypsy. She only ever wore jeans and a t-shirt, a black leather jacket and black boots. There was no obvious security and Fetije didn't think they were locked in although she never tried the door. They were warned not to leave the apartment and they were all happy to cooperate.

'Yesterday morning, they were woken before dawn by Branka and two men. They all got their things together and were leaving the apartment when Branka spoke to Marta evidently telling her she wasn't going with them. Marta was very upset, crying and talking loudly in a language Fetije didn't understand. She considered staying to help but was led away by the men and given no choice but to go downstairs and straight into the van outside. They were in the city streets for around five minutes making several turns then the road got smoother. They drove at medium speed for around three hours stopping for fuel and for a comfort break in some woods. Then they drove for a few more hours before parking up for around half a day a few metres from where we intercepted the van. That's all consistent with our working hypothesis that they were being held in Niš.'

'Did she know what was going to happen to Marta?'

'No, she was just told to stay in the apartment. I asked the Serbian girls and they confirmed that Branka just told her she was staying where she was. None of the other girls could provide any more information except to say that Marta seemed in some kind of trouble. They tried to help her and encouraged her to eat, but she was always miserable. The only other information I got was that late on Wednesday evening the woman had come to the apartment and taken Marta away with her. They were gone around 30 minutes and no one was certain whether they got into a car outside or not, but they thought probably yes. When she came back, she was shaken up and crying but didn't appear to have been physically harmed.'

'So now she's on her own in an unguarded apartment that we can probably locate if we hear a clock and see a gypsy. Are you thinking we could carry out some sort of snatch?'

'Alec, this is not The Equalizer and you're not Denzel Bloody Washington, neither are you Liam Neeson in Taken or any other stupid action thriller you've been watching. Niš is a small town and you're talking about grabbing someone from under the noses of a violent criminal gang who have the police in their pockets. Even assuming Marta is still in the same place, someone's got to locate her and get her into a vehicle then reach the border with half the Serbian underworld on their tail."

'Ok, so you don't rate me as the action hero, but you know someone who is right?'

'Let's just say, I'm making enquiries.'

'Boom! Get in. I knew it.'

Chapter 21

1.55pm

'So, as the clock ticks round to 70 minutes that's going to be a yellow card for Stevie Mac. It was a clumsy challenge rather than a malicious one, wouldn't you say, Barry?'

'Absolutely, he's just mistimed his tackle and the player's gone down. Nothing in it, as you say, but a yellow is the right decision from the referee. We've seen McBrien commit worse fouls and, I have to say, we should perhaps be more surprised that it's taken until this late in the game for him to pick up a card given his recent form. He must be giving the manager some sleepless nights.'

'Quite. He's always been a physical player but, as he's matured, what he's lost in guile and mobility he seems to have made up for in brute strength and aggression. And with the score poised at 1:1, the last thing his team needs is for Stevie Mac to have a rush of blood to the head and they're down to 10 men. As it is, they've got a free kick to deal with in a dangerous area and it will be Emanuel Boloré to take it. He's waving his arms and urging his teammates forward, but in the end the ball goes through the pack and bounces away harmlessly for a goal kick.'

A flurry of interest greeted Stevie Mac's card in North London and in Niš as Alec Munday and Marko Vasic simultaneously tried to calculate what his misdemeanour had earned them. Alec had worried that Stevie might have forgotten his commitment but caught the look in the player's eye as he stared down the lens of the TV camera picking up his discussion with the referee. This was a favour Alec wouldn't be allowed to forget.

3.03pm

'Rutgers passes out to Kevin Mooney who misreads the pass and catches the ball with the outside of his foot sending it out across the side line for a throw-in to the visitors who take it quickly but only succeed in giving it back to Mooney who drives it forward more positively now.

There is a lot at stake for both teams in this game but, if what we've seen so far is an indication of the sort of football we can expect, then I'm afraid it's going to be a long afternoon.'

Mooney to give away a throw-in in the first five minutes – check. 3.40pm

'Diego's on the ball and he's made it into the box. A neat dummy and he's beaten the first man, oh, but he's brought down by the second, and the referee has no hesitation but to point to the spot. The Brazilian let the ball run across his body leaving the defender completely wrong footed. All he could do was to stick out a flailing leg and Diego goes down for a certain penalty. Some might say he could have stayed on his feet there. Robbie, what's your view? Is that a penalty in your book?'

'Well, there's no question that he might have stayed on his feet, but he's been tackled in the box and he's entitled to go down when he's through on goal, and I don't think the ref's got a choice. For me, that's a penalty all day long and the defender can count himself lucky he's not been red carded.'

'We've seen them given, haven't we, Robbie? Looking at the replay, though, I can't see much contact there at all.'

'I think the lad has a right to feel he's been harshly treated. Definitely a soft pen.'

'Well there's no sign of injury as Diego lines up to try and convert. Oh, and he's missed it! For a player of his class, I have to say, that was woeful. He didn't seem to approach his run-up with anything like his normal confidence, he completely scuffed the shot and the goalkeeper can't believe his luck. The player looks furious and upset and his teammates aren't exactly rushing over to console him. We've seen some terrible penalties over the years, but that one is right up there, Robbie.'

'It was a complete shocker, Jonathan. He hasn't got his head together at all. He's practically telegraphed which side he's going to, he miskicks the shot and the keeper's gone "thanks very much," and just gathered it in. Now he looks distraught. He's got his face buried in his hands and

he's shrugging off his teammates who are trying to get him back in the game.'

'Well that's a penalty that will be remembered for all the wrong reasons, and coming just before half time, it might have a decisive influence on this game which has been crying out for a goal. Anyway, we're off again, the goalkeeper's playing it out from the back and Diego's immediately in the face of the opposition's defence. He's won the ball and he's skipping past the defenders perhaps looking to make amends for that terrible spot kick. He must have gone past three players, now he's one-on-one with the keeper, a quick sidestep and it's an easy tap in but he's absolutely drilled it into the underside of the net, Robbie. If ever there was a goal to lay the ghosts it was that one which, I reckon, came less than a minute after that awful missed penalty.'

'And look at his reaction. He's got his hands cupped behind both ears daring the crowd not to cheer him and they're loving it. Talk about zero to hero, and the manager's thinking if that's what it takes to get him firing, then I'll take a missed pen any day of the week.'

'What we've seen in that four-minute passage of play could form the basis of an entire thesis for a sports psychologist and, as the ref blows up for halftime, Diego heads down the tunnel with the cheers of the crowd ringing in his ears.'

Alec glanced over at Michaela who was sound asleep on the sofa, before rewinding the passage of play on his Sky box and reviewing it several times. The penalty was terrible, but Alec knew the miss would soon be overshadowed by the way Diego bounced back to score. He was more concerned about what the whole episode said about the player's state of mind. He looked fragile and close to a meltdown and that was soon going to draw the attention of the club and who knows who else. He pulled out his phone and sent the player a text.

'gd game 2day mate call with M at 8 2nite cu l8r'

The teatime fixture was supposed to feature Nikolai committing a classic striker's foul and getting a yellow card. But, as the teams were announced, it was clear the Russian would be coming off the bench if he played at all. Alec checked back in his messages and saw that the player had said the incident would be in the second half but his failure to start added an unwelcome element of doubt that Alec hadn't considered. There was no such thing as a dead cert in sport and everything needed to go smoothly with Marko this first weekend to bring him fully on board. He spent the next forty-five minutes attending distractedly to a series of social media posts on behalf of his clients with more than half an eye on the TV action. When the players emerged for the second half there was no sign that Nikolai was being brought on, and Alec could feel his palms sweating. As the fourth game of five this weekend he was sure Toby would have got as much on in bets as he could and he stood to lose a fortune alongside his credibility with Marko.

He needn't have worried. True to form, the manager rang the changes bang on 60 minutes and the big Russian was on the pitch. He had hardly touched the ball when he earned his yellow card with a needless mistimed sliding tackle forty yards out from his own goal. The TV commentary put it down to 'taking a while to adjust to the pace of the play' and Alec was amazed once again at how easy it was to pull the wool over the eyes of some of the most experienced watchers of the game. The subsequent free kick led to nothing and the game carried on with the card destined to be a minor talking point at most for the various highlights shows.

Alec breathed a sigh of relief and the enthusiasm he put into his final flurry of tweets and posts was genuine. It had been a great afternoon's football so perhaps it was true what they say that "it matters more when there's money on it", although he did consider contacting Toby to reduce the amount of risk for the Sunday game. He had learned the hard way that the money taps turn off far quicker than they turn on.

With the business of the day successfully concluded, he turned his attention to the evening. They had been invited to one of his client's birthday celebrations at Hedonista in Mayfair, and he had persuaded Diego to go with them. With most of the London teams having played at home that afternoon, the West End was going to be hosting quite a party with players and dozens of their friends hitting the clubs.

Now she was refreshed and awake, Michaela was more than up for a night on the town. She went to shower and change while he poured them both a drink and sat back down in front of the TV determined to pick up any hint that the pundits found anything amiss with the afternoon's games. When she came back into the room to ask him to do up her dress he was blown away. She had clearly picked up some tips from the French fashionistas and looked fabulous in a black lace LBD.

'Wow, you look a million dollars. You smell great too,' he said, nuzzling her neck. 'I'm not sure whether to zip up the dress or try and talk you out of it.'

'Why does it sound like you've used that line before? Anyway, you couldn't if you tried. You promised me a big night out so now it's your turn. I've heard you footballers scrub up ok.'

An hour later they emerged from the house looking like the perfect couple and ducked into a waiting taxi which whisked them towards the West End.

On the other side of Europe, Marta was lying alone in the apartment that had been her prison for almost a week. Today had been the worst since she had been taken hostage and she was close to despair. The other girls had gone and Branka had not shown up with any food leaving her alone, cold and hungry. With too much time to think and little idea why she was being held, her mind started to fill in the blanks. She became convinced that she was being left to die and tried to find ways of attracting attention. She had tried screaming and throwing objects around the apartment. Then she squeezed some plates through the only window she could open, a quarterlight in her bedroom, sending them crashing to the street below. The sound of smashing crockery echoed up to the window but that was the only response she got.

By the time the key went in the lock just before 8.30 in the evening, she was frantic and practically fell on Branka when she came in with pizza. She ate quickly, her back to her minder who waited while she finished. As she wiped away remnants of cheese and tomato Marta turned to face the other woman wondering why she was still there. As she did she saw that Branka's face was badly beaten, her mouth swollen around a split lip where a dark scab had formed. The white of one of her eyes was blood red with heavy bruising spreading to her nose, and she looked like she had been dragged some distance by her hair. Despite her recent despair Marta responded with concern and asked, 'What happened to your face?' She received only a shrug by way of reply.

'I am very cold. Could I have a coat?' she persisted.

'I bring tomorrow,' Branka said speaking with difficulty. 'Now we go.'

The pair got into her car and took the same short journey across town arriving within minutes at the sports stadium where Marta had spoken to Diego soon after being captured. That call felt like a lifetime ago but maybe now they would speak again. Her hopes were raised as told Marta to go up to the office as before but, as she entered the building, the sound of a man shouting echoed around the stairwell. She waited outside the office unsure whether she was walking into even more trouble. After four or five minutes it seemed like the man wasn't going to stop so she entered nervously. As she did so a dozen pairs of eyes turned suspiciously towards her. Marko peeled off from the group and pushed her back through the door. The shouting continued as the pair waited awkwardly for Diego's call to come through. When Marko's mobile finally rang he spoke only a few words before handing it over. She tried to talk for as long as possible but Marko was in impatient mood and the call was ended all too soon. She started crying and pleaded with the Serb to help her but Marko, unmoved, just took back his phone and re-entered the office leaving her in the lobby alone.

She had time to compose herself once again and took the opportunity to explore her surroundings. On the opposite side of the lobby there was a bar with windows through which she could just make out stadium seats and the football pitch beyond. There were large posters and memorabilia on the walls and a glass cabinet containing a small collection of trophies and medals. With the shouting still continuing in the background she tried a couple of the doors that led off the lobby but, finding everything securely locked, she had no choice but to go back downstairs and out to Branka's car.

There was no conversation between the two women on the return journey but when they arrived back at the apartment building Marta felt somewhat more emboldened and sat tight refusing to move. Branka looked weary but resolved to show she could dish it out as well as take it. She walked around the car, opened Marta's door, grabbed the girl's ear and twisted her from her seat. She marched her into the building and up the stairs releasing her grip just long enough to open up. Marta was pushed roughly through the apartment door but resisted and spun round to face her jailer who hit her hard across the face. Without a word the older woman turned and walked out, locking the door firmly behind her.

The shock of the slap was greater than the pain and Marta soon recovered herself buoyed by a tide of anger coursing through her tiny frame. At that moment she made up her mind she would do whatever it took to get through the ordeal, and put herself to bed feeling more positive than she had for days.

Back in London, Alec had booked dinner at an Italian restaurant owned by a former footballer who was front of house when they arrived. He greeted them warmly, clapping Alec on the back and kissing Michaela on both cheeks before showing them personally to their table. Michaela took in the décor which was an unlikely combination of Italian marble, renaissance art and football memorabilia which one reviewer likened spitefully to 'opening a sports bar in the Uffizi Gallery'.

'It's like there's a football subculture I had no idea existed,' said Michaela, as two flutes of champagne arrived.

Alec shrugged. 'It starts out as a trust thing. Players are so used to being ripped off by estate agents, car salesmen or whoever, so they tend to go with who they know. Then it's like a village: there's always someone who can help you with whatever you need, whether it's a holiday home in Spain or a decent bite to eat. It's not an easy club to get into but, once you're in, there's no reason to leave.'

'I have to say I hadn't ever expected I'd be spending an evening with a bunch of WAGs. Are they all total bitches?'

'The girls are generally what you'd expect when you get to know the player. If he's a shagnasty, then she's likely to be either a gold digger or a doormat. Deano's an all-right guy and I've met Lauren a couple of times. She seemed like a good sort to me but I know you ladies always see things that us blokes don't pick up on. I've meet most of the others and, for what it's worth, I'd say they were really nice too, but actually it's not the wives and girlfriends that are the problem. Whenever the guys are out they're the target of female attention, whether they're with a partner or not. I know the players get a hard time in the press but some of the girls they come up against are completely outrageous, and it's even worse when the boys are on their own. I've seen fights breaking out between them over some totally ordinary-looking guy just because he's a footballer.'

'Maybe I'm getting old but I can't see the attraction. What makes them do it, do you think?'

'I suppose some of them genuinely imagine they'll end up in a relationship with a player although I don't know many that have lasted beyond the night. Others see the lads as trophies and want to shag a player for the bragging rights, so you can see why it sends some of the boys off the rails.'

As they tucked into Osso Buco Alec relayed some of the tamer experiences he'd had in the company of partying players, all the while hoping this evening would not get too messy.

They met Diego and the rest in the Aurora Bar where Deano had a half a dozen magnums of champagne in a giant ice bucket. Spirits were high after a successful afternoon on the pitch and Diego batted Alec aside when he tried to have a quiet word about how it had gone on the phone. The player seemed full of energy and was laughing loudly at every opportunity. Overcompensating or high on something? Alec didn't know but his media management instincts kicked in. Tonight was not a night to let Diego wander off on his own.

After a couple of hours the group were starting to draw attention to themselves and the management were not too disappointed when they moved on from the Aurora snaking their way around the corner to Hedonista. Their arrival had been pre-arranged and the bouncers quickly waved them past the queuing punters installing them in a roped off VIP area inside. Barely had they taken their seats when all the lights went out. After a few seconds of screaming a single spotlight flooded one corner where half a dozen girls wearing little more than dental floss and a smile carried bottles of champagne aloft on silver trays. The soundtrack was the intro music to the Premier League and the signal was a clear one. Within seconds the VIP area had turned into a seething mass of female flesh.

The club's security was already struggling to keep order but a misplaced stiletto in a rival's foot and an elbow connecting sharply with an overinflated breast quickly turned the scene into chaos. The air was thick with hair extensions and clawing finger nails as the bouncers waded in calling desperately for the house lights to be turned on. Part of being a successful team is knowing when to fall back and defend, and the footballers and their partners escaped through a discreet door leading to an upstairs lounge. Several of the boys were still laughing if only nervously while they waited for the melee to die down below them. The girls did their best to look shocked and appalled although Alec knew for a fact that at least three of them had got up to similar tricks.

'Hey, isn't this the place where we did MDMA on Danny's birthday last year?' piped up Deano, but he shut up quickly when Lauren shot daggers in his direction.

The other players were tempted to share their recollections of that evening but thought better of it as they remembered a few hazy details of a lad's night out that had got dangerously out of hand.

'I'm sure they've got the dance floor back under control by now,' said Alec, getting the evening back on track. 'Let's go down and party.'

A couple of hours later he and Michaela were cooling off in the night air having put Diego in a taxi with strict instructions about where he was to be dropped.

'That scene earlier was like Saturday night in Tottenham Nick,' she said. 'But then I was being paid to put up with it. Why would Deano and Lauren even want to be in that situation let alone celebrate his birthday there?'

'It's not easy for the guys sometimes. They just want to go out and have a good time like anyone else but, I have to say, whoever set up that whole lights out thing should be fired. You know, it's flattering for the younger players to have girls falling over themselves to get off with you, but that went way too far, especially in front of Lauren.'

'I'm not sure that's really the point. How does she feel knowing that he's going to be in that situation every time he's playing away from home?'

'They don't call it 'playing away' for nothing.'

Chapter 22

A buzz from Alec's phone woke him up just before midday. He glanced at the screen to see he had a text message from Andy Grubber. He clicked on the notification to reveal a photo of Diego, clearly the worse for wear, with a girl on each arm falling out of the last night's club.

'Shit,' he muttered under his breath.

Michaela turned over and looked at him sleepily. 'What's the problem?'

'Fucking Diego,' he said showing her the picture. 'I can't believe what I have to deal with sometimes. I'd better call Grubber.'

'Maybe you could try and bring him onside. Couldn't the press help in some way?'

'At some point going public could be a useful option but not Grubber and not yet. Morning Andy. How's it going?'

'In my experience, Alec, there are two types of people in this world: honest open souls, brave and decent, up bright and early on a Sunday morning with a clear conscience, some of them have even been to church. They call me Grubber. The other type has either got a favour to beg or something to cover up and based on what I just sent over to you, I'm guessing in your case it's both.'

'Just being cautious, mate. After the last time we spoke my client's intimate finances were in print the next day.'

'Yeah, I remember thinking it was funny how easily that little fart of information squeaked out. Anyway, this time he's gone completely open kimono all by himself. That was taken at 4.30 this morning outside Hedonista. Nice girls, Stacy and Nikki if you're interested. We caught up with them a few hours later. We're already pumping them for details about their, err, night of shame, but probably not quite as hard as your boy was pumping them a few hours ago.'

Alec winced at the terrible banter. He knew there was no point telling the journalist the truth, that he'd put Diego in a cab over an hour before the picture was taken. It would only suggest he knew more than he was letting on and he was happy to keep the nature of his relationships with players ambiguous as far as Grubber was concerned. Time to go on the offensive.

'You're a rancid little shit Grubber. What are you planning to do with this scoop of yours?'

'Duh! It's going live on the website in about 40 minutes and, assuming Trump doesn't nuke the fucking Chinese in the next few hours, it will be our lead story tomorrow morning. Unless of course...'

'Unless what?'

'You know I like Diego, always have. He's a good boy and he has the makings of a great player, but I reckon there's something going on with him. You know what I think, Alec? You spunking details of his finances was a classic diversion. I spoke to Stevie Mac again and he as good as confirmed the lad's in trouble. So, I'll tell you what I'll do. You get me a sit down with Diego, get him to open his heart, and I'll make sure Stacy and Nikki forget last night ever happened.'

'Stop bullshitting, Grubber. There's not going to be any deal. All you've got is a grainy picture that could have been taken any time in the past two years. If Stacy and Tracy, or whoever they are, were actually talking you'd have already handed over oh, what's it going to be, twelve grand or so? And your editor would have your balls on a plate before he pulled that story. You publish your picture if you want, but you can piss off if you ever want anything about my players again.'

'Nice work,' said Michaela, with genuine admiration as he hung up. 'I particularly liked 'rancid little shit'. Sounds like quite a good description.'

'Grubber's a real lowlife but he's got an instinct for a story. I've probably done enough for now but he's not going to give up. At some point this one is going to get out.'

'So, what now?'

'I'm sending that picture on to Diego. He needs to get those girls out the tradesman's entrance before any more denizens of Her Majesty's free press get the scent of scandal and turn up on his doorstep.'

Alec made coffee and brought it back to bed where Michaela was waiting, ready for him. The call with Grubber had started the day with a jolt and, rather than let the energy go to waste, they were both happy to expend it on each other. Dozing later, they were disturbed again by Alec's phone as Diego came back with a series of apologetic emojis.

'Sometimes I feel like I'm running the world's most expensive babysitting service,' said Alec, showing Michaela the player's latest messages.

'Whatever you have to put up with, I think you'll find it's a whole lot better than running the world's cheapest babysitting service.'

'Yeh, I suppose. Anyway, I going to need to get over there and see him. There's a risk the photo will make the papers and I'll need to persuade him to let the club know first.'

'You enjoy that. I've got a meeting in town.'

She wasn't prepared to elaborate further so he fixed some juice and eggs for breakfast then took her to the station on his way to Hampstead. He arrived at the wrought iron gates just in time to see the two girls, in the same outfits they had been wearing in the photo, clambering into a taxi.

Diego looked sheepish when he saw Alec. 'What can I tell you man?' he whined. 'It's hard to sleep on my own.'

'You better hope that your wife doesn't have the same kind of problem. Anything could be happening to her right now and you're out shagging some slappers. I put you in that taxi for a reason 'cos right now the last thing you need is the press all over you. Wouldn't you even like to know where I got that picture from?'

'Did you sort it out?' Diego asked distractedly.

'I don't know, but I don't think you're taking this anything like seriously enough. At best it's going to be in the Mail's snack bar of dirt ready to be dished out at when you really won't want it, but if it's a slow news day you're going to be click bait on their website within the hour. We need to let the club know before they start taking calls.'

The player shrugged and walked into the house. Alec swallowed hard and tried to remind himself how much pressure his friend was under but made a mental note to increase his retainer nonetheless.

Had Michaela's employers been tracking her movements over the past few days it is doubtful that they would have found any sort of pattern, but they would have known for certain that she was operational. She had told colleagues that she was spending time with her parents in Kent and today was the closest she had got since arriving in London. She emerged from the tube system at Canada Water, a stone's throw from Rotherhithe Police Station but didn't slow down or even give it a sideways glance as she walked past.

Back in the day, Rotherhithe was a colourful elbow in the Thames where roughneck dockers traded insults with cheap prostitutes. Generations of both had plied their trades in the heyday of the British Empire but the closure of the docks in the late 1970s started a transformation of the area. That process was completed at the end of the Century by the extension of the Jubilee Line through Rotherhithe to neighbouring Canary Wharf. Warehouses were converted and pubs gastrofied to serve a braying horde of incomers whom the dwindling indigenous tribe referred to as yuppies.

The faded ghosts of a once thriving criminal fraternity still hung around Whelan's pub on the Old Road, but their manor was now unrecognisable. The old police station had been turned into an arts centre and a new purpose-built nick was opened serving a very different community. But, much like the criminals they fight, Police officers are creatures of habit. Most of those stationed at the new station still frequented the Farriers Arms, a traditional old boozer less than a hundred yards from Whelan's, squeezed between a launderette and a Chinese takeaway. The two pubs had been the informal power bases for those on opposing sides of the law with operations both large and small inspired by the beer served under their roofs. The Farriers was still known locally as the Old Bill's pub but there were no police officers in evidence on a Sunday afternoon as Michaela pushed open the door. The warm fug as she approached the bar was a welcome contrast to the bracing chill of November by the river. Although tempted to try her luck and order coffee, she opted wisely for a bottle of diet coke and settled herself at a corner table. The table was well chosen and she had a clear view when two casually dressed men in their mid-thirties came in and ordered pints of lager. They were both lean and clean shaven, one sallow, the other fair with close cropped hair and square shoulders. They greeted Michaela like an old friend as they took their places at the corner table. An hour and a half and a couple of drinks later the trio emerged into the deepening gloom outside and went their separate ways. She retraced her steps to Canada Water and they disappeared in the streets towards Deptford.

Meanwhile, in Hampstead, Alec was in Diego's subterranean man cave. He had persuaded the player to come clean with the club and texted Vic Vickers who had been over to check everything was actually alright.

'The picture makes it look worse than it was,' Diego had mumbled, knowing he would be in line for a proper ticking off from the boss in the morning.

'It is true,' Alec chipped in. 'I was there, and these girls just latched on to Diego for the cameras. And the half-closed eyes? That's just a natural reaction to all the flashlights going off.'

Vickers shook his head at the player. 'In the words of that well-worn phrase, I'm not angry, just disappointed, but I warn you, Diego, the boss is unlikely to be as understanding tomorrow. I strongly suggest you make it a quiet one this evening. If this photo is actually in the papers tomorrow, you can expect to have to answer a good few questions. As for you Alec, I'm beginning to have my doubts about whether you're a good influence or actually the cause of some of Diego's problems. Can you both just try to go a few weeks without any incidents, accidents or injuries please?'

Once the Player Care man was out of the way, the pair caught up on Diego's conversation with Marta the previous evening.

'She just wants to know what's happening and when she's coming back home. She was with some other girls but now she's all on her own. She kept saying that she is really cold. She started telling me about where she was but there was a lot of shouting in the background and then Marko took the phone away.'

'Do you remember if she said anything useful?'

'There is a woman called Branka who comes each day with food. She didn't arrive yesterday until it was time to collect her for our call, but she looked like she'd been beaten up with blood on her face and a black eye. She was speaking from a football stadium, the same place the call came from on Wednesday. There was a whole bunch of guys having a big fight but Marta didn't know what it was about. The only new thing she said was there were a lot of posters and signs for Rad-nički.

'Ok, that may be interesting. Did Marko say anything about letting her go?'

'I just said only a few words to him. He said we were doing good with the network and that she would be home soon but he never said when.'

'Well, I'm talking to him tomorrow so hopefully I'll be able to give you some better news after that. But stay positive, mate. We've made loads of progress so it shouldn't be too long now.'

He tried to sound upbeat, but privately Alec was becoming more and more concerned. The gang's treatment of Branka showed the kind of people they were dealing with and Marta would be safe only for as long as it suited their purposes.

An intercom sounded and Diego buzzed open the gates watching the screen as a Bentley Coupé, two pimped out Range Rovers and a Ferrari swung into the drive. Alec's BMW looked a long way out of its comfort zone as various of Diego's teammates powered down their supercars and trooped into the house. Officially, they were there to watch the five o'clock game but, like many professional footballers, they were not really interested in watching televised sport, preferring to lark about in Diego's pool or his home gym.

Alec googled Radnički on his phone and quickly confirmed Michaela's working assumption that Marta was indeed in Niš. Digging deeper he found that not only did it seem the Belovic Clan had their office in the team's stadium, but they had also been its main benefactors over recent years. Their investment had seen the team win promotion to the Serbian SuperLiga after nearly a decade in the wilderness. The stadium was completely rebuilt to international standards and the team, boosted by imported talent from Belgrade and Novi Sad, had started winning at the top level. There were constant rumours of match fixing swirling around Serbian football but Alec could find nothing specifically implicating Radnički Niš. From Michaela's insights into the Belovic Clan he thought it was likely that the team was a front for money laundering, but that didn't really add much to what they already knew. It did, though, show they were familiar with the world of football and perhaps even explained an interest in the Premier League.

With the players comparing six packs next door, Alec had the TV to himself to watch his Midlands goalkeeper ship the agreed four goals in the evening fixture against the League leaders. He felt a twinge of conscience over the performance as Darren's side had defended well. The first two strikes at least would have tested the best keepers though, and in the end the challenge was to keep the score to only four. The game done, Alec rejoined the players who were in the middle of a lively discussion about what to order from the Deliveroo menu. Some were being asked to watch their weight while others were trying to bulk up so choosing was not easy. In the end, they just ordered way too much of everything and turned their attention to weightier matters like the venue for the next road trip.

'I'm working on something special,' said Alec, 'but it's not going to be this side of Christmas. Let's get the New Year out of the way then you guys will have a mini break and I promise I'll have something lined up.'

There was some grumbling but most in the team knew that the period ahead was going to be decisive for their standing at the end of the season. The guys started trading ideas for where they would next like to test their supercars with Alec filing away their suggestions for future reference. From remote racetracks to winding mountain passes the propositions got more and more outlandish so, when Diego suggested the 'Road of Death' in Bolivia, everyone in the group just laughed. None of them suspected there was anything amiss or that the tours had got him into so much grief, but Alec was beginning to wonder whether there was more to the death wish than the player would like to admit.

Chapter 23

At just before 5.30 on Monday morning, an unremarkable white van approached the port of Dover and lined up for an early crossing to mainland Europe, a small ripple in the daily tide of commercial vehicles that washes back and forth across the Channel. Presenting nothing which would raise any concerns, the van was waved through security by French border control personnel nearing the end of their shift.

Had they pulled it to one side for a random inspection, officers would have met with two tough-looking men traveling on regular UK passports which gave their names as Christopher Tyler and Neil Edward Fleetwood. A perfunctory search would have revealed nothing more than a consignment of electronic equipment with paperwork indicating delivery the following day to an office in Lyon. Had anyone ventured into the darker cavities underneath the van, however, they would have found a pair of Glock 17 compact pistols, two Hechler and Koch MP5 sub-machine guns and a cache of ammunition. At that point the two men would have produced UK police warrant cards together with their Authorised Firearms Officer certification and European Firearms Passes. In the event progress through passport control was so routine that officers would have struggled to describe either the van or its occupants five minutes after it boarded the Pride of the Seas bound for Calais.

Two hours later Alec woke up next to Michaela and slid out of bed trying not to disturb here. Despite knowing they were illegal, he could not help but be excited as he went online to check his winnings. Adding the various accounts together the total soon shot through £1 million even allowing for Hugo Ashburton's 5%. It was a sum of money he hadn't expected to see in his name since the end of his footballing career and Alec was elated. He knew he should feel a measure of personal guilt or shame but, if he was honest, he was struggling to find a downside. Michaela would no doubt see things very differently, so he slammed the lid of his laptop shut as she walked into his office.

'I'm not even going to ask,' she said flatly, putting a crease in his smile.

'How did you know?'

'I'm trained to know these things and you haven't exactly made it difficult. You've been glued to every football match this weekend and now you've got a stupid grin on your face. Like I say, I don't even want to know how much you've won.'

'Sorry. I know I promised I wouldn't put you in a compromising position but I needed to have something to convince Marko to give Hugo's outfit the gig. I'll try and be more discreet. By the way,' he said, trying to change the subject. 'I didn't tell you that Diego got a couple of useful bits of information from Marta last night. She said the stadium where she speaks to him from is decorated with images and memorabilia from Radnički Niš football club, so that proves she is where you thought she was. The Belovic Clan are the team's owners and use part of the stadium for their offices. Apparently when they spoke on Saturday night there was a lot of shouting in the background and Marta said that Branka's face looked all messed up. It sounds like news of your operation got back to head office and the boss was going mental.'

'It's always nice to know they're hurting. When is Diego's next call with Marta?'

'Err, not sure. Up to now they've spoken after matches where he has delivered a fix and I think his next game is on Wednesday. Why?'

'Marta is obviously looking for things which could be helpful and I'd like to think about any questions he could be asking her.'

'Ok, I'll firm it up with Marko when I speak to him this morning.'

She walked over, put her arms around his neck and kissed him full on the lips with an intensity Alec hadn't felt before. He responded by trying to ease her out of her bathrobe but she pushed him away.

'Don't get any ideas. I just wanted to let you know that we're on the same side even if we are coming to it from very different places. I'm going to need some privacy today so I think I'll work from my flat in Shoreditch. It's between tenants at the moment and it will give me the chance to see what state it's in too.'

'Sure. Will I see you tonight?'

'Why don't you come to me? We can do something in town.'

Alec slipped on a tracksuit and made coffee while she showered and dressed, then he drove her to the station. It was still too early to call Hugo when he got back so he took the opportunity to use the treadmill and multi-gym in his spare bedroom and burn off some nervous energy. He was on the phone to NumbersGame soon after nine and was greeted by Hugo's voice booming down the line, clearly delighted.

'I'm just running the numbers now, but I think we've turned your £10,000 into just shy of £1.9m. Amazing really. I mean, I know how the system works but I have to say I'm still rather pleased with myself. Some of the accounts have yet to pay out but that will be available to you in the next few hours less my commission of course. What are you going to do with the money?'

'I've got a vague plan for when this is all over but it'll stay in the bank for now. Do I need to tell my accountant?'

'Up to you of course but that's the sweet thing about our kind of investments: returns are yours to keep untaxed and you don't even have to declare the income.'

'Good to know. Listen, I'm calling Serbia after I get off the phone to you so you can expect to do the same thing again for the midweek games.'

'I'll be ready and waiting; I may even have a flutter myself.'

'Isn't that like a publican drinking the profits?'

'More like a banker putting his money where his mouth is in a proprietary trading account. Anyway, I've already told you I'm not a gambler.'

'Well, the priority is to give Marko something to show his bosses so we get the whole crew on the hook.'

'Understood, dear boy. I'll be waiting for your call, breath appropriately bated.'

Alec had run through in his mind how the conversation with Marko was going to go, but he couldn't have anticipated the reception he received. The Serbian was putting on what passed in his case for charm and was more than receptive to Alec's suggestions.

'I hope you've got good news for me, Alec. My associates experienced some, err, disruption to their supply chain over the weekend and they are concerned there may be, what I think you English would call, a fox in the henhouse. I need to be able to show results to convince them this thing is going to work to their benefit.'

'So if I told you I turned £10,000 into the best part of two million quid over the five games do you think your associates would be interested?'

Marko couldn't help but sound impressed. 'That's a lot of money and the kind of amount that they would take notice of, for sure.'

Alec sensed a window of opportunity. 'Everything's in place to deliver,' he said. 'The players are up to their necks in it so I can turn the network on and off at will. We don't need to get greedy but you should be able to wash around a million per game through the markets and double your money each time. By the way, how much did you make this weekend?'

'I did ok but, as you warned me, it is not so easy making lots of big bets on sure-fire winners. Bookmakers are so suspicious: two are still threatening not to pay out at all.'

If that was what Marko was admitting to then Alec suspected the reality was much worse. It would have been hard to actually lose money but it seemed highly unlikely that he had done enough to make his bosses certain he wasn't the weak link in the chain. Now was the moment to get a deal for Marta's freedom.

'The guy I'm using can work incognito, get all the money on and guarantee a payout. Now that the network is in place we can do that every week but if we're going to do this for you, we need to take Marta out of the equation. You need to let her go now.'

There was a moment of silence on the line before Marko said, 'You have picked a good moment to ask, my friend. My associates are keen to focus back on their main business so, if you can convince them that our arrangement will continue, then this should be possible.'

Marko paused again, reviewing his options then said, 'There are a few midweek Premier League games this week, I think. Let's say I convince my associates to allow your friend to invest some of their money. If the returns are good then they will invite you and your colleague to a meeting here. If that goes well then, why not? Maybe you will be able to take the girl home with you.'

Alec knew they would be putting their heads in the lion's mouth but he could see Marko's logic, and Michaela would be sure to have some ideas to improve their chances of coming back in one piece.

'That sounds like a plan,' he said, crossing his fingers that Hugo could be persuaded. The former banker was happy to operate in the shadows but Alec suspected he had a streak of pure piss running through him. 'First things first. Let me have a conversation at this end and we'll get you set up on my friend's system. How much do you think your associates would be prepared to put up?'

'The recent supply chain disruption cost my associates around £2m so let me turn the question back to you. How much do you think they would need to invest to make their money back?'

Alec did a quick calculation. If he could influence events in three midweek games that would be three opportunities to get a bet on at say, 3:1, so in theory they could comfortably get to £2m with £40,000 up front but, with two games happening simultaneously and no way of getting all the winnings re-staked, it was going to take a lot more than that.

'If your associates would put up £200,000 then I'm confident they could expect that sort of return, plus their initial stake of course. But I'm guessing that might be a bit rich for a first-time experience of working together, am I right?'

There was silence on the other end of the line so Alec ploughed on. 'Look, I'll tell you what I'll do. I'm so confident in our system that I'll put up half of the stake myself. It will all be in a bank account that you can control; your associates will see my money there too and they can track their winnings in real time. If they can match my investment with £100,000 of their own, then they'll make the £2m at half the risk. Just two things, though; I would ask you to return my stake at the end and to pay my colleague a small commission of 2% out of the winnings. Do we have a deal?'

'I will need to discuss this with my associates but I think I can persuade them.'

'You let me know and I'll send over access details for a bank account that will already have my stake deposited in it. One last thing; Diego wants to speak to Marta again after the game on Wednesday. I assume the usual arrangement is ok?'

Marko agreed and, as he hung up, Alec jumped off his seat punching the air. It was the closest he had ever been to having Marko over a barrel. Offering to stake them was a stroke of genius and it felt good to know that the tables had been turned for the first time since Las Vegas. He was still buzzing as he picked up the phone and called NumbersGame where, as anticipated, Hugo was rather less ebullient about the prospect of a visit to their client.

'I've always been more of an office warrior,' he confessed. 'I mean, I can buckle a swash with the best of them but I find I tend to lose a bit of my swagger when actually staring into the whites of their eyes, you know. Wednesday's fine, of course and thank you, by the way, for negotiating a tiny slice of the action for yours truly. But I have weekend plans, and a trip to Eastern Siberia isn't on the agenda, I'm afraid.'

'It's Serbia and I need you on that plane. If these people invite you to a meeting it's not the kind of invitation you can turn down.'

'Alec, you have no idea how much I hate the sight of blood, especially my own. I'm really not your man for this one.'

'Look, you must have known when you set up NumbersGame that you were likely to rub shoulders with some pretty moody characters, so look at it as the best new business opportunity you're going to get this year.'

The call ended with Ashburton still muttering but Alec needed to turn his attention to the players in his network. He had a player in only two of the six teams playing midweek so needed a new recruit more quickly than he would have liked.

As he was flicking through the contacts on his phone the white van was circumnavigating the orbital motorway around Brussels. The driver, Chris Tyler, had deviated from the main road only once since they left Calais, pulling into a quiet and windswept lorry park outside Dunkirk. Carefully avoiding the gaze of any CCTV cameras, he and Neil 'Mac' Fleetwood had replaced the van's English licence plates with a set liberated from a Serbian-registered car, then retrieved their weapons from underneath the spare wheel, stowing them in canvas holdalls tucked behind the front seats.

Fleetwood and Tyler were officers with the Met's Specialist Firearms Command, SCO19, but Michaela had known them since they were beat officers in Tottenham. Her career had followed a radically different path from the men but they had stayed vaguely abreast of each other's progress. When Dave Prentice, her old station sergeant, brought a get-well card from Tottenham Nick after her accident, he also filled her in on developments with her former colleagues. They were all frustrated, he'd told her, that no one had been charged and if there was anything they could do to bring her attackers to justice, then all she had to do was say the word.

She wasn't surprised to hear that Chris Tyler had been accepted for firearms training. He was already a keen marksman and a member of a shooting club and breezed the police tests. He was also a disciplined and experienced officer who had worked with armed backup on several operations, so he knew what he was getting himself into. Mac Fleetwood's route to SCO19 was less predictable although his career seemed to have reached some kind of fork in the road. As a graduate it was assumed that he would become a detective but, in the choice between remaining a 'lid' or joining the ranks of the 'suits', he chose to stay in uniform. Now several years into their careers as police shots the men split their time between active deployment in Armed Response Vehicles, training new recruits to the unit and regular joint exercises with military Special Forces.

When Michaela had contacted the pair she explained that there was no evidence of a link between the gang in Niš and her accident, but the chance to get back at some Serbian criminals was enough for them. When she mentioned the link to a high-profile footballer they were practically biting her hand off to let them go. With Fleetwood due some leave and Tyler suspended from active duty pending the outcome of an IPCC enquiry, they were ready and willing. The hardest part had been acquiring the guns. Although they were routinely armed the Met got distinctly queasy about its officers taking their weapons on holiday with them. However, members of their unit and others like it tended to have similar private and professional interests. A word in a few ears and they were soon kitted out with small arms that were practically identical to those they used on the job with no questions asked. The van had come from one of the Met's car pounds in Charlton, South East London and the Serbian plates had been removed from a car at the same location. By the time they had met with Michaela the previous day, they were fully mobilised and ready to go.

Chapter 24

Alec had two out of three of the midweek fixes sorted when his front door bell rang. He assumed it would be a delivery or, at worst, Jehovah's Witnesses but opened the door to a worried looking Vic Vickers.

'Vic, come in. Oh, shit. I haven't checked the papers. Is he plastered all over the Mail?'

'Diego? No, it's nothing like that Alec. Seems like you did a good job there although no doubt that picture will surface from the swamp at some point. No, it's just, well, he didn't show up for training this morning. Apparently he had some of the team round at his place after I left there yesterday, but they all reported that he was in good shape when they left at around 10.30. I've been round this morning myself obviously and got no reply. I rang his mobile and got no joy there either, so I called Marta and, as I suspect you already know, she wasn't ever going to answer. When he did finally answer his phone he sounded like a completely different person. He was croaky and wheezing and when I asked him what was wrong, all he said was that you knew all about it and to talk to you. The boss is one more slip away from putting him up for sale so, here I am, and I need to know what's going on.'

Alec was caught off guard. 'Well the whole Marta situation. It's complicated. She hasn't left him as such but...'

'Listen Alec, I've been in this job a long time and I've been with the club even longer. I've seen everything the lads go through. They get their hearts broken, their heads turned and their moral compass totally fucked, if you'll pardon my French. But it's obvious that this has nothing to do with some sort of domestic bollocks. So, stop treating me like I just stepped off the banana boat, and start talking.'

Vickers had an instinct for when to put an arm around a shoulder and when to go for the jugular, which was part of the reason he was so good at his job. Alec knew there was no pulling the wool over his eyes anymore. 'Right Vic, I'm going to tell you the truth as far as I can. You're not going to like it but, believe me, it's all I can give you. Diego and Marta are in serious trouble. Serious. Trouble. It's bigger than the club can sort out and it's bigger than Totò can fix too. Marta's life is in danger and Diego's playing career is on the line because of something he's done, so you can understand that it's tearing him apart. I've done my best to help him keep it together, I really have, but the strain is beginning to tell. That stuff over the weekend was just the pressure release valve going off. As it stands, we've got a plan, we're working through it and I'm pretty confident it's going to work. If you'll just play him on Wednesday and play him again on Sunday, then we're done.'

Vickers thought for a moment, then the penny dropped. 'Match fixing, that little bastard. I fucking knew it. I said after the Saturday game there was something wrong with that penalty. And the way he reacted afterwards: we could all see that wasn't on the level. This goes right to the heart of the club's values and no player is bigger than the club. I've got no choice but to take this to the board.'

'Vic, this is about more than the club; this is about the integrity of the game itself which is why the club can't fight it on its own. Unless you're certain you can bring the whole League with you, then the club needs to be as far away from this as possible.'

There was silence and Alec's words hung heavily in the air. Then Vickers said, 'You're a football man, Alec. You know what the game means and the damage a scandal like this would cause. So, I've just got one question for you: can I trust you? Can I trust you with the players, can I trust you with these games coming up, and can I trust that, when all this comes out, which it will, people are not going to turn round and say, "the game is fixed, and we can't trust what we're watching?"'

'Believe me, Vic, those are the questions I keep asking myself and I can only say that the answers matter as much to me as they do to you. So, yes, you can trust me and I give you my word I won't let you down.'

Vickers paused a moment fixing Alec with a stare, then nodded and said, 'Well then, we can't play him if he doesn't turn up for training, can we? So let's go and see if we can't find some sort of miracle cure that's going to get the little dickasaurus out of his pit and onto the pitch.'

Half an hour later both men were standing in Diego's huge hallway as the player hurried to get his stuff together. Vickers had given him a pep talk telling him he understood that life was difficult but trusted that Alec had the right plan to get him out of it. Alec really wasn't sure what his comments were based on but they seemed to have the desired effect and Diego rallied. The club man also promised to move into the Hampstead mansion and not to let Diego out of his sight until Marta was safely home, and the pair drove off together with smiles on their faces. Watching them go Alec was touched by their confidence but left with an almost overwhelming sense of responsibility to them both.

On the other side of London the weight of responsibility was also hanging heavily on Michaela. Tyler and Fleetwood had taken on the job partly due to a misplaced sense of guilt they felt over what she had gone through at the hands of Serbian organised crime. Now, though, the pressure of a live operation hundreds of miles away was bearing down on her and she was having real regrets over what she was asking them to do. She wanted to be as sure as she could be that the risks were minimal, but the more she turned the facts over in her mind, the more out of control the situation seemed to become. When she had briefed the two policemen the plan had been to spend a few low-profile days in Niš trying to identify the apartment where Marta was being kept. They had a reasonable description of the woman she now knew as Branka and the town was a small one. Once the address was located, the men would stake it out and work out whether there was way to rescue the player's wife on the assumption that she was only lightly protected.

Now they had information as to when and where Marta would be, dramatically increasing the chance they could attempt a snatch. However, the fact that it was right at the heart of the Belovic Clan's operation made the risks of doing so enormous and the consequences of failure too costly to contemplate. She had to find a way of loading the odds back in their favour or stand the men down and call off the entire operation.

The first decision she faced was their route home. If the men did manage to grab Marta off the street, they needed to know they had a clear exit route. Niš had an international airport, the Constantine the Great, and there were regular services to major European capitals. But there was a strong chance that customs or security or both were in the pay of the Clan so she would be sending the trio straight into the jaws of a trap. Belgrade's Nikola Tesla airport was equally well connected but that could simply be a case of out of the frying pan and into the fire.

From Niš by road Serbia's nearest neighbour was Bulgaria whose capital Sofia was barely 100 miles away. They could be at the border in under an hour but checks were known to be thorough and the team would have to ditch their weapons rather than risk a search. There was no way she could gamble on them getting stuck at customs with Belovic just a few minutes behind. Romania was to the north but it's main cities, Bucharest and Timisoara, were over two hundred miles away over some of the worst roads in Europe. Kosovo was out too, its border effectively closed due to a historic dispute between the two countries.

In the end she settled on Skopje, capital of Macedonia, whose airport connected with a range of destinations in Western Europe.

Macedonia's border with Serbia was primarily there to deter migrants coming north, so those going south into the country could go largely unhindered. At 120 miles, Skopje airport wasn't the closest but it offered the clearest run.

Having identified the best point of departure the next thing to look at was flights. The call between Diego and Marko would take place at around 11.30 local time so the trio would not arrive until 1am or later which was too late for a scheduled flight out. Diego would no doubt pay for a private jet but that would mean he'd have to be brought in on the plan. It was really too much of a risk to leave them in the area overnight when Belovic's men would be all over them so it looked like there was no choice. But telling Diego could have unpredictable consequences. He was going to be talking to Marko and who knows what he would reveal and, if he told Marta, how would she react?

And what about the rescue itself? The key might be to grab not just Marta but Branka too, at least for the first few miles, so as to gain maximum time before a crew could be alerted and mobilised. Could Tyler and Fleetwood do that just the two of them? Marta could be expected to cooperate but Branka would no doubt put up a fight, so there had to be a plan B in case they didn't get clean away.

This was new territory for Michaela and, experienced as she was, she could feel herself starting to panic. Apart from planning a failed raid on a bank she had spent the past eight years chasing shadows in financial cyberspace. She'd accused Alec of watching too many cop dramas but she was in danger of falling into the same trap. Fleetwood and Tyler could handle a gun and look after themselves, and they had dealt with hostage situations before, but SCO19 would only ever act if a negotiator lost control and there was an imminent threat to a hostage's life. She badly needed advice but she knew her old boss would blow her plan full of holes before she'd even had time to explain it. Instead she called Alec whose line was engaged, so she texted instead. 'Can you get over here early. I need to talk to you.'

Alec was just finishing up a long call with a client from one of the South coast clubs. It had taken 20 minutes but the lad was now persuaded as to the benefits of giving away the first corner of his next game making the web of fixed events complete. He texted Marko to pile a bit more pressure on: 'Midweek setup complete with odds currently 4:1, 11:3 and 3:1 so we'll make a killing. Let me know when you're in.'

He sent a three-word text to Michaela then set off. An hour-and-a-half later he was sitting quietly in her flat as she told him about Fleetwood and Tyler.

He reacted as she knew he would. 'This is bloody brilliant; I knew you'd be able to do something. Diego's going be ecstatic knowing there are guys out there trying to get Marta back.'

'The prospect of you telling him was one of the reasons I didn't bring you in on what I was setting up. We can't risk Diego letting on to Marta and her giving Marko the hint that help is on the way, so you're absolutely not going to tell him. Anyway, I'm having serious second thoughts about the whole thing. My men may be among the Met's best shots but the last thing they actually want to do is kick the doors down and get into a firefight. Their entire modus operandi is to use the threat of lethal force to contain a situation without discharging their weapons. When I sent them out on the road I had planned for an easy exfiltration from an unguarded apartment and now we're looking at a snatch from the gang's stronghold itself. There's no way I can ask them to do that.

The room went quiet before Michaela said, "Did you make any progress with Marko that might give us an alternative?"

Alec relayed the details of his call earlier.

'Ok, so at least we have a couple of choices,' she said, when he'd finished. 'I think I should pull the guys back and see how your plan plays out.'

'Hold on a minute. As it stands, Marko hasn't confirmed his bosses are on board yet and, even if he does win them over, there's still the small matter of a meeting and walking away with Marta. As you so kindly pointed out, I'm no Captain America and Hugo's already told me he's going to be about as much use as an inflatable dartboard. At the moment we're relying on a good line in chat and an honest face, so I'd say if there's a chance of getting her out another way we should take it. At least get your boys in situ and let them make the call. They're the pros, after all.'

They both stopped talking, trying to think through the best way forward.

'In this kind of situation, you know, when there's a range of plans and possible outcomes, my old coach used to say, 'let's hope for the best and plan for the worst'.'

Michaela shot him a glance. 'I've got three lives at stake here and we're relying on footballing wisdom.'

'No, think about it. Best case, your guys have a clean shot at grabbing Marta and you've got a plane waiting for them 120 miles away. Or, they haven't, they back off, follow her back to the apartment and collect her later on and they can still make that plane. Worst case, they simply abort and they're out of there anyway, nothing lost'

'No, that's it, you've got it. Why didn't I think of that? There's no need for a snatch or a private plane. My team will simply follow them back to the apartment, pick up Marta when it's quiet and we're back to the original plan.'

'So, what were you saying about footballing wisdom?

'You just got lucky, that's all.'

'Anyway, I'm glad we're not talking about a private plane. I don't think Diego can cope with any more at the moment. He didn't show up for training this morning and I've got the club's Player Care man camped out at his house for support. He needs Marta home but he could go to pieces completely if he's on the rollercoaster ride that it's going to take to get her back.'

Michaela didn't need any reminding of how serious the position was. 'I haven't said this before, but I'm sure you know that hostage situations never get better over time, only worse. If we could find a way of bringing things to a conclusion this week then you know...' she tailed off.

'Yeah, I know. I got the distinct impression from Marko that everyone on their side wants to get out of the kidnaping business. We just need to find a ladder they can climb down that keeps Marta alive before they do something stupid.'

'The guys are on course to arrive in the area tomorrow afternoon which means they will have 24 hours to get dug in and assess the situation. Give me five minutes to get an update on their progress then you've earned yourself dinner.'

The road around the Belgian capital had been slow going but once they were back on the E40, Chris Tyler picked up speed. An hour down the road he pulled into a service station for a brief pitstop to take on fuel and coffee. Fleetwood replaced him at the wheel rejoining the thin line of traffic and keeping the van to a steady sixty-five mph. Outside, the landscape was relentlessly drab as leafless winter woodland gave way to bare fields, but inside the chat was colourful covering everything from First World War battlefields to the quality of continental roads. As the clock on the dashboard registered midday, they crossed the invisible border into Germany on the outskirts of Aachen. Lunch was an hour later just outside Bonn, after which they swapped places again for the penultimate stretch of the day. One comfort break and five hours further on, they reached the suburbs of Regensburg, 70 miles short of the border with Austria. They had just pulled into the carpark of a Mercure Hotel when Michaela's call came through.

The conversation was brief but informative on both sides. The men confirmed their location and greeted her summary of the new information with a simple acknowledgement before clicking off. They would have all the following day to work through the implications and prepare a response. For now, it had been sixteen hours since their journey started on the other side of the Channel and the pair were looking forward to tucking into schnitzel and some German beers before turning in. They checked in to the hotel then retrieved the black canvas holdalls from the van taking them directly to their rooms. Once inside, the men removed the weapons and stashed them under their beds then stuffed the bags with their remaining content in a wardrobe before adjourning to the bar to catch Monday Night Football. If either of them wondered why a German hotel was screening English football when they had a top league of their own, they didn't remark on it. Nor did they make any connection between the Premier League's ability to extract enormous sums from global TV networks, the consequent tide of money in the English game and the mission they were on.

Chapter 25

Time slowed to a crawl over the next 48 hours. In Niš, Marta was joined by two new girls and, although communication was just as difficult, it was a relief just to have other people to share her prison. By now she had a good idea why the girls were there and what they could expect in their futures but did not have enough common language to challenge the wisdom of their ambitions. Branka's visits resumed their regular pattern although the two women eyed each other warily following their confrontation at the weekend. Marta took quiet satisfaction from charting the progress of her minder's black eye which went from livid red to dark purple, green then yellow. Following through on her decision to try and take some control of her situation, she began exercising in the tiny space available. To the bemusement of the others girls she passed the hours doing a combination of yoga and HIT training until she collapsed in an exhausted heap. The exercise improved her mood and her appetite recovered too. She borrowed a hairbrush, scraped her hair back and tied it in a ponytail. Then she washed and dried her few clothes as best she could. Although she had no idea of the chain of events going on around her she was sure the next few days were going to be make or break and was determined to be prepared.

As the hours went by one link in that chain was moving closer to completion as Fleetwood and Tyler drove along the banks of the Danube before piloting the van round Vienna and branching off for the Hungarian border. The initial buzz of their first foreign mission had long since evaporated and the two were preserving energy in anticipation of the long job ahead of them. The atmosphere was one they were all too familiar with; in their line of work, they joked they were always either bored shitless or scared shitless. They had another 750 miles to go but Michaela had been clear about the need to reach their destination by the end of the day. Tyler was driving, taking the second stint behind the wheel while his colleague relaxed in the seat beside him. Michaela had not been specific about the information that had been obtained but she had said they now knew with a high degree of certainty where Marta would be on Wednesday evening.

Fleetwood was the first to mention the operation. 'What do you think about Dagg's new intel then?'

'I'd like to know where it comes from, but having a location and a window of time has got to be a good thing. I had visions of us trailing around the city for days on the hunt for some mysterious gypsy woman.'

'I was never too happy with us wandering the streets. Niš is a small town owned by the Belovic gang and we'd stick out a mile. I reckon they'd have known about us from the time we ordered our first coffee in whatever the local version of Costa is. At least this way we can do a recce then keep our heads down somewhere out of the way.'

'Agreed. Do you reckon she's thinking about some sort of snatch?'

'It depends where the girl is but it's not going to be easy with just two of us. We'd need to improvise at the scene, maybe use the car to block off the exit while we grab her. No, I don't think it's a runner: too much to go wrong.'

'What we do know is we can get eyes on her and take it from there.'

'Do you remember that snatch job we did on the tube? You were pumped up like a junkie; I thought you were going to shoot the whole place up.'

'As I remember it, the report afterwards stated that I showed admirable restraint. At least he didn't end up like that other poor bastard.'

'You just didn't have a clear line of sight, that's all.'

'Well, maybe I was lucky, but that was one of my first live fire ops, and anyway I wasn't the one who ended up sitting on his head.'

'Do you remember the curry house siege where that little scrote was holding the kitchen staff hostage? I was in the corridor outside and it suddenly went worryingly quiet. I remember behind me the phone went and all I could hear was you picking it up and saying in your best Bangalore accent, 'Coriander Restaurant, how can I help you?' I pissed myself laughing, the kitchen porter threw a pot at the guy and it was all over. Decent Madras afterwards too.'

The reminiscences about past conquests and cock ups were a welcome distraction from the reality that they were a long way from home, under strength and unprepared, but as the miles passed, the exchanges grew more infrequent.

The communication between Marko and Alec was also close to zero except for a two-syllable message from east to west, 'You're on.'

The text triggered a short burst of activity as Alec first confirmed that another £100,000 had been deposited alongside his own, then called Hugo to get everything lined up for the following evening's betting action.

'Can we also create some sort of digital totaliser on a website somewhere that we can show Belovic?' he asked. 'I'd like to get the boss engaged and most people get excited when they can see the money starting to roll in.'

'I'll see what my Hungarian programming chums can come up with. They may be able to put some middleware between the bank and some sort of graphic generator.'

'It doesn't have to be linked automatically, in fact, thinking about it, it's probably better if it isn't. As long as it matches up to what's in the bank and gives the impression that the two are connected, that should be enough.'

'I'll see what I can do. Are you grabbing a piece of the action for yourself again this time?' Hugo enquired.

'I don't know, I'm already keyed up enough as it is. But let's put another £10k on in case they decide to hold onto my stake and your commission.'

'Good plan. I'll do the necessary and you should easily get back your £100,000. And if your chaps do keep up their end of the deal, we can look at it as danger money for when we actually go out and meet them.'

'Glad to hear you're on board with a face-to-face, Hugo.'

'Don't think for a moment that I've put my reservations aside. It's just that, between you, me and GCHQ, these are the only clients I've got on the hook at the moment and beggars can't be choosers.'

'We'd better give them some good reasons to invite us out there then,' said Alec, as he hung up.

With everything now in play, he turned his attention to the next Direct From The Dressing Room. Half an hour later he was still sitting in front of an empty screen, the pressure in his brain preventing him from stringing a sentence together. Abandoning the column, he tried to focus on his clients. One or two had been with sponsors in the past week, but even the short attention span required to bang out a few status updates, tweets and Instagram posts seemed beyond him. In the end he did what he always did when he was stressed. He had never been keen on running for the sake of it but an hour or so of repetitive pavement pounding would take his mind off everything else. He slipped into his gear, plugged in his headphones and headed out the door.

Michaela, meanwhile, retreated into the world inside her head and could feel herself tumbling down the dark rabbit holes she had stumbled into after her accident. She thought back to the moments before the hit and run and tried to rediscover the person she was then. That woman had a glittering career ahead of her; now Senior Agent Dagg was haunted by the knowledge that her time with the job was coming rapidly to an end. Even if they did by some miracle reunite Marta with her husband, Michaela had crossed too many lines for things to go back to how they were. Life for her had always been black and white: she had seen what happened when officers entered the grey zone of pragmatism and compromise and knew it wasn't a world she could operate in.

She lay down on the bed in Alec's spare room and stared at the ceiling contemplating life without her police badge and warrant card. At some point in the future she might look back on this moment as a turning point but, for now, she struggled to see beyond the loss of status and purpose. She must have slept because the next thing she knew he was back from his run. He showered then made lunch while she dragged herself off the bed, splashed her face with water and forced down a couple of mouthfuls before they took off to meet Diego.

Alec's BMW arrived at the player's Hampstead mansion just as a lurid orange McLaren P1 was pulling into the drive. Diego got out laughing as Vic Vickers struggled to prize his ample frame from the car's bucket seats and haul himself to a standing position.

'What do you think of it, Alec? It just got delivered this morning.'

'Very nice, mate. How's it going for you, Vic?'

'Bloody uncomfortable,' Vickers grumbled, half-heartedly but with a smile. The two were clearly getting on well. They all went inside the house where Alec and Michaela paused awkwardly.

'Ah, right, need to know basis is it?' said Vickers. 'I'll make a brew.'

'If you wouldn't mind. Sorry mate, we won't be long.'

The three of them entered Diego's office where his mood switched abruptly. 'I need this shit to be over man. What's going on now?'

'Just hang tough for a bit longer,' said Alec. 'I think we're nearly there. I spoke with Marko and he's got his bosses on board for a deal.

We've got a lot riding on the games tomorrow but, if all goes well, then I'm hopeful we'll go out and meet with them at the weekend and bring Marta back with us.'

'So that's like two more games and she's coming home, right?'

'That's what we're hoping but negotiations are at a very delicate stage. We're trying to give ourselves the best shot so Michaela just wants to go through your calls with Marta to see if there's any little piece of new information or anything we've missed.'

The interrogation lasted well over half an hour with Diego losing focus regularly. Michaela kept pulling him back, going through the details he knew about the apartment and the stadium several times. She pushed him to remember as accurately as possible the precise words that were used, whether he had heard any other people in the background and even the acoustic of the room they spoke from. She pushed to the point where every signal being transmitted by Diego's body indicated that he was about to lose it, then finally she wrapped up.

'Diego, thank you. I know this hasn't been easy, but we're done. I'm going to work on some thoughts and I may get you to ask Marta some specific questions on tomorrow's call. One last thing: has Marta's passport been returned to you? I'm going to arrange for an Interpol notice to be issued and they'll need her documents.'

The player stumbled over to a cupboard within which was a hotel-style safe. He opened it and removed a little blue book embossed with gold stars handing it over without making eye contact.

'Thanks. If I think of anything else, Alec will text you, but meanwhile, we'll get out of your hair.'

Vickers was waiting on the stairs. 'How did that go?' he asked.

'It was heavy going but I think we've got everything we're going to. He's in a bit of a state so you may have a job with him, sorry mate.'

As they showed themselves out they heard him saying: 'Right, are we going to put some miles on the clock of this new motor then?'

'I hope that was worth it,' Alec said, when they were back in his car. 'Talk about sweating the details.'

'It was that fucking car that flipped me out. It's like he has no concept of how much people are risking to sort out his shit. I've got two men who, as we speak could be, well, you know, and it's like he's just floating off somewhere above it all.'

'Yeah, I know, but you have to remember he leads a weird life and he is a victim here too. Do you think you learned anything new?'

'I don't know, I'll have to look back through my notes, but probably not. It's not necessarily about new information but trying to get as full a picture of what my team and potentially you are walking into. There are still a lot of gaps which hopefully the guys on the ground will be able fill in.'

The guys concerned had made good progress. Lunch had been at a service station well to the south of Budapest and they were now approaching Szeged, the outer limit of the Schengen area and the same border crossing where Michaela had spent the night seventy-two hours ago. It would be their first checkpoint since Dover and, while they were not anticipating any problems, they had pulled off at a remote spot several miles back to stow their weapons. It was a sensible precaution but one that was not tested. The border guard waived them through with no more than a glance at their passports. The motorway signs had been counting down the kilometres to Belgrade since the Hungarian capital but, as they crossed into Serbia, they saw the first mention of Niš. Neither of the men said anything but their eyes darkened as they drove on towards their goal. The risk would increase with every hour on this road and Tyler knew immediately why Fleetwood exited the highway and pulled into a lorry stop a few miles beyond the border. Wordlessly, the weapons were reclaimed and checked before the pair were moving again. They followed the two-lane highway until they were past Belgrade then swapped seats again for the final 140-mile push to Niš. The density and quality of traffic had been declining ever since they had left Austria. Now, apart from the occasional German saloon, most of the vehicles were either elderly Yugos or smoke-belching Kamaz trucks. The road narrowed to a single carriageway, slowing their progress considerably, but the surface was passable and they overtook where they could. The van ate up the miles remorselessly as the two men stared dead ahead in silence.

Michaela's call jolted them into life half an hour down the road and they both listened intently. After a brief status enquiry, she said, 'We got information over the weekend indicating there may be a window of opportunity tomorrow evening, that's Wednesday, between around 22.00 and 23.30. We don't have a fix on the apartment where our hostage is being held but we do know that she has been taken twice to an office in a stadium where the Radnički football club plays. She gets from the apartment to the stadium in a car driven by a single female, the gypsy lady by the name of Branka who, by the way, is currently sporting an obvious black eye. You'll need to conduct a thorough review of the access around the stadium but there has been no mention of security outside. It may be the Clan feels they have such a secure grip on power that no one would dare attack them at their base. For us, though, it could be just the kind of opening we need. The girl is next due to speak with her husband after his game on Wednesday evening and the moments after the call should be your chance to get eyes on her.

'Don't get any ideas about snatching her off the street though; it's way too risky and, anyway, I don't have any transportation for you until Thursday morning. At the moment I'm working on the basis that you'll tail the car back to the apartment and review whether you think there is an opportunity to retrieve her later. Meanwhile, I know it's already been a long day, but tonight is the only time to find out what you'll encounter at the stadium at the time you'll be there tomorrow. Radnički are not playing either this evening or tomorrow so you should be able to get a sense of the kind of default security levels they employ. The electronic gear you've got in the back there can actually tell you how many mobile phones are within an area and the stadium being isolated from surrounding buildings means you should be able to find out what you're up against in terms of manpower. A word of warning, though. You'll need to be close and stationary for at least a couple of minutes for it to work so don't attempt a scan unless you're sure you're not going to be seen. And, of course, it goes without saying that however few men there are in the stadium, the last thing we want is a firefight.

'Do we know any more about the apartment?' asked Mac Fleetwood.

'Not much, but we may get the chance to ask? We know it was occupied by a dozen young women before all of them bar Marta were trafficked on last Friday. It is likely that some of them may have been replaced but I'm hoping it will only be one or two. He's a bit flaky but I'll get the husband to try for some more info and text you so you've got as clear a picture as we have. After that, it's up to you and what you find out locally.

'Assuming we can grab her from the flat, what's our exit route from there?' Tyler asked, revealing where his mind was going.

'That's a big assumption, and I repeat, we will need to work out the details together before you consider making any attempt at a rescue. But, speaking purely hypothetically, I do have an overland route going due south from Niš and crossing over into Macedonia. Skopje, where the main airport is, is less than two hours beyond the border and, if you are able to grab Marta, I would be there to meet you with her passport and your tickets. In the case of that happy eventuality, 36 hours or so from now, we could all be on a plane back home.

'Let's try and refine a plan based on that then,' said Fleetwood. 'We'll look at the options but getting her onto a plane would definitely be preferable to this van: the sooner we're off these roads the better.'

'I'm going to travel to Skopje tomorrow afternoon anyway, so I'll give you the next 24 hours to assess the situation then we'll reconvene by phone to go through what you've learned. For now, I'll text you the details of a hotel I've booked you a bit out of town. You should be there by early evening so get a couple of hours kip and only drive into town once its dark. No heroics, understood? Don't take any unnecessary risks and I'll speak to you tomorrow.'

She didn't need to add that she shared their concerns about them being spotted. The closer they got to Niš, the clearer the risks were becoming to all three of them. The two men pushed relentlessly on towards their destination pondering what they had just heard, meanwhile, Michaela was stressed and restless. Despite the long months she had had recovering from her injuries, patience was not a strength. She would be better once she was traveling, but that would not be until tomorrow. For now, she needed Alec beside her: she craved his body and needed a complete distraction from the riskiness of the operation. She was pretty sure he wouldn't object to a few hours spent banging their brains out.

He was happy to oblige and didn't question it when she got out of bed and left the house in an Uber shortly after 2am.

Chapter 26

Left undisturbed, Alec slept deeply and woke up to find it was after midday. He felt strangely calm and achieved a remarkable amount in a few hours setting up some media briefings with his Premier League clients, investigating arrangements for a Friday departure to South Eastern Serbia and even making progress on his next column. His chosen subject this week was touring and he spent a remarkably worry-free couple of hours reminiscing about dodgy roommates, foreign food and the world's longest coach trips, synthesising his own experiences with those of other players whose boasts were legendary. He was pleased with the end result and sure it would generate a lot of correspondence from readers which the paper always seemed to appreciate. *The Guardian* had had a change of sports editor recently and it never did any harm to give the new guy some good news. After all, he was paid to pull back the curtain on life as a pro footballer although there were some stories that he hoped would never be told.

The column done, he pulled out his mobile and messaged the players reminding them of what they had agreed to do in the evening's games and of just how grateful he was going to be. Then he called Hugo Ashburton for reassurance that everything was set up. It was probably nerves, but Hugo was in danger of becoming a caricature of himself.

'To misquote our American cousins, 'E unum pluribus', he quipped. 'Assuming your footballing pals deliver the goods, we're looking at a return of around £3.2 million which should more than satisfy the Serbian chappies. What?'

'Err, yeah. Just keep up the good work, Hugo.'

Finally, he sent a text to Michaela wishing her luck. She had not told him in any detail what she was about to do but he knew enough to realise she would not want to be disturbed. There was a lot riding on tonight for all on them.

Now that what passed for the work of the day was complete, Alec could feel the tension starting to rise inside him. He pulled on his gear, ran to the gym and worked out harder than he had for years. By the time he got back home there was still two hours to go before he was due at Diego's, so he whiled away the time absent mindedly exploring options for the next driving tour. There were some circuits in Southern Spain that looked good from a racing perspective but he quickly dismissed them as the destination lacked the 'wow' factor he knew the boys would want. The Nürburgring was rejected for similar reasons but maybe Monza would fit the bill if he could secure them exclusive access to the F1 works at Scuderia Ferrari. He made a note to see if he could pull a few strings.

1400 miles away two loose ends of the thread linking London and Niš were tantalisingly close to being united. Marta was continuing her exercise regime oblivious to the presence just a couple of hundred metres away of her potential rescuers. Fleetwood and Tyler had spent the previous evening staking out the Radnički stadium and were using the time they had left to get acquainted with the streets of Niš. As a precaution their weapons were once again behind their seats but they had no reason to expect they would be needed.

The two men had learned little from their observations the previous evening except to confirm that the stadium was indeed being used as an operation centre for a group of men they had to assume worked for the Belovic Clan. They took up a concealed position eighty metres from the office entrance and watched as a total of five men in dark suits came and went over the course of the evening. Once nightfall had given them full cover of darkness, they scanned the building using the kit they had been given confirming what they had already seen: five suits, five phones. Two left shortly after 11pm then, at 11.40, the final three exited the stadium leaving it in darkness. Apart from keeping late hours, there was nothing about the men to raise any suspicions.

They scanned again to confirm there were no remaining mobile phones on site then drove past the building to get a closer look at any external security. There were cameras at key vantage points around the entrance and a video access control system to enter the office itself. As they drove away, they agreed that there was no possibility of a rescue attempt from outside the stadium and determined to get to know the city thoroughly the following day to prepare themselves for a discreet tail operation that evening.

Wednesday had been spent cleaning and checking weapons and trying to second guess the various eventualities the night ahead might bring. In London, SCO19 operations were planned meticulously with maximum use of intelligence to prepare for the full range of possible scenarios. Planning was one thing but years spent in ARV's had taught the pair the kind of flexibility they would need in abundance on an operation like this. That and an instinct for danger kept them and the public safe as well as ensuring offenders were for the most part apprehended without injury.

On their first daytime visit to Niš the pair had acquired a detailed city map as well as a smaller scale regional one together with supplies of water and food. Back in their hotel room, they reviewed Michaela's choice of Macedonia as the best safe country to aim for and made a note to check routes from different parts of the city onto highway south. They were keenly aware that it had been a very long time since she'd done anything operational so preferred to rely on their own expertise. An hour or so was sufficient time to study and memorise the geography of the city then they checked out of the hotel and set off to drive the routes they had chosen. They passed near enough to the stadium to confirm no visible change from the day before but not close enough for the van to be picked up by the building's security cameras.

By the middle of the afternoon they were confident that navigating the city would pose very few problems. Tailing Branka's car would have to be done at a distance but, unless she was taking evasive action, they should be able to follow unseen. The main problem they could foresee was identifying the actual apartment where Marta was being kept.

'We need to ask whether Diego can help us out a bit when he talks to his wife later,' Fleetwood said. 'She must be able to tell him what floor she's on and maybe even the number of the apartment.'

'Agreed. We also need an update on the number of occupants in there and ideally where they are all sleeping.'

In her London flat, Michaela had tried without success to get some sleep then spent the day cleaning the place from top to bottom. It may have been displacement activity but it served a purpose. Nevertheless, she was relieved when the clock reached mid afternoon and it was time to get going. She packed a small bag with a phone charger, basic toiletries and a change of clothes for Marta, then picked up the Brazilian's passport along with her own. She used her phone to download boarding passes for a Lot Polish Airlines flight from Heathrow to Skopje via Warsaw, then grabbed her purse, credit cards and Interpol ID and took off for the station. It would be well into the evening before her arrival in the Macedonian capital giving her plenty of time en route to catch up with Fleetwood and Tyler. This point in the mission was crucial if their findings were to be translated into an effective operational plan. Alec's 'good luck' text came through as she sat on the tube to the airport. She glanced at it but didn't reply. Trusting to luck in a situation like this was not going to be enough and the thought of it only served to remind her how exposed her men were.

Michaela spent the first leg of her journey preparing for the call with her operational team, running through in her mind what they knew. By the time she entered the transit lounge at Warsaw airport she had reached broadly the same conclusions as they had. She called the two men and listened as they updated her on their activities of the past 24 hours. She understood completely why they wanted more information from Marta but was hesitant to get Diego to ask her too much.

'I'll see if he can feed in some casual questions. If I give him a list it would be too obvious what was being planned and we can't risk either of them giving you away. Unless there's an opening to improvise, let's reset expectations as to what can be achieved tonight. We know she's not in imminent danger, so if we can discover which building she's in and on which floor, then we'll find another opportunity later on.'

'Ok. Text us through any intelligence that does come out of the phone call and an indication of the girl's state of mind.'

'Don't worry, you'll have a full sit-rep as soon as I do. I'll be out of contact for the next couple of hours but I'll check in with you when I land in Skopje.'

Alec arrived in Hampstead shortly after seven and was let in by the housekeeper. She was preparing food for her boss's return home but clocked off a few minutes later leaving him alone in the Diego's mansion for the first time. With the evening games not starting for another forty minutes he had time to explore the house which had clearly been treated to the loving attentions of a highly-paid interior designer. The ground floor was home to a huge kitchen with dazzling chrome and white fittings that looked as though they'd never been used. The room opened out onto a comfortable living space with leather sofas and rugs artfully arranged with more than a nod to the residents' Brazilian roots. For any normal family this would have been the heart of the house, but it looked like it had come straight out of the designer's artbook. There was no mess, no clutter, nothing at all in fact to suggest that anyone even lived there. The wall art was tasteful but impersonal as if it was the kind of thing a house like this ought to have rather than anything the young couple who owned it had chosen.

He opened the double doors to the formal reception room and found it completely empty. Not only did the huge space have no furniture; there were no curtains, carpet or light fittings and the walls were bare plaster. It was early days, he thought, although he had known footballers live for years in a place and only decorate the den.

Upstairs two distinct wings led off a gallery landing overlooking an enormous chandelier which hung down three metres towards the floor below. He carried on wandering and found four bedrooms in the east wing each kitted out with an en-suite bathroom and fitted cupboards but otherwise empty and devoid of any sign of life. It occurred to him that it would be possible for an entire family to live here completely undiscovered, but there was not a sound as he passed from room to room. He located Vic Vickers' room from the collection of trainers and kit draped on and around a velvet ottoman which was the only piece of furniture apart from a single put-you-up bed. At the far end of the landing, he stumbled into a box room containing a trophy cabinet full of assorted Brazilian team caps, winner's medals and almost a dozen match balls.

Back across the gallery landing he put his head around the door of the master bedroom in the opposite wing feeling progressively more uncomfortable about intruding into Diego's private space. The room was pristine with a huge bed adorned with crushed velvet scatter cushions and a throw giving the room a dash of colour in contrast to the Farrow and Ball shades of grey on the walls. There was an extensive dressing area with minimalist white wardrobes and straight ahead of him one of the largest panoramic windows that Alec had ever seen. The only thing which gave away the recent presence of another human was a small dent on one side of the bed and Alec suddenly felt very sorry for his friend.

The feeling brought him back sharply to the task at hand and he went down the two flights of stairs to the subterranean living area to watch the evening's football. Diego played a storm scoring a hattrick before picking up the second-half yellow card that he had committed to. He was voted man of the match and Alec watched for any signs of mental turmoil in the post-match interviews, but whatever the player was really feeling, viewers were left none the wiser. By the end of the evening the other two fixes had come off and Alec was looking forward to hearing Marko confirm that their weekend meeting was going ahead.

Diego made his excuses early although not so early as to avoid showering and changing into a personally tailored Lanvin suit. He went ahead of Vic Vickers and his car pulled into the drive shortly before 11.00.

'Great game, mate. That's another match ball to add to the collection,' said Alec, regretting it immediately. He eyed the player for signs that he registered the obvious admission that he'd been snooping, but there were none.

'They were shit, man. We should have scored another four. Anyway, let's do this call.'

'Do you mind if I have a word with Marko first? I need to see how things stand for the weekend.'

'Yeah, for sure. Take my phone and call him now.'

'Marko, it's Alec. How's it going?'

'I can tell you that my associates are impressed. I am sure they will want to review the bank accounts in the morning and move some money around but, assuming all is well, I think we can all be confident that a meeting at the weekend will happen. We have some international guests in town so they want to lay on some special entertainment.'

'Good news. I'll call you tomorrow then, to make the arrangements. I was going to suggest we come on Friday to explain more about the system and give your associates and maybe their guests the opportunity to consider how much to raise the stakes by.'

'Alright, I'll set it up, but now put Diego on. I've got his bitch here.'

Alec handed the phone to the player and the conversation proceeded in Portuguese for a few minutes until someone in Niš got bored and the call was ended.

It was well after midnight in Serbia when the rear office door of the Radnički stadium opened and a tiny woman emerged. Mac Fleetwood had a pair of British Army issue Steiner binoculars trained on an old white Yugo parked near the entrance and got a good look at the girl as she passed through the arc of a security light before getting into the passenger seat.

'We're on,' he said, and Chris Tyler shifted in the driver's seat. He waited until Branka had joined the trickle of traffic on the road before starting the engine and moving off. She was 250 metres ahead of them as Tyler eased into the road behind another car turning on the van's headlights only once he was fully obscured. As he did so Fleetwood's phone buzzed with a text message from Michaela.

'Apartment is on the third floor. Two other occupants, both female, early twenties. Marta seems in good physical and mental shape. No other useful intelligence obtained. No risks.'

He acknowledged the message and relayed it to the driver who was closing the gap with the white car as the traffic thinned. Five minutes later they both watched as it turned into a neighbourhood of apartment buildings. They passed the turning then doubled back quickly and followed still at a distance until they saw Branka pull into the side of the road. They kept looking straight ahead as they passed taking the first opportunity to divert into a side road and out of view.

Fleetwood grabbed a pack of water bottles and one of the bags of supplies and got out of the van and onto the street. As he rounded the corner Branka was out of the car and pulling Marta who had clearly decided to make things awkward again. Carrying his load, he approached the main door of the apartment block just as Branka was opening it and nodded to her as she held it open to let him pass. He noticed she kept a firm grip on the girl who was resisting.

Knowing the apartment was on the third floor, Fleetwood took the stairs two at a time moving quickly to the fourth where he put down the bags. From the gloom of the stairwell, he could observe the two women's laboured progress. They reached the third floor landing and opened the internal door and he edged himself into a position where he could see them entering the corner flat at the back of the building. He shrank back into the shadows again until Branka came back down the corridor, retraced her steps down to the lobby and out onto the street. Through the thin exterior glass he could hear her battered Yugo struggle to turnover then splutter into life and pull away. Branka turned the corner at the end of the street then picked up her mobile phone and made a call.

Chapter 27

The sound of the Yugo faded and Neil Fleetwood waited a couple of minutes listening for any signs of life before moving silently down the hallway to examine the apartment door. It was cheaply made and secured with a deadlock but he put his shoulder up against it satisfying himself that it would yield when the time came. He retrieved his parcels and descended to the lobby where he squatted down and disabled the lock on the external door before leaving the building and rejoining his partner.

'I'd say we're where we thought we would be but with the advantage of knowing exactly where the girl is,' he said. 'There's no security in the flat and I didn't see any movement on the street either. It's after midnight now so I say we suggest to Dagg that we'll come back in two hours and, if it's all quiet, we go in.'

'Agreed. By my estimate it will take us four hours to reach the airport, so we need to tell her to line up tickets for that flight too.'

Michaela insisted on going through in detail what they'd found out and what they planned to do next but, in the end, she concurred with their analysis. The prospect of discovery would only grow the longer they stayed around, so tonight was the moment of opportunity.

'Ok, I'll see you in around 5½ hours,' she said, 'and please be careful. Anything changes, you bail and get the hell out of there. Right?'

The men spent the next two hours parked up in a quiet spot on the edge of town dozing uncomfortably before returning just after 2.30. They stopped the vehicle one hundred metres away from the base of the building and scanned the street watching and waiting for a full five minutes. Seeing no movement and feeling no presence, hostile or otherwise, they inched the van forward cutting the engine thirty metres out from the main entrance. The pair removed their handguns from behind the seats, tucked them into the back of their jeans and walked briskly towards the door. They were off the street and inside within three seconds using the cover of the lobby to check the street outside for signs of any unwanted company.

They moved noiselessly to the third floor and checked again. Drawing their weapons, Tyler went first onto the landing where he drove his foot forcefully against the lock of the door while Fleetwood covered the corridor. The door gave way on the second kick and Tyler was through it quickly leaving his colleague to deal with any reaction outside. There was no response from the neighbouring apartments where residents had learned over the years that nothing good could come from investigating the goings on in apartment 3C.

Inside Tyler pulled out his Maglite and shone it into the faces of the startled girls until he found the one he was looking for.

'Marta?' he said clearly. 'Let's go.'

She hesitated momentarily but was jolted into action as he followed up with a sharp, 'Now!'

Marta grabbed a small pile of clothes and followed him through the open door. All three of them hustled down to ground level where Tyler signalled to her to stay with his partner. From the safety of the lobby he checked it was still clear outside then exited to recover the van. He pulled the vehicle parallel with the building and Fleetwood covered the street while the girl threw herself inside. In one smooth movement they were away, the most dangerous part of the operation complete. They had been in the building less than four minutes.

The men scanned nearby cars and apartments, checking whether they might have been observed, but saw nothing. They controlled their breathing and their speed, determined to make themselves as unobtrusive as possible. At the end of the road they turned into an almost deserted shopping street. As they did, a black BMW started its engine and glided out of the mouth of an underground parking garage behind them.

In the van, the men were concentrating hard, neither of them speaking to Marta. Tyler's internal map of the city was faultless and he guided them steadily towards the city limits checking his mirrors frequently. Fleetwood peered into side streets checking the cars they passed as the built-up streets gave way to low rise dwellings and on through a semi-industrial region to farmland beyond. No one spoke until the van had crossed the iron girder bridge over the Juzna Morava river fifteen minutes later and joined the A1 for the hundred-mile run to the border with Macedonia.

'Sorry about that, Miss,' said Fleetwood at last. 'Bit busy back there.'

'I am get used to many things,' said the diminutive Brazilian woman. 'Who are you?'

'Yes, well, sorry again. My name's Mac and this here is Chris. We're British police officers. We're taking you to an airport where you'll be flown back to London.'

Outside Skopje, Michaela was tracking the van's movements on her phone and called when she saw it had left the city.

'Have you got her?' she said as Fleetwood answered the call.

'Yes Ma'am.'

'Any problems?'

'It went like clockwork.'

'Good work. I'm at the hotel Mirabel near the International Airport in Skopje. I'll be waiting for you here. Can you put her on?'

'Sure.'

'Marta? My name is Michaela. I am a friend of Alec Munday and your husband.'

'Alec? I knew he bring trouble.'

'Well you're safe now. The two men will look after you and I will be waiting when you arrive at the airport. I've got some clean clothes for you and you can have a shower then we'll soon be on a plane out of here, ok?'

She handed the phone back to Fleetwood who said: 'Tyler's got his foot down so we should be with you in two hours tops.'

'Ok, thanks Neil and well done again.'

Fleetwood hung up and said: 'I can always tell when the brass are happy 'cos they call me Neil.'

'Whatever. I thought that all went bloody well mate.'

'Yes, although I'll be happier when we're out of this van and on a plane.'

Tyler kept the vehicle at a steady eighty and the two men started to relax. He could see Marta's face in his mirror, tired looking but still wary as they ate up the miles towards the border. Suddenly her face was replaced by a blaze of lights.

'Whoa shit. What've we got here?'

The men tensed as headlights appeared closing rapidly behind them and two black BMWs overtook at speed disappearing into the night. Neither man spoke but they reached reflexively for their guns. A mile later the road narrowed to a single carriageway and turned sharply as it crossed back over the river. Ahead of them Tyler saw the two black limos stationary, bumper to bumper, blocking the road. In his headlights he picked out the shape of four men using the cars as cover, handguns pointed directly at them. He braked sharply and spun the van through 180 degrees, desperately looking for a way out. As he did so another set of lights caught his face blinding him momentarily. He flailed at the wheel but the spot was well chosen. With barriers on either side of the bridge and cars to the front and rear there was nowhere to go.

Ninety miles away Michaela was searching on her phone for flights leaving the next morning, tabbing between the Lot Airlines website and the tracking app she was using to follow the van's progress. She was at the point of confirming four flights when she realised it hadn't moved for several minutes. Her stomach lurched, bile rising in her throat. She switched all her focus to tracking, hoping vainly that the signal was just affected by patchy mobile coverage. Five minutes later the van still hadn't moved then, without warning, it disappeared completely and she knew the fate of its occupants was sealed. She let out a brief howl of rage and grief then brought herself under control and snapped into action.

Whatever the cost to herself, there was no way she could leave her men out there without at least finding out what had happened. She left the hotel room and moved quickly to reception which was closed. The Mirabel was an unofficial carpark for the airport with keys held in the office. She forced open the door and picked the lock of the key cupboard within selecting a new-looking Mercedes fob. Outside she clicked in the direction of the parked cars until there was a response and she was soon pointing a silver C-Class saloon towards the Serbian border.

Just over an hour later Michaela reached the point where the phone signal had failed. She slowed and commenced a search of the area, first in the car and then on foot. It took less than half an hour to locate the van which had been driven beyond the bridge and a few metres into the woods at the side of the road. She had prepared herself for the worst but the sight of the men when she opened the van caused her to stagger back and vomit. Both had been shot through the head, their bodies dumped in a twisted heap in the back. Marta was not with them.

Michaela fought against the stench of death to ID the men, searching for passports and weapons and finding neither. She spent a further hour looking methodically in the immediate vicinity of the van but again found nothing. She planned to continue when the day dawned, but for now she slumped back exhausted in the Mercedes and wept.

Marta was less than twenty miles away but the distance was immaterial. She was locked in a storeroom at the Radnički Stadium where she sat alone on the floor listening while a fierce argument raged outside. She could understand none of what was being said but was certain her fate depended on the outcome. In the end the shouting stopped and she was left in the dark, silent stadium.

At that moment Alec's mobile went off beside his bed in North London.

'What the fuck was that stunt about, you little shit?' came the voice on the line.

'What? Marko? What time is it?'

'You're just lucky that bitch is still alive. I'm telling you, if it wasn't for me, she would be as dead as those two cops.'

The realisation of what Marko was talking about rapidly dawned on Alec, but he needed to keep up the pretence of ignorance.

'Look, Marko. I don't know what you're talking about. Has something happened?'

'No, you know what? Nothing happened, thanks to me, but the price just went sky high. You need to get your ass over here tomorrow and make sure it's a fucking big weekend for my associates. We're gonna have a party and you're the entertainment.'

'What, I don't get it. You've seen what we can deliver but how big the prize is depends on what your boys are prepared to lay out. What stakes are we working with?'

'Believe me, the stakes are the highest you've ever seen.'

Chapter 28

The line went dead leaving Alec to wonder what they would be walking into in Niš. With sleep now impossible, he tried to imagine the likely chain of events leading up to the call. Michaela's team, whilst no doubt experienced and well prepared, had evidently failed and paid the ultimate price. He had known what kind of men they were dealing with but the death of two policemen brought home the stark reality that Marta's life hung in the balance. From Marko's comments he guessed she had been the subject of a power play between him and the Belovic brothers, the latter presumably wanting her dead and Marko, still desperately trying to earn his way back into the fold, trying to trade her for a huge pay out. Alec had no idea of their definition of a big party but he and Hugo would be walking into a hair trigger situation. What he was certain of was that the girl was now toxic and her chances of surviving the weekend were zero unless they were successful.

With some trepidation, Alec tried Michaela's mobile but the call went straight to voicemail. He hadn't known what he was going to say if she'd answered and didn't have the words to leave message. Instead he made a start at planning the fixes he would need to have in place for the weekend. Marko's words rang huge alarm bells and if the price was as high as the Serbian claimed, they would need to offer up something spectacular. He would have to find a series of spot fixes where not only could he guarantee the event, but which would give Belovic the opportunity to bet enough money to make a massive win. The more he thought about it, the more certain he became that he was going to need to recruit a referee.

Many international criminals use the betting markets to launder money. They know it's a mug's game but it also offers the anonymity and tax advantages they need. That said, they don't just accept losing as an occupational hazard; they try all manner of schemes to influence the outcome of the games they bet on. In general, though, they are reasonably sanguine if they end the weekend even, but this weekend would be different. Alec needed to be able to guarantee the actual result of a Premier League game and an unlikely one at that to get a large enough sum bet at the kind of odds that would deliver. That put him in a moral and practical dilemma. He had meant what he said to Vic Vickers when he swore that The Game was safe in his hands. This was stepping over a line he had promised himself he would not cross. Practically, it was impossible to recruit enough members of a single team to ensure they threw a game. A goalkeeper could improve the odds of losing a game if he had the chance, but only a referee had enough decision-making power to absolutely guarantee a result.

Premier League referees are normally announced on the Monday of each week during the season, so he pulled up their website to see who was officiating where. His eyes flicked down the list and one name caught his eye: Keith Stiles. The man had refereed Alec's last ever game of football and here he was on this week's list of officials. He'd assumed Stiles had long-since retired but dug a bit deeper and found he had been selling his soul in the All Stars League in Qatar. Now, it seemed, he was back from the desert tax haven and handing out dodgy decisions in England again.

Leading referees earn about the same in a year as a top player earns in a week, so they would appear to be eminently corruptible. However, where footballers are risk taking and reckless, your average English referee is among the most anally retentive individuals on the planet, with an obsession for rules bordering on the insane. Alec didn't hold out much hope of picking up the phone to Stiles and getting a result, but he was reasonably sure he would get an audience if he was in front of the man himself. The pair hadn't spoken since his career-ending injury but Alec had never forgotten him. He would be interested to meet if only to satisfy his curiosity as to how the guy could sleep at night.

If you asked the average football fan to describe what they thought a referee's house would look like, then, chances are, they would come up with something like chez Stiles. He lived in a three-bedroomed semi- in Milton Keynes with a modest four-year-old family saloon in the drive. It was identical to the house next door and, like all the others in the street, its front garden was fenced off by a privet hedge. In estate agent speak, the accommodation benefited from recently fitted UPC double glazing, a neatly presented kitchen with modern appliances and a 60ft garden to the rear laid mainly to lawn with some mature plants. Privately they might also say that it lacked a woman's touch Mrs Stiles having long since left for the brighter lights of Leighton Buzzard.

It was just after 8am when Alec pulled up outside number 29 Acacia Avenue and looked for signs of life. Chances were high that the referee hadn't had a big one the night before, so he rang the door-bell. The man who answered was already in his black kit and looked like he could brandish a whistle and cards of both colours without his feet leaving the welcome mat.

'Can I help you?' he enquired formally.

'Mr Stiles? You may not remember me. Alec Munday. I was a footballer.'

Stiles paused then said: 'Yes, of course I remember you. How have you been Alec? Perhaps you'd like to come in.'

The pair went inside where tea was poured and Stiles said, 'You may not believe this, but I often relive that game. I could see you running rings around their right back and I genuinely thought it would be to the benefit of your football education if you got a taste of the harsh realities of life lower down the football hierarchy. I'm sure it doesn't help now, but I had just decided to myself that I would blow up the next time he had a nibble. Then that tackle came in and it was all too late. You were a decent player and I do wonder what might have happened had I called a foul a few seconds earlier.'

He paused wistfully, then said, 'You've never come looking for me before, so I assume you have a particular reason for doing so now.'

Alec took the comments of the man in the Specsavers shirt as a good sign and launched into his story. He chose the details he revealed with care, trying to avoid giving any impression that he had become a career match fixer. Without naming names or clubs he painted a picture of a defenceless young girl at the mercy of east-European gangs who were intent on destroying the Premier League.

'I know what I'm about to ask you to do goes against the grain,' he said, as he reached the end of his tale, 'but I'm going to ask it anyway. You're officiating at a game in South London this weekend where the hosts are up against a well-known northern powerhouse. The locals are the underdogs, obviously, and the odds on them winning are 4/1. I was hoping you might help them to get the result.'

The referee flinched like he'd been slapped. His face whitened and a spot of bright red appeared on the end of his nose.

'Munday,' he said, his voice strangled into a half scream, 'as a recognition of the history between us I am not going immediately to the authorities to report this approach, but I warn you, if I ever hear your name in connection with attempts to corrupt the English game of football in the future, then I will gladly summon their full weight to bear down on you. Do I make myself crystal clear?'

Alec nodded, got up and walked out of the house without a word. As he drove through the checkerboard grid of Milton Keynes he had to admit to a grudging respect for the incorruptibility of the referee. In a sport where everyone seemed to be permanently on the take it was reassuring, if monumentally inconvenient, to come across an individual with integrity. Nevertheless, the encounter had left him feeling grubby and bruised, angry that the referee who had cost him his career had once again put principal and rules above his personal welfare.

He retraced his route London bound on the M1 with the radio turned to a tinny whisper while he weighed up the predicament. He sat in traffic for well over an hour but, by the time he turned onto the M25, he thought he might have the answer. He called Numbers-Game.

'Do you want the good news or the bad news, Hugo?'

'Oh, dear boy, I'm not sure I know the difference these days.'

'Well, the good news is that we're on for this weekend.'

'Hells teeth, the bad news must be apocalyptic.'

'Yeah, well it seems something has gone on in Niš and Marta is now a liability. We've got one shot and we need to make it count. We've got to deliver the biggest win they've ever had if we're all going to walk away. And the bad news is that the referee I thought I could rely on for a one-off fix has just told me my fortune in no uncertain terms, so I can't guarantee a result.'

'Don't worry about that. It's just the kind of challenge we're here to meet. Win, lose or draw isn't ultimately where the best action is.'

'I was hoping you might say that, but we need a plan. I'm coming over to your office later to see what we can come up with.'

'You're welcome to drop by of course, Alec, but what skills exactly do you think you'll add to my algorithms?'

'Once a banker, always an arrogant bastard,' came the testy reply. 'I'll tell you what I add; lateral thinking. And that's what's going to make this trip work not you fucking around with algorithms. I'm pretty clear what we're going to do but I need to go through it with you to make sure we're on the same page. I'll see you in after lunch.'

Chapter 29

Alec pulled into his drive, outwardly calm but raging on the inside. The coffee he had abandoned three hours earlier was beyond redemption but he brewed a new pot then dashed off the quickest Direct From The Dressing Room column he'd ever written. The subject? The bull-headed intransigence of referees. The quotes were all his own but the subject was raw and close to his heart. Having unburdened himself on the page he started to feel better and got down to work on the weekend's fixes. Reviewing the fixture list again he decided to pile everything onto the Saturday afternoon and evening games. That way the timeframe would be compressed and hopefully they would walk away while the party was on a high. On the flip side, if everything went to shit, then at least it would be over quickly.

He looked down his list of players to see who he could rely on then waited until morning training was over before calling them. By now the lads had got used to his calls and most were amenable. It was good to be able to promise them that this would be the last time and that he would then be taking them on the trip of a lifetime. The news went down well with everyone except Kevin Mooney who didn't hide his disappointment.

'That's a right shame Alec, so it is,' he said, the harsh tones of his Ulster accent giving the statement an undertone of menace. 'I thought we had a good thing going there for a while. But I'll tell you what I'll for you. I'll do this last fix for you but, in exchange, I'm going to want the details of the other fixes you're running for this round of games. Seems only fair, eh? What do you say?'

Alec knew him well enough to be certain the player wouldn't budge, but he hid his annoyance well. You could never tell when you might need a Premier League footballer on your side.

'No, don't worry, Kevin. Let's just leave it mate. We'll catch up soon right?'

'Oh, you just suit yourself now but don't be leaving me out of your travel plans in future. And if you get a text from me come Saturday afternoon, get yourself a wee bet on. Do you know what I'm saying?'

Alec forced a laugh. 'Yeah, good one, mate. I'll look out for that.'

He had deliberately left Diego out of his weekend fixes but, with Kevin off the team, he was going need him. It had been a couple of days since the pair had been in contact and Alec decided to pay him a visit later in the day to update him on the forthcoming trip to Niš. He would need to keep the conversation light with no mention of the failed attempt to rescue Marta or the fate of the policemen involved. Diego was stressed enough as it was and that conversation could wait until they were all safely back home.

With everything in place he got back into his car and headed over to NumbersGame where he was equally circumspect about the latest developments. He outlined his plan to Hugo who, for once, seemed impressed and the pair spent a productive couple of hours refining the details. Faced with the seriousness of the high stakes game they were playing, Hugo's normal bluff and bluster deserted him. Alec saw his mood change and tried to stiffen his resolve.

'This is going to work, you know, Hugo. I've covered it from every angle and the more I think about it, the more I'm convinced we've set this up right. We've got them just where we want them.'

'I do hope you're right,' Hugo came back, grimly. 'I'm with you on the money; I think we can deliver on a big haul. But what's to stop them simply shooting us when they've got it?'

'If they had any intention of killing Marta they would have done it by now; they've certainly had enough provocation. We're going right into the heart of their territory and I just don't think they'll shit in their own backyard. We give them a big enough prize then, even if they don't have any leverage over us for the future, they'll be happy to see us walk away and get Marta out of their hair without any comeback.'

Hugo's expression was enough to reveal his concerns were far from being allayed, but he said nothing. They booked flights to Niš for the following day and a single night's accommodation in a hotel near to the Radnički stadium. There were no return flights leaving the city on Saturday evening so Alec called a contact at Air Charter Services, a company well used to extracting football teams and players from locations around Europe. He made a spur-of-the-moment decision to go for a mid-sized jet on the basis that it was capable of repatriating Michaela and the bodies of her two colleagues. The bill for the charter came in at over £17,500 and that would almost double if they had to stay over until the Sunday, but he was confident that Diego would be more than happy to pay to get Marta safely back home.

As he got off the phone Alec could see that Hugo was still looking worried. To avoid any danger of cold feet he arranged to pick him up for the airport the following morning. As he walked back through the Plexal complex he was as certain as he could be that none of the bearded, laptop-toting liggers were living life quite as far out on the edge as the portly former banker. He drove through the Queen Elizabeth Olympic Park putting a quick call through to Diego telling him he was on his way, then took a deep breath and called Michaela again.

Her broken voice came on the line. 'Oh, Alec, it's a total disaster,' she croaked. 'They were ambushed and murdered in cold blood. What am I going to do?'

'Marko called me at 4am this morning in a complete rage. I think his life and Marta's were on the line too but he seems to have done enough to buy them an extra day or so. Are you ok; physically I mean? You weren't hurt.'

'No, I'm ok but I just don't know what to do. I'm sitting in a car in the middle of nowhere with the bodies of two English policemen whose deaths I'm responsible for. I can't go to the authorities in Serbia as we're all illegals; I don't dare go back across the border to Macedonia in a stolen car as I'm almost certain to be stopped and searched. What am I going to do Alec?'

'Alright, take it one step at a time,' he told her, trying to sound more confident than he actually felt. 'Hugo and I will be in Niš tomorrow and I've booked a charter flight to get us all back home the following evening. For now, just find a hotel somewhere well away from the City and keep your head down for a couple of nights. I'll keep you updated on the details as they emerge but get yourself close to Niš airport on Saturday evening and I'll be there to meet you. Hold it together and connect with that plane and, in forty-eight hours, we'll all be out of there.'

Michaela seemed grateful and slightly buoyed by the prospect of a plan although Alec could hear the vulnerability in her voice.

'Ok, I'll try,' she said. 'Whatever you do, don't leave me here. I can't make it on my own: I'm relying on you Alec.'

'I'm not going to leave you anywhere. We've been in this together from the start and that's not about to change.'

He continued to reassure her hoping his own fears were not obvious from his voice. They both knew that getting home would be only the start of another whole heap of trouble, but for now he was just determined they would make it that far. Alec ended the call and spent the rest of the drive to Hampstead preparing for his conversation with Diego. He decided he needed to bring Vic Vickers into his confidence so he would be able handle the player as things came to a head over the weekend.

The three of them sat in Diego's den as Alec brought them up to speed with the latest developments and his hopes for the weekend. Vickers was visibly shocked as he learned for the first time the full extent of Marta's predicament. For a man who thought he had seen everything a young footballer could get caught up in, he was wide eyed as Alec relayed the story of Marta's kidnapping. Diego just looked thoroughly miserable but eventually asked,

'Do you know if she's ok?'

'She is for now, mate. I spoke to Marko early this morning and she has been brought to the stadium where they have their offices. I do think her time there is getting short though, which is why we have to go to Serbia this weekend.'

He went on to give a few more details of his arrangement with Marko, aware that a great deal had changed since it had been agreed. By the time he left Hampstead and returned home, it was late evening and the early wakeup call was starting to take its toll. He would need to be on his toes over the next couple of days, so he briefly checked his messages and watched some mindless TV to try and distract himself before turning in.

In Serbia, Marta was spending a second night in the stadium store cupboard. Branka had brought food to her earlier in the day and she had been allowed the run of the offices although she took care to avoid its regular inhabitants. In a stroke of luck, she had even managed to raid the club shop grabbing a bright red Radnički hoodie and a pair of sweat pants so she was better equipped than she had been since her arrival. Having seen first-hand what her kidnappers were capable of she was careful not to stir up trouble, but she did ask Branka what the plan for her was.

'Your friends come tomorrow,' was all that she had been able to discover but, after the crushing disappointment of the failed rescue, those four words were enough to send her spirits soaring. As she settled down to sleep among boxes of t-shirts and stationery she felt more positive than she had for many days.

Marta's mood was in stark contrast to Michaela's, who lay with her eyes open on a single bed in a hotel a few miles away. She had forced herself to eat something earlier in the evening but, now every time she tried to sleep, she could see the vacant eyes of her two dead colleagues. Worse still was the smell of death which accompanied the picture inducing waves of nausea. Assuming she was even able to get them home, Michaela was then going to have to face the men's families. Neil Fleetwood she was sure was unmarried but, the last time she had worked with him, Chris Tyler had a wife and kids. There would be an inevitable disciplinary and dismissal from the Met and the long trip to Lyon to clear out her office at Interpol. She felt exhausted and desperate for a night of uninterrupted oblivion. In the end she took herself downstairs to the tiny hotel bar where the night porter served her a large measure of Rakjia, the local plum spirit, in a brandy glass. Back in her room she took out a Fentanyl tablet left over from the early days of her accident and popped it under her tongue, relying on the drink to wash away the taste. Within a few minutes she was dead to the world and did not regain consciousness for almost 15 hours.

Alec's first task of Friday morning was to call Marko who answered almost immediately.

'Just checking we're on for today,' he said. 'My friend and I should be with you by late afternoon. Is there an office somewhere we should go to?'

'No. My associates have some guests in town and have asked you to join them for dinner. I am working very hard to keep them focused on the big win they're gonna enjoy this weekend rather than the fact that they were attacked on their own soil. You are just lucky none of our men was killed.'

'Sounds to me like we're all lucky.'

'Don't try and be clever, Alec and I'm sure I don't need to tell you that any tricks would be suicide for you and a long and painful death for the girl which at least one of my associates would take great pleasure in. So, I've done my part, it's all set up and now it's up to you. You will join Mr Lech Belovic and his brother Arkan and their guests in the rear dining room of the Kafana Mrak restaurant from eight this evening. I am sure they will all be very interested to hear how you are going to make their fortune this weekend. One thing between us: if these winnings are as guaranteed as you say I need you to cut me in too. Get your friend to set up an account for me and I'll see how much money I can pull together. It won't be a very large amount but it should be enough to give me a personal insurance policy.

'Good thinking,' he said, happy that Marko would also have some skin in the game. 'I'll text you the details in a while. How's the girl?'

'The bitch is getting on everyone's nerves. We're gonna be glad to see the back of her.'

'Well I'm very happy to take her off your hands.'

'One way or another, Alec, that's how the weekend will end up.'

Alec's next call was to NumbersGame where Hugo confirmed that he would be ready to be picked up from the office at 10.30. Alec packed a small overnight bag and set off into the Friday traffic. He arrived at the Olympic Park forty-five minutes later and just ahead of Ashburton who was hauling a large backpack across the carpark, his lungs heaving.

'I hadn't quite realised how much gear I'd need,' he said, panting.

'What the hell have you got in there?'

'Tip I picked up from my years in investment banking: it's all about the show. No good hunching over a silly little notebook if we want our new friends to spring for a large wager, so I've brought along a projector to give them some big screen action.'

Alec was impressed and pleased that they were on the same wavelength although he suspected Mrs Ashburton may also have insisted that her brave hubby pack a Kevlar vest too. The journey, via Gatwick and Zurich, was a smooth one but the pair felt their stress levels rise as they passed through passport control at Constantine the Great airport. They emerged with the other passengers into a modern concourse and were relieved to find there was no reception committee holding up a board with their names on it. They used a nearby ATM to withdraw some Serbian dinars and followed the signs for local taxis. So far, so good: perhaps Serbia wasn't the Wild East they feared. Any negative preconceptions they had were further dispelled as their English-speaking taxi driver pointed out local landmarks on their way into the city with his meter apparently running at a normal speed.

'Well, bugger me,' said Hugo after they handed over a modest sum for the ride. 'I fully expected to be robbed at gunpoint but this all seems very civilised.'

'There's plenty of time for that especially if you're going to insist on being buggered.'

'Just a figure of speech, of course, but I do take your point though.'

Alec had chosen not to tell Hugo that two policemen had been shot in cold blood by the group they were on their way to meet judging, correctly, that he would have bailed at the airport. As a result, he did not share the former banker's confidence in their safety although he too was pleasantly surprised at how normal the place seemed to be. They had time to check into their hotel rooms and drop off luggage before taking another taxi to the restaurant an hour ahead of the main party. Their arrival caused some consternation among the restaurant staff who insisted on calling the owner. A portly, moustachioed local who, judging by his rather grubby whites, also doubled as the chef, arrived on the scene carrying an impressively large meat cleaver. He stiffened at the sound of the Belovic name and explained that the party was for his most special customer. His staff were, he assured them, only trying to make doubly certain that the evening would go without a hitch.

The two foreigners were poured beers and, with some effort, Hugo manged to explain that he would need access to WiFi. The restaurant was a traditional Serbian establishment where the guests were encouraged to focus on the food and the company rather than their social media status, and it offered no such western luxuries. Instead he logged on to a connection in the flat above and soon established a link between his laptop and the programmers in Hungary. He picked a large blank wall at the end of the private dining area and projected the image of a set of dials onto it.

Pleased with his work, Hugo said, 'For the purposes of tonight's demonstration you just need to use your phone to make a couple of transfers in and out of the account I set you up with. My Hungarian chums will monitor it and the balance will update in close to real time.'

'Do you think that will be enough to convince them?'

'I don't see why not. Each of our new clients will have his own dashboard and can cash out at any time before bets are placed if he gets cold feet. We will need to remind them that not all bets are settled instantly but as long as they can see the total keep on rising and they know it's only going to increase, I'd like to hope they'll take the bait.'

As they were talking a large black BMW pulled up outside and two dark-suited thugs emerged from inside.

'I think this is the advance party, mate,' said Alec. 'Looks like we're getting close to showtime.'

The mobsters gesticulated to the restaurant staff who immediately snapped into action. A heated conversation in Serbian ensued during which it became apparent that Alec and Hugo were to be treated with extreme suspicion. Without any discussion the men approached, indicating they would be searching both them and their gear. Coward that he was, Hugo was immediately ready to drop his trousers and quickly assumed the position. Alec was more reluctant and waited until he received a request in broken English before complying. These men almost certainly had two British policemen's blood on their hands and he was damned if he was going to make their lives easy.

The unpleasantries out of the way, one of the men made a call and ten minutes later three more large black saloon cars pulled up. The restaurant staff made a great show of welcoming the evening's guests while the Englishmen waited in the bar area. First through the door was a modest-looking man, slim and clean shaven, wearing glasses and a grey suit to match his neatly cut hair. He was greeted respectfully as Gospardin Belovic by the patron, now in a clean pair of whites. Following the man who Alec took to be Lech Belovic was a slightly younger character who was his polar opposite. He was large in every dimension and at least a foot taller than his compatriot. He had three-days growth of beard, a big belly and huge hands which he used to grab the restaurateur in a bear hug, his voice roaring a coarse greeting in his native tongue. Michaela had said that both of the brothers were former paramilitaries and it was easy to imagine Arkan Belovic toting a Kalashnikov. By contrast Lech Belovic, while he had enough ice behind his eyes to suggest he was capable of murder, looked more like an accountant than a soldier.

Once his brother had been persuaded to release his grip on their host, Lech Belovic said, 'Brother, we must change to English in honour of our guests.'

He stood to one side as two Chinese men entered with bodyguards in tow. One was overweight and puffy and wore a red t-shirt under his jacket; the other was slight with angular pointed features with slicked back hair and a dark suit. They were both offered drinks and, as they reached out for a glass, Alec caught a glimpse of a snake tattoo extending from under the slim one's cuff. They Chinese men moved through into the body of the restaurant and were followed by a tanned man in an extremely sharp grey suit with brown shoes and flanked by two bodyguards of his own. Alec recognised him immediately. It was Totò Diaz.

Chapter 30

Alec stared at Totò, his face a mixture of shock and incomprehension, but he received an indifferent glance from the Brazilian in return. He simply glided past, into the room ignoring the simpering restaurant staff, and took up his place as part of the party. Marko was the last to enter locking eyes with Alec as he did so. He whispered in the ear of the older Belovic brother who took his cue.

'My friends, let us give our staff the opportunity to withdraw and I will introduce Mr Munday and Mr Ashburton, the two Englishmen who will be joining us for dinner. As I told you earlier I think you will find they have a fascinating proposition to share with us.'

The bodyguards shuffled off to the cars outside and he continued, addressing Alec and Hugo directly.

'Gentlemen,' he said, in very precise English. 'I am Lech Belovic, this is my brother Arkan and these are Mr Lau and Mr Tang. I believe you may already know Mr Diaz.'

Alec was still recovering from the shock of seeing Totò leaving an awkward silence until Hugo jumped in, covering smoothly.

'It is our great pleasure to meet you, Mr Belovic. We are grateful to you for your hospitality and hope that our little piece of business will not cast a shadow over the evening.'

'On the contrary,' said Totò, looking directly at Alec. 'I am sure we are all extremely interested in what you have to show us.'

'In that case,' said Hugo, looking to Belovic senior for approval, 'perhaps we might start with a short presentation and answer any questions over dinner?'

He got a nod and launched into his pitch. 'Thank you. Now gentlemen, you may be familiar with the old English phrase 'a licence to print money'. Well, what we would like to demonstrate to you this evening is that printing is now an unnecessary expense with a scheme that returns a potentially limitless amount of money deposited direct into your bank accounts.'

Alec had pulled himself together and was starting to appreciate the polished presentation skills that had made his friend such a success in his former career. He took up the story outlining how, through a combination of leverage and persuasion, he had recruited a number of Premier League footballers into a network which could deliver certain predictable events in the upcoming matches.

'Certainty of outcomes on which wagers are placed is the foundation upon which our scheme is built,' Hugo continued, warming to his theme. 'Put, simply, we have the players in our pockets but I'm sure you don't need me to tell you that that is just part of the story. Despite being the widest and deepest betting product in the world the football authorities' and betting companies' fraud detection systems mean it is not easy to win enough money back to make it worth the effort: if markets look like they are being manipulated the system simply shuts them down. However, what my company provides is a solution using to this dilemma; a hybrid of a bank's trading platform and a hacker's distributed denial of service software. In simple terms, this allows us to place thousands of anonymous bets in markets around the world that fly beneath the radar of the fraud detection systems and deliver consistent, guaranteed winnings. In normal operations we can promise you a positive return on your stake but, with Mr Munday's contacts and talent for persuasion, we are offering you the chance to win every bet you make.'

He had the room's rapt attention and cut quickly to the chase.

'You had no intention of listening to me for the evening, I'm sure, so let me lay out what Mr Belovic thought might be an amusing diversion for the weekend. Mr Munday has arranged for a number of events to take place during tomorrow's Premier League games upon which we plan to place bets. I will make available a series of untraceable offshore bank accounts to which only you have access.'

He pointed to the dashboard on the screen as Alec moved some money into the account and out again with his mobile. 'You will have the numbers and access codes of your individual account and, as you can see, our system is completely transparent: you can cash out at any time. To further give you confidence, we will place an initial $100,000 in each of the accounts which is yours to play with. If you would like add to your pot you should transfer the amount of money you would like to invest into your account. We will place the total in the markets on your behalf guaranteeing you a return of at least twenty times your stake by the end of the final match.'

The group stood in silence as the characters around the table absorbed what they were being offered.

Alec tried to pre-empt their questions saying, 'I know what you're thinking; why should you trust us? So, let me just say that we know a little of your reputations as businessmen and of the consequences should our scheme fail to deliver, and yet here we are. I would also add that we had the opportunity to lay on a personal demonstration for Mr Belovic earlier in the week and I believe he was happy with the result, isn't that right?'

The grey-haired Serbian nodded and gestured to them all to sit down.

'Let's eat, my friends. I am sure we have much to discuss with our new acquaintances.'

As the wine flowed the men relaxed and so did the conversation. The Chinese pair demonstrated a thorough knowledge of the workings of the gambling markets and confirmed Hugo's description of the challenges of betting on the Premier League. Their questions were precise and detailed but Hugo was more than able to satisfy them with his answers. By the time the post-prandial cognacs were being served there was only one thing left to decide and Lech Belovic took the lead once again.

'Mr Munday, Mr Ashburton, this has been a fascinating conversation. I have the advantage of having seen your scheme in operation so I should like to show my confidence with a commitment of $1m.'

'One fucking million, you mean bastard,' Arkan interjected, noisily. 'We made $2m two nights ago and we're gonna be betting more than that this weekend anyway. I say we go for a big win and make it $10m.'

His brother winced but deferred nonetheless.

'Thank you, Arkan, for giving our guests such a revealing insight into our business,' he said, to general laughter.

'Mr Ashburton, do you really think you can turn it into $200m?'

'I can practically see it sitting in your bank account, no printing required,' came the reply.

'Then, Arkan, you have your wish. $10m will be coming out of your personal stake in our operation.'

The giant Serbian roared with laughter and prepared to raise his glass in a toast.

'Not so hasty, brother. What about our guests?'

Lau and Tang exchanged a few words in Chinese then Lau said, 'My partner and I will also invest $10m. Each.'

Arkan roared his approval and turned to Totò. 'Put me down for $10m too,' said the Brazilian, not taking his eyes off Alec. His face showed beyond any doubt that he was playing with his own money and $10m meant rather more to him than it might to the others around the table.

'So, brother,' came another roar. 'It seems you are the only one with no money on the table and that is very bad manners.'

Lech held up his hands in surrender: 'Ok, ok. I too will put up $10m.'

The cheer went up around the room and Arkan grabbed the brandy bottle. He spilled large slugs into everyone's glass and proposed the first of a series of increasingly wild toasts. Hugo meanwhile got to work pulling off the details of an offshore bank account for each of the men which he wrote on the back of his business cards before packing away his projector and laptop.

He distributed the cards discretely saying, 'Mr Belovic, thank you for your hospitality and your confidence which will soon be handsomely repaid. Here are details of your personal offshore accounts, gentlemen, and, as soon as you are able to transfer the money, we will start our operation running. Meanwhile there is much to do so we wish you all good night and look forward to celebrating with you tomorrow.'

Marko followed as the pair left the restaurant with Arkan still roaring his toasts.

Alec asked, 'How did we do?'

'You're still alive.'

'That's setting the bar quite low. Arkan seemed to like us.'

'He'll also be the one to put a bullet in your brain if you fuck up tomorrow.'

'You're just a happy go lucky ray of fucking sunshine, aren't you,' Alec shot back, keeping up the bravado. 'Tell me, what's the story with Totò? You know who he is right? He's the last person I expected to see here.'

'We know he's Diego's agent, if that's what you mean. He also controls a slice of the trade in a very lucrative commodity that we import from Latin America.'

'So, he fucks over your London operation and kills your crew and you have to suck it up because he can deliver regular shipments of Columbian nose candy.'

'If it was down to me he'd already be in a box but, for my associates, business is business.'

'Shit, you must be in more trouble than I thought. Seems to me you're right out on a limb and it's as likely to be you who's taking a bullet if we don't come through. So, how about you put me and my colleague in one of your fancy cars and drop us ever so gently at our hotel.'

Marko didn't reply but nodded towards one of the waiting limos which pulled alongside. He said a few words to the driver then watched as they pulled away.

'What was that all about?' asked Hugo. 'Was that really your chap's agent?'

Alec shook his head still struggling to believe it himself. 'All I can say is the world of professional football is a smaller and more toxic swamp than even I knew. But let's focus on the big picture; he may be the most dishonest, disloyal and devious agent in the world, and believe me, the competition for that honour is fierce, but it doesn't change anything for us. Assuming they make the transfers overnight then your job is just the same.'

'Understood, but, I mean, fuck me with a claw hammer, this is even more iffy than I thought.'

'Maybe, but look at it this way; it removes a layer of uncertainty on their side. With Totò there we have to assume they all know about Marta and the leverage the Clan has over us. That's the kind of power they understand so they know we're not going to just walk away. With the possible exception of Arkan Belovic, these guys are totally addicted to money and we're offering them the biggest, quickest fix they've ever had. So we do our job, give them their drug and walk away with the girl. Simples!

At the hotel they agreed that Hugo would text as soon as he saw any money hit the bank accounts and the two parted company.

Once in his room Alec sent a quick message to Michaela. 'Stage one complete. The fish are nibbling.'

He could not have known but at that moment she was so deeply comatose it would have taken an all-out war to wake her up, so Alec didn't get the reply he was after. He knew there would be all sorts of pieces to pick up when they got home, but for now, he needed to know that Michaela was getting through.

Chapter 31

The first text from Hugo reached Alec's mobile at 5am. 'The Chinese are in.' They had already exchanged the details of the afternoon's spot fixes and, with the first punters on the hook, he could make a start in the markets. For Alec, though, the morning was going to be a long one. He was confident that the Belovic's would come through as they had already seen the system in operation. That just left Totò. He tried to go back to sleep but his nerves were shredded so he slipped into his gear and hit the hotel gym. After a workout, a shower and some coffee he went through his normal matchday routine checking in with the players, not that he had any worries. This was the third round of fixes and the guys were getting worryingly good at it. As professional athletes their success tended to be the product of an unhealthily obsessive streak: they were trained to be the best at everything they did and fixing was no different.

Mid-morning Hugo confirmed that a further $20m had been deposited which meant that, even if Totò didn't come through, the party was going to go with a swing. He was hunched over his computer in the hotel business centre working the NumbersGame algorithms like his life depended on it which, to be fair, it almost certainly did. The first game of the afternoon was a 12:30 kick off so they headed over to the stadium in a taxi for 1pm local time to get set up. They received two messages en route: one a simple 'good luck' from Michaela and the other an alert for Hugo telling him that Totò's $10m had been transferred.

'That's bloody late in the day. Barely gives me time to get the bets on. What time do you estimate the first fix will take place?'

'Do you even look at the bets you're placing? I deliberately set up Nikolai to give away a corner within five minutes of start of the second half so you're looking at shortly after 1.30pm UK time.'

'Yes, of course, right. Well, just get me onto some WiFi.'

It was matchday at the Radnički stadium too, with the local team hosting fierce Belgrade rivals, Partizan. Security was tight with armed police checking bags to try and reduce the number of flares and glass bottles entering the stadium. Crowd trouble was a given, but death and serious injury were at least reduced through their efforts. Upstairs the stewards were crammed into the office receiving their pre-match briefing and it was a few minutes before Alec was able to locate Marta. He found her in the small office kitchen looking stressed and gaunt but otherwise unharmed. Coming face to face in such a strange situation, he didn't know what to say. She had no such difficulty.

'What the fuck, Alec?' she yelled. 'Totò here last night, now you. What is going on and when am I going home?'

The meeting outside went quiet and Alec held his hands up quickly and patted the air in front of him, gesturing to her to keep calm.

'Hi Marta. It's really good to see you. We've all been so worried about you. Just hold it together for a few more hours and we'll all be on the plane to London tonight.'

'I have heard this before,' she continued, her voice barely modified from a shout. 'Those guys are dead. Why should I believe you?'

'I know it's been a terrible time for you but we've got a deal we're going to deliver on this afternoon. Then we're all going to walk away and you'll never see these people again. Just trust me.'

'You have no idea what hell it's been for me and, I'm telling you, if we escape, you and my fucking husband will never stop hearing about it. But now, I have no choice. I'm not going nowhere so you just do what you're gonna do and tell me when it's time.'

It was the biggest speech he had ever heard her make and every word was dripping with fury, but he was still happy to hear it. He smiled broadly and was about to speak when she slapped him hard across the face.

'Fair enough,' he said, still smiling. 'I knew you were a fighter, Marta and I'm glad to see you've lost none of your spirit.'

'Get out or I hit you again,' she said, blinking back tears. He didn't need to be asked twice and left to join Hugo at his laptop.

Outside the stewards had gone and Belovic and his guests had taken up their places in the hospitality suite which doubled as a boardroom. One wall was made entirely out of glass offering a panoramic view of the pitch below, but all the chairs and eyes were directed towards a wall at one end of the room on which hung a television and a projected image of five identical dashboards all but one showing a zero balance. Alec assumed this represented Totò's account where Hugo was still scrambling to place all the bets. In any event, the sum was rapidly ticking down and the dial would soon hit empty. The atmosphere was as tense as an England penalty shootout with Totó especially looking like he was about to throw up. All the conviviality of the previous evening had gone and deep suspicion had taken its place. It was one thing to understand the concept that their money was being put to work in the international betting markets; it was quite another to see $10m disappear under the control of two complete strangers. The next hour was going to go extremely slowly indeed.

'Do you guys have a TV station that shows the Premier League?' he asked, his voice ringing loud in the silence.

'We have Sport Klub but it will only show the evening game,' said Marko. 'We should be able to get a satellite feed from beIN Sports in Qatar but I'll need to get a technician on it.'

'Ok, you do that, and can you get some drinks served in here too? It might calm a few nerves. Not that there's anything to be nervous about,' he added, hastily with what he hoped came over as breezy confidence.

'Perhaps it would help if I shared with you what we're going to be seeing this afternoon.'

Blank faces all 'round except for Arkan whose expression said very clearly that 'yes, sharing the fucking story might, just might, help him repress the urge to rip Alec's throat out'.

Alec breezed on. 'So what's happening right now is that my colleague has placed thousands of small bets in the markets at odds ranging from 4:1 up to around 7:1 on the number 9, Nikolai Ruslanov, giving away a corner at the start of the second half of the game that kicked off a few minutes ago. He's a good guy, one of the best. I was with him recently; he's got some great stories from the last World Cup and a very interesting collection of Russian porn.'

Alec's attempt at levity fell flat. There was silence in the room.

'Anyway, as I say, the game has just kicked off so we're looking at just under an hour to wait. Good timing for Mr Diaz as it gives Hugo time to get his bets on, but I'm sure we'll all be a bit happier when the ref blows up for that corner. I'm sure I can find some radio commentary until we get the feed set up, or you can follow along with the score and text commentary on the Eurosport mobile app.'

Silence in the room. The door opened and a waiter brought in a tray of bottles of beer and glasses of wine. The distraction of drinks being distributed around the table was a welcome one but it was over much too soon.

Silence in the room. Through the glass, players appeared on the pitch outside and did a few stretches and warm ups. Some of the hardier members of the crowd were making their way into the stadium selecting strategic positions dotted among the empty seats. The stewards took up their stations.

Alec struggled on gamely. 'For this first round of bets my colleague is favouring betting platforms that pay out instantly. They won't necessarily offer the best odds but it means we will have the maximum funds available for the three o'clock games where most of the action is concentrated. By that point you won't even be able to keep up with the fixes and the money rushing in and out of your accounts, so I'm not even going to tell you what we've got set up. I'd be interested to know at the end what you think you've spotted. My guys are getting pretty good at this stuff by now.'

Silence in the room. He excused himself and took as long a comfort break as he dared. He knew better than to look over Hugo's shoulder while he was at work, so he spent half an hour locked in a toilet stall praying that Nikolai would come through. When he re-entered the boardroom the air was thick with cigarette smoke, sweat and the sharp tang of fear. The technician had rigged up a television feed and the onscreen time registered 45+2 minutes.

'Not long now,' he said, looking around the room. He caught the mood and immediately abandoned the joke he was going to tell about Arkan growing a beard while waiting. Alec had warmed the bench on plenty of occasions, but this was probably the longest half-time he had ever experienced. He asked for more drinks to be brought in, handed them around and finally it was time for the second half to begin.

The fix, when it came, was almost a non-event. The Russian's team kicked off, the opposition pressed them immediately and the ball started to go backwards. Nikolai dropped back in support and passed clumsily back to his keeper who let it roll out for a corner. Job done. In Niš nobody spoke but their attention switched from the screen to the dashboards showing the funds available in their off-shore accounts. After an agonising five minutes the needles started moving steadily upwards. There was an audible sigh of relief as the dials went comfortably past the $10m point and kept on going, climbing through $20m, then $30m and $40m before each account hit $45m and levelled off. As they realised their money was not only safe but significantly enhanced the mood switched abruptly. Arkan roared and clapped his mighty hands ordering shots of Rakjia for everyone. The others played it more coolly but they shook hands congratulating each other as if their personal brilliance was responsible for the win.

Alec decided that now was not the moment to burst their bubble, so he said, 'Well done gentlemen, well done. Now, if anyone wants to leave it there you can cash out and take your profits before Hugo reinvests for the next round.'

He saw Totò hesitate but by now fear had given way to bravado. Arkan roared that there was no way he was pulling his cash out and looked threateningly around the room for dissenters. It would have taken a particularly courageous and single-minded individual to go against him and, in the end, everyone agreed they were still in.

Alec thanked them for their confidence then said, 'Obviously you're going to see your accounts empty out again but this time it will be rather less predictable. Money will flow in and out quite quickly as our systems execute the instructions they have been programmed with. Once the three o'clock games start things will get fast and furious as we try and place as many bets as possible in the limited time available.'

Although they were still paying attention the mobsters were reassured enough to give Alec and Hugo the benefit of some operating room. The Belovic contingent were at least partly distracted by the match taking place behind the glass and Alec reminded himself that their interest in the local outcome was likely to be financial as well as tribal. As the afternoon's football action progressed and the Rakjia kept flowing the party gathered steam, fuelled by regular injections of cash into the bank accounts they saw represented on the wall.

The stadium rang with celebrations at a Radnički win and the crowd dispersed into the evening gloom. By contrast, the mood in the hospitality suite was sunny and Arkan opened up the party to the heavies that the brothers relied on to give the Clan its muscle. Lau and Tang had been hitting the spirits hard and were happy to have more Chinese company at the party so invited their bodyguards in too. Totò was more restrained and, as the group started to become less formal, Alec took his chance to approach the Brazilian.

'I thought I knew some dodgy agents, but being involved in the kidnap of the wife of one of your own players? You are a real piece of work.'

'I had no involvement in what has happened to Marta. It is pure coincidence that she happens to have fallen foul of a couple of business associates of mine.'

'But what about your duty of care to your client? You should be trying to help him get her back rather than cashing in on her misfortune.'

'You're a football man, Mr Munday; I'm a businessman. I'm not so naïve as to think Diego will have any loyalty to me, that's if his playing career even lasts for another few seasons. There are times when dealing with these jumped up little pricks becomes a very tiresome and unreliable way to make a living, so excuse me if I look to diversify my business interests. Now, if you'll excuse me, it seems my colleagues are also invited to our gathering and I must let them know.'

Alec shook his head as he watched the Brazilian snake his way across the room returning seconds later with his henchmen who were soon tucking into the hospitality. Alec left them to it and sought out Marko to clinch their imminent exit.

'The afternoon is going well, my friend. My associates are content and their guests are enjoying the entertainment. We have one more Premier League game for you to make good on your promise of a return of twenty times their stake. If you come through, then you will all walk away without a problem.'

By the time the teatime game rolled around the party had been going for almost five hours. The effects of the alcohol had created a hair-trigger atmosphere: superficially good natured but stretched tight like a drum skin over an underlying threat of extreme violence.

At this point there were fifteen men in the room, at least half carrying firearms, and all at different stages of intoxication. A spilled drink here or an accidental stumble there could be the spark that would ignite a bloody shootout and Alec was nervous for everyone's safety.

The Chinese group were steaming and Arkan was trying to instigate a knife game with a vicious looking hunting blade pulled from somewhere under his jacket. Only Lech Belovic and Totò were focused on the screens and they tensed as the bank balances fell from an average of over $100m down to a fraction of that total. Their tension spread like a bush fire around the group and the noise level dropped to a low murmur.

Then, midway through the first half, a clumsy challenge went in and the referee produced the first yellow card of the game. Totò glanced quickly at Alec then back at the dashboard which stayed stubbornly close to empty. Ten minutes later another reckless challenge from the same player, the ref reached for his pocket once again producing yellow then red and the player was soon walking down the tunnel. This time more eyes were on Alec but still the needles didn't move. Anyone knowing the consequences of a team going down to ten men would have realised this was unlikely to be fixed but that didn't stop the irrational comments from coming.

'How many more cards before I get my money?' shouted Lau.

Arkan joined in, 'Yeah, what the fuck's going on?'

In the end it was Lech who silenced the room.

'If Mr Munday had placed wagers on those bookings then we would have won our bets. Am I right to assume that you have something else arranged?'

Alec nodded and pointed at the screen as Darren, his tame goalkeeper, appeared to lose his bearings and stepped out of his area to catch the ball. He was only over the line for a fraction of a second but the linesman's flag was up, and the ref blew his whistle for a free kick. The misdemeanour might have gone unnoticed in the room if Alec hadn't pointed it out and, by the time the wall was in place and the spot kick taken, the dials had started to climb. There was a cheer as the balances smashed through $100m and kept on going. The room clapped in rhythm willing the needle on through $150m, $180m then erupted as the $200m threshold was passed. The levels peaked at almost $210m apiece and, when the noise had subsided, Alec addressed his hosts while Hugo packed away his laptop and projector.

'Congratulations gentlemen. A very good afternoon's work. We must do it again sometime but. Meanwhile. we wish you a very pleasant evening.'

The pair received a cheer and entreaties from Arkan to carry on the party. True to his word Lech came to their rescue.

'Mr Munday, Mr Ashburton, you have done excellently this afternoon and fulfilled your part of our bargain. That brings our business to a successful conclusion and my brother and I send you on your way with the girl and our good wishes. Now, some more drinks for everyone.'

The two saw their opportunity and made a rapid exit waving and shaking hands as they did so. Once in the office suite Marta joined them and soon all three were in one of the BMWs speeding towards the airport. Inside, Alec called his contact at Air Charter Services and was told they would make a take-off slot at around 9.30. Then he called Michaela.

'We're on our way to the airport. Are you somewhere close?'

'Wow, well done, yes' she said breathlessly. 'I'm parked up outside. I've got the consignment that I need to see onto that plane.'

'Ok I'll get the charter service to make arrangements. See you in five.'

Passengers on private charter planes are afforded privileges not available to regular users of the airport and the BMW bypassed the terminally completely, driving straight up to the plane where it stood in a remote corner of the airfield. A member of cabin crew was waiting to welcome them onboard taking their passports for checking by the authorities before they were cleared for takeoff. Marta, who had been tense and silent in the car, got herself up the aircraft's retractable steps but her legs buckled as she went through the cabin door. She was caught by a hostess who lowered her gently into a chair where Alec put an arm around her and held her close.

'You're safe now, I promise,' he said, as she sobbed into his shoulder.

Hugo bundled clumsily into the cabin with his backpack and went immediately to work hunching over his laptop which was tethered to his mobile phone. Once he was sure the passports were back and they were preparing to leave he hit a button on his keyboard and slammed the lid shut. He settled back into his seat, the immense relief at having made it out of the lion's den written all over his face.

'I know we all have good reasons for being pleased to be on this plane but, fuck me, am I glad that's over. I can honestly say that's the closest I have ever been to the genuine prospect of death and I have no desire ever to do it again. I was convinced they were going to kill either us or each other in there.'

Alec was equally ecstatic at the outcome. 'No question they would have done had things not gone to plan. Good work, by the way.'

He looked out of the plane's porthole windows and saw a van pull up alongside. Michaela got out of the passenger side while ground crew carried two 6ft black bags from its rear doors to the luggage hold under the tail.

'Hey look, the band's back together,' Hugo said in surprise as her face appeared in the cabin door. She looked tired and drawn but smiled weakly and took her seat as the stairs were pulled up and the door closed.

Unconsciously, they all held their breath as the plane taxied onto the runway then accelerated hard quickly leaving Serbia behind. Once at cruising height, the air hostess offered them drinks and something to eat and the cabin started to relax. Alec went over to Michaela and held her hand without speaking. There would be time for words later but, for now, they were on their way home.

After a few minutes he took the seat next to Hugo while Michaela checked in with Marta.

'Everything in place?' he asked.

'All done, dear boy, just before takeoff. You are now a very wealthy man.'

'You too, I'm sure.'

'Oh, you know, I'll have enough to survive,' he said, unable to suppress a broad grin.

'There is something totally exhilarating about pulling off a sting like that right under their noses.'

The two men fist pumped each other awkwardly and toasted their success while on the ground far beneath them a scene of murderous carnage was playing out. The dials projected on the wall were stuck firmly at well over $200 million but, when Totò tried to move the money out of his offshore account, he came up dry. His cries of dismay alerted Tang and Lau who, despite their drunken state manged to login and confirmed the same result. Accusations flew and guns were waved around wildly. Who fired first would never be known but in such close quarters an accident was the most likely catalyst for the ensuing bloodbath.

After the shooting stopped Totò waited for a few minutes then extricated himself with difficulty from underneath his sacrificed men to survey the scene. The suite was a sea of red with spatters of blood on every wall and the carpet oozing stickily. Without waiting to establish whether anyone else was alive, he did what he could with his blood-soaked clothes then quit the scene hastily departing by taxi directly to the airport. The last outbound flight of the day had left, but he secured an online ticket to Zurich for 5am the next morning and settled down in a quiet corner to wait. They picked him up as he approached security and walked him to one of the airport's business entrances where he was handed over to the occupants of a large black BMW

Chapter 32

'Get out of the water kids; it'll be 30% piss and 40% lager by now.'

Kevin Mooney's unique parenting style was enough to shake Alec from a recurring dream in which he was running to catch a plane and never quite making it. He sat up and rubbed his eyes. There were over forty of them around the executive pool at Dubai's Jumeirah Beach Hotel, taking full advantage of his long-promised hospitality during the post-Christmas mini break. If the players felt aggrieved that they weren't getting a high-octane lads' driving trip, they were prepared to put their gripes aside when they found out he was offering a four-day all-expenses-paid jaunt to the sun with partners and kids invited too. There had been some resistance from the usual suspects who saw the chance to get away from their better halves as a big upside of previous excursions. But Alec had been insistent: hedonism was so last year and it was a lot safer for everyone if the group turned over a new leaf for the New Year.

From Alec's lounger, he could see more designer gear than Paris Fashion Week as the girls struggled to outdo each other with out-landish beachwear, silk sarongs and more than a few pairs of Daisy Dukes. Their children too, were dressed for the occasion and it may have been the thought of damage to those Vilebrequin and Valentino swimming costumes that brought on Mooney's outburst. As he sipped his Mojito Alec was satisfied that his debt to the players was being amply repaid. They had flown Emirates first class, enjoyed chauffeur-driven limousine transfers and luxury accommodation at one of the world's leading family-friendly hotels. He had block-booked the beachcomber rooms on the ground floor for the families while those who had yet to replace themselves luxuriated in exclusive duplex suites at the crest of the hotel's landmark wave.

The boys had just come back from a round of golf on the Ernie Els-designed course and earlier that morning he had organised an 'impromptu' media appearance with tame paparazzi for those players and their partners who were looking for a boost to their public profiles. There was a 4x4 desert drive scheduled for the next day, the evening meal programme took in Dubai's hottest nightspots and he had even laid on entertainment for the kids to give their parents a break. All in all, a job well done, he thought.

He had originally been planning to ask Blandine to make the arrangements but she gave him short shrift:

'I'm not in that business any more, darling,' she said, managing to make even a flat rejection sound sexy, 'but I'm sure I'll see you around.'

He had worried momentarily about how Nikolai would take it when he found out she wasn't going to be involved, but put the thought to the back of his mind and moved on. Now, as he looked across the pool, Alec could see the pair of them 'packing on the PDA' as the Daily Mail would no doubt describe it. He could only guess at how they had got together but the scratches on the footballer's back told him as much as he needed to know about how the relationship was going.

So Alec had been left to organise the party himself although, in truth, it turned out to be a useful distraction. The reunion at Gatwick airport had been an emotional one with tears, laughter and more than one attempt by Marta to slap her husband's face. Diego declared himself 'more grateful than words can say' to Alec, Michaela and Hugo and invited them to 'party like we won the World Cup'. But Michaela had already made herself scarce and the flight had been long enough for everyone else's adrenaline to disperse leaving just a heavy feeling of fatigue to fill the vacuum.

'We're not exactly going to be the life and soul of the party tonight, mate,' he had told the player. 'You enjoy yourself and we'll make up for it in a few days when I've had chance to think about just how grateful I need you to be.'

The two embraced, Diego with tears in his eyes. He started to speak but Alec stopped him. 'Remember this moment,' he said, 'and just make sure you don't fuck it all up again. We got really lucky this time but I can guarantee your luck won't hold if anything like it happens again.'

As he said the words, he thought about Totò and the inevitable fallout in Brazil that events in Niš were going to bring but tonight wasn't the night. In fact, Diego's agent and his commercial interests in the player were not even close to the top of the list of things that would need to be resolved in the aftermath of their foray into the Serbian underworld.

By the time he checked in with her on Monday morning, Michaela had used her Interpol credentials to clear Tyler and Fleetwood's bodies with the border authorities, and had them collected from the airport by a government approved undertaker. Now it was time to break the news to their families. She had personal addresses from the men's files: Tyler had divorced from his wife and the mother of their two children a couple of years ago and was shown as living in a flat in Lewisham. The ex-wife's address was also listed, reasonably close by in Plumstead. Fleetwood, who had never married, seemed to live with his parents as both his address and that of his next of kin was the same; a house in Greenwich.

Michaela had wanted to visit the families alone but Alec insisted, and they were now sat in his car driving towards South London. As they drove he volunteered that, one way or another, there would be a fund set up to support the relatives. Diego would see to that and the club would probably want to help too but, either way, there would be significant compensation for their loss.

They started at Tyler's Lewisham flat, Michaela hoping there would be no answer. She got her wish and posted a card through the letterbox just in case there was a new partner on the scene. The house in Greenwich had seen better days but was still a substantial property. They rang on the door and waited. It was answered eventually by an elderly woman.

'Mrs Fleetwood?' said Michaela.

'Yes, dear,' came a frail voice. 'What is it?'

'I'm afraid I have some very bad news about your son. May we come in?'

Neil Fleetwood turned out not to be the woman's son but her grandson. His parents had been killed in a car accident when he was small and he had been brought up by his grandparents until Mrs Fleetwood senior's husband had died fifteen years ago. Since then, it had been just the two of them.

Alec and Michaela left Greenwich a long hour later leaving the old lady in the care of a neighbour but promising to return soon. They arrived in Plumstead late on in the afternoon and rang the door of a Victorian terraced house. It was answered by a hassled-looking bottle blonde.

'Oh shit,' she said when she saw Michaela's badge. 'Chris hasn't gone and got himself killed, has he? What am I going to tell the kids; they adore the bastard.'

Michaela had been practising the words she needed. 'I'm afraid I do have to tell you that Christopher Tyler was killed earlier this week while on an unofficial operation overseas. His body was repatriated last night and is with an undertaker pending the family's instructions. I'm very sorry for your loss.'

The former Mrs Tyler went quiet for a moment processing what she had been told, then her eyes narrowed. 'Unofficial?' she asked, a decade as a policeman's wife giving her an instinct for the operative word.

'It was an off-the-books operation which the Official Secrets Act prevents me from discussing with you.'

'So why are you mentioning it?'

'It is unfortunate in that, as he died in the circumstances he did, he cannot be said technically to have been killed in the line of duty.'

'Oh, this gets worse. You're bleeding telling me I'm not going to get a pay out, right?'

'There will be no official compensation over and above his pension however, there will be a significant hardship payment to ensure that you and his children are not left worse off by Chris's death.'

'How much? He was many things but Chris always made sure me and the kids didn't want for anything.'

'The figure has yet to be finalised but we can say it is likely to be more than one million pounds.'

At this news the mood brightened considerably.

'Well, that puts things in a bit of a different light, doesn't it? Said the ex. 'We had our differences but he was a good man and I know he would never have left us out in the cold.'

'There will be some papers to sign in the next few days,' Michaela went on, officiously, 'but meanwhile, can I ask, would it be you that would be taking care of the funeral arrangements?'

'I suppose it would be. His parents both passed a few years ago.'

'I appreciate this news will have come as a shock but I have details of the undertaker here. Perhaps tomorrow, when you've had some time to recover, you could call them and discuss arrangements. Here's my card: you can contact me too if you need to, and I will personally be in touch again in the coming days to confirm the hardship payment.'

'That went well,' Alec said as they drove away from the house. There was no reply and as he glanced at her, he saw Michaela's face was set in a grim mask, eyes staring straight ahead but seeing nothing. Her next piece of official business, with her bosses at the CoLP, would be harder than almost anything she'd faced so far. After ten minutes on the road Alec tried to break the silence again.

'My mum bought me an elephant for my room once. I said, 'thanks very much' and she said, 'don't mention it.''

'Alec, I know you really want to help but I've got to deal with the job on my own.'

'I know,' he said, quietly. 'Have you any idea what you're going to be facing? I mean, what can they do to you?'

She didn't reply and they drove the final few miles to the station in silence. As he pulled up, she leaned over kissed him and hugged him briefly but tightly.

'I'll call you,' she said as she walked away, not looking back. The draft caught his shirt and he felt the damp chill of her tears. Every part of him wanted to run after her and hold her in his arms but he resisted, and simply watched as she disappeared behind the ticket barrier.

It was their last contact for almost four weeks. He had the Dubai trip to arrange which occupied some of his time with the rest of it taken up a lot of new work: he seemed suddenly to have acquired a reputation for his expertise on match fixing. He knew how the bush telegraph worked in football and was worried at first that Diego's cover might be blown around the industry. All his concerns that the Premier League would brush any hint of corruption under the carpet were quickly dispelled as club after club called him for advice. Once a signed non-disclosure agreement guaranteed them his discretion he found them ready to open up, and gain the benefit of his recent experiences. They talked about the environment around specific players, the dubious company some of them kept and the thrill-seeking habits that could lead to their entrapment by fixers. The one area that was off limits was betting sponsorship: although an obvious inconsistency, official gaming partners were here to stay in an era when all but the top clubs struggle to find brands to prepared to pay top dollar for sponsorship.

With all the calls on his time it took a while to absorb the fact that his own financial situation had been completely transformed. The balance in his offshore account showed $102m and change, or 10% of the total winnings Belovic and his guests thought they had made. The rest of the money had been split between Hugo and eight of his most affluent or risk-hungry friends and clients. Working as a syndicate they had put up enough funds to make a market providing a counterparty in a series of outrageous spread bets courtesy of Hugo's access to the offshore funds. An hour after the final game had finished, losses and winnings were calculated and a margin call made on the gangsters' accounts wiping them out completely.

For the first time since the end of his career as a footballer Alec had back his sense of financial indestructibility, re-experiencing that carefree feeling that, whatever things cost, there was always going to be enough. If he experienced a twinge of conscience, he eased it by reminding himself that he had taken money off some very bad players, money which would otherwise be funding bigger and more audacious criminal acts.

He thought about Michaela often wondering how she was coping with being the subject of police enquiries rather than the one doing the enquiring. She had said she would call and he had to give her time to sort things out, but if he was honest with himself, he missed her and felt a huge unpaid debt of responsibility. Then, late on Christmas Eve, out of nowhere he received a text message:

'Merry Christmas. I'm still standing but I miss you loads.'

Her words opened the floodgates of both messages and emotions. Within four hours they were in each other's arms, their bodies entwined in a Gordian knot pulled tightly together until dawn on Christmas Day. The intensity of feeling was not something Alec had experienced before and he was not about to let her go again.

When they did start to talk it became clear that the past few weeks had been everything Michaela had dreaded and more. She had been suspended pending the outcome of two separate enquiries, but told to be in no doubt that her police career was over. She would in all likelihood face disciplinary action for bringing the force into disrepute and criminal charges were not being ruled out. Much worse was being frozen out by former colleagues whom she had previously looked on as friends. No one had a problem with the guys doing a bit of freelance work on the side but she was held to have been responsible for the deaths of two effective and popular officers. That put her beyond the pale as far as the fraternity of old bill was concerned and they were determined to make sure she knew it.

The funerals had been the worst. She had attended as a mark of respect and support for the relatives whose grief she shared. But, as well-liked and respected officers, SCO19 colleagues were out in force to give Fleetwood and Tyler an appropriate send-off along with dozens of others who had served alongside the pair over the years. Their expressions of outright hostility were chilling and Michaela was physically shaking as she fled the packed church unable to make it to the end of the memorial.

News of her persona non grata status had travelled as far as Lyon too, so that when she visited Interpol headquarters she faced similar treatment. Police the world over share a lot of the same characteristics and she felt the cold heat of disapproval stab her repeatedly in the back as she walked through the open-plan office. Relief came briefly when she was alone and closing up the French apartment in which she had passed many a happy evening, but, when she drove the long road back to the UK with all her possessions in the back of a hired Renault, it seemed like her life was over.

24-hours later she and Alec were together and it felt as if a huge weight had been lifted allowing her to breathe again. Christmas passed in a blur and was followed by some extensive retail therapy as prescribed by Alec who insisted she fill at least two suitcases with designer swimwear and clothes from Selfridges and Harvey Nichols.

Now, a week later, the change of scenery and the chance of a bit of escapism had given her some perspective. When she wasn't by Alec's side, Michaela found herself drawn to Marta. The Brazilian had recovered well physically from her ordeal but the carefree indifference to her husband's comings and goings had been replaced by a new wariness in her eyes. The two had the kind of bond that comes from a shared experience but it soon turned into genuine and warm affection too.

The sun was setting as Alec got up from his lounger and looked at the group spread around the pool. The waiters had strict instructions to keep the drinks flowing but the party had started to drift to the margins. The parents had kids to turn around into another new set of clothes for the evening and the others had some serious grooming to do before hitting the town. He was just about to invite Diego and Marta to join them back in their suite when his phone went with a number he didn't recognise.

'Hello, Alec? My name is Simon Cauldwell. I represent some key interests in the British establishment. Are able to talk?'

'I guess so,' he said, immediately suspicious. 'What's this about?'

'Your recent adventures have come to our attention, Alec; yours and Michaela Dagg's that is. I understand you're in Dubai at the moment but my associates and I would like a conversation when you're back. It's a matter we think you'll both find of considerable interest. You've got this number now. I'd appreciate it if you would give me a call in the next few days.'

Write a review

If you've enjoyed Kick Back then the biggest compliment you can pay me is to leave a review on Amazon. I read every review and always learn something from my fantastic readers.

Kick Back is my first novel and it is really hard to get started as an author. So, I would hugely appreciate it if you could leave a review and lead others to the world of Alec Munday. As an extra incentive, I'm offering you another book absolutely free. There is no obligation to review Kick Back before you download the next book in the series. I just hope you'll think I'm a generous guy and feel like doing the same. It would also be great to have you as part of the Alec Munday Reader's Club so do take advantage of that offer.

Phil Savage

Readers Club Download Offer

Free bonus book. **Give Back** is the next episode in the Alec Munday series and is available to you now as a free download. Get your copy of **Give Back** by Phil Savage absolutely FREE.

Get your free no-obligation download today. Find out more at www.philsavage.org

About the Author

Phil Savage has worked in sports journalism and publishing for almost two decades. He has covered corruption, match fixing, illegal gambling and doping as well the many positive aspects of sport.

Many of the stories he has come across could never be reported but they have been reimagined and worked into his fiction writing.

None of the events in his novels are true - but they very nearly could have been.

Read more at www.philsavage.org.

Printed in Great Britain
by Amazon

14647371R00164